TORRENT OF TEARS

SCOURGE SURVIVOR SERIES – BOOK THREE

JL MADORE

To those who love the Haven gang, Fate's Journey continues. Without you, there would be no adventure.

To my Writers' Community of Durham Region family: You are without question, the greatest and most talented community of writers ever assembled. You energize me. I'm honored every day to be your President, your peer and part of the group. Rock on WCDR!

To my editors, Ruth and Gwynn of Writescape: Lexi's story took a bit more work to tighten. She's a free-wheeling character and went off the rails a few times. A huge thank you for pulling things back into order.

To my writing circles/guides, Critical Realm, BookEnds and the gang at 20Books: your critiques are invaluable, your support immeasurable, and your friendships irreplaceable. Much love.

CHAPTER ONE

I flailed. Reaching behind my head, I clutched for the handle of what could only be the blade of a battle axe lodged between my shoulder blades. Early-morning sunlight pierced the blue sky above. Pain burned though me. It blinded. White spots and tears obscured my vision. Let death come. I was done anyway. They were dead because of me.

I couldn't make out their faces in the fading reality of my vision, but the loss of lives hollowed my heart and left me feeling drained and desolate.

A ragged breath rushed from my lungs as my consciousness returned. Gods, what did I do wrong? No—what would I do wrong? My butt slid off the snow-covered log and I slumped to the side. Winter wind whistled over my body, across the forest clearing, and rattled the weathered boards of our childhood clubhouse. Unable to move until the effects of the vision wore off, I laid on the ice-crusted ground and blinked up at our motto carved and painted above.

Shitstorm Survivors: Come in peace or leave in pieces.

Almost two decades and it remained. Scrawled in the chipped, slime-green paint Bruin had 'borrowed' from the maintenance room of Haven castle.

The numbing dread of the vision drained away as my mind filled with memories of the four of us here, playing, training and holding strategy sessions on how to avenge our dead. Painful as it was, life was simple then. We were a team. A united force of four orphans against the evil of our realm.

The Scourge.

When the shakes passed, I hauled my ass back onto the log and dropped my head between my legs. The melted patch of snow where I'd fallen, exposed the unyielding, packed dirt and leaf detritus beneath. When had life come between the four of us? I wanted it back . . . that sense of belonging to people who gave a shit. That's what had always made the killing and fighting and training worthwhile. My family.

The *crunch* of heavy footsteps from the forest path had me breathing deep. The breeze, crisp and fresh in my nostrils, held the bite of winter that wouldn't relent. No stanky rot of Scourge. I let my gloved hand relax from the hilt of the new Guardian double-edge sheathed to my thigh and waited. Only a half-dozen people on this mountain knew the location of our childhood sanctuary. Sadly, I wasn't inclined to see any of them at the moment.

"Princess?"

Reign's gravel voice made my chest tighten. I leaned forward and picked up a chunk of snow and cupped it between my palms. It was spongy and packed into a tight ball under my fingers.

"Mind if I join you?"

I scootched to the side to make room. "That bad, is it?"

"What?" He lowered himself, knees cracking as the log groaned under his weight.

"I'm such a train-wreck that my father tromped through the forest during school hours to find me?"

"You missed your morning training session with the third years and then your one o'clock battlements class. You're pale, Lexi. You have a vision?"

I nodded, tossed my snowball into the skeletal scrub and rubbed my gloves together.

Reign reached into his wool trench and handed me a chocolate. Each member of my family carried a stock of treats to ease the after-effects of my gift. He was quiet a long time, sitting with his elbows on his knees, turning the massive platinum ring on his thumb. In the chill of the afternoon, warmth oozed off him. It leeched into my hip and shoulder where his frame touched mine. "Wanna talk about the vision?"

The grieving ache of my dream lingered too fresh.

Close like this, him six-foot-six and two feet taller than me, I waited for the security to come like it always had. When I was a kid, he'd scoop me up like a doll and make everything right again. If I didn't have that, what did I have?

Just the black void of nothingness that was my life before Maximus Reign.

"Can't you fix this?" I pressed my fingers into a fist, the *pop-pop-pop* of each knuckle breaking the silence. "I thought he'd get over it by now. It's been months. I've said it a thousand times. I didn't mean to hurt her."

Reign shook his head, his brindled hair rustling off his shoulders, longer than he usually let it grow. There was more salt than pepper in it these days, but he wore it well. "All intentions aside, you *did* hurt her. Bruin has every right to be pissed. If Jade wasn't there that afternoon—"

"But she *was*," I choked, surprised at the wave of bitterness washing over me. "She always is. Everyone plays their part. Jade's the savior, Bruin's the fighter, Julian's the genius and I'm the spoiled screw up, right?"

Reign's square jaw clenched tight. "Just because you screwed up, doesn't make you a screw up, Alexannia Grace."

I laughed, a white cloud of breath escaping my lungs. "My full name proves it's really bad."

"You smashed Mika's head into the marble floor. Brain bleeds are really bad."

I sighed, sick of this convo. "Please. Talk to Bruin again. Make him accept my apology." Reign made a noise which indicated that he might as well have been trying to teach Savage to sing. "Do you think he'll get over it by my party? I want him there."

"Them," Reign grumbled. "You want *them* there. Mika is his mate, you have to get used to that. And no, I don't think he has any intention of coming to your birthday celebration."

An anorexic squirrel with a patchy grey coat dug for some forgotten cache of food on the edge of the clearing. It searched here and there, uncovering fallen leaves and bits of dead forest, then shimmied up a redwood, empty handed.

"Do you ever regret adopting me?"

Reign kissed the top of my head and got to his feet. "Not for one second in sixteen years." He stepped over to the clubhouse and knocked his scarred knuckles against the writing on the wall. Without looking back, he strode to the path and left me to myself.

I stared at our faded, slime green promise to each other and the world. *Come in peace or leave in pieces.* Yeah, well the irony of that statement just sucked.

"Am I boring you?" Tham nipped at the soft curve of my breast and raised an elegant blond brow. "Where are you this afternoon, *neelan?*"

I shrugged.

He propped himself up on the bed beside me and pulled me against his smooth chest. Highborne skin was the palest ivory and Tham's smelled like the suede of his buckskins. Golden waves fell loose around his gently pointed Elven ears and down his shoulders to tickle my nose. "It will work out, Lexi. No one can stay angry at you for long."

I snuggled closer, idly thumbing along the defined ridges of his stomach to his tight, pink nipple. "You're still going to be my date for my birthday, right?"

His chin rubbed the side of my head as he nodded. "We shall dance the night away." He gave me a squeeze then pulled back. "What exactly is a bacchanalia?"

A flutter of excitement had me smiling. "Originally, it was a wild and mystic festival dedicated to Bacchus, the Greek god of wine. Now though, it's a big fancy ball with gowns and masks and drunken revelry. It's going to be amazing."

"If you planned the event, it could be nothing other."

I kissed Tham's chest and sat up, gathering my t-shirt from where it had fallen beside my bed. As always, Tham had lifted me out of my malaise and I could breathe again. He had that gift. No one could spend five minutes with him and not be drawn out of their wallowing.

"What did I pull you away from when I called you? You sounded busy."

Tham lifted up the sheet and winked when he found the lost sex toy. It was a shame that Highbornes saved their virginity for their one true mate, but the two of us excelled at creatively making do. I bit my lip as he sauntered across my suite to the bathroom and flashed me a glorious view of his carved physique. The way the muscles pulled and stretched as he practically glided across the floor was an actual thing of beauty.

"Galan and I went through the Gate to the village," he said. His charismatic blue gaze met mine in the reflection of the mirror. "We spent the afternoon with the Highborne Elders."

"Is it already time to update them on the progress of your Ambar Lenn?" I rolled onto my stomach and propped my chin in my palms. "Let me guess. They fell over themselves praising Galan for how well he's done for himself, proving himself a true male of worth, while condemning you and Aust to the rank of worthless failures."

Tham flashed me a devilish smile. "It's like you were there. No matter. I work very hard to be known as the grandest disappointment in Highborne history. Though, it hurts Aust to be exiled and have his mother alienated from her friends in the village."

"Yeah, well, their loss is our gain. Aust's affinity with animals is something to be praised, not judged. He's thriving here with the Weres. I wish Lia was doing half as well."

Tham finished rinsing the rubber phallus and bounced it against the edge of the sink a few times to knock off the water. "Galan gathered some belongings for her while we were there. He hopes to bring her back to herself before the young are born."

Ahh. I flopped back against my pillow. Jade and Galan were sickeningly happy these days. Jade was expecting twins. How could life be anything but glorious when your husband is perfect and your long-lost biological father turns out to be the most powerful man in the two realms?

Oh to be the lost love child of the god of gods.

I clenched my teeth. Jade deserved all the happiness the two realms could offer. It would be petty and wrong to begrudge my sister that. Yeah . . . well, color me petty.

"Hey Hotness," I said, sitting up. "Do you want to pilfer the kitchen and hole up with me tonight? I'm thinking we lock the door, lounge around naked, and have a Lord of the Rings marathon. I'll even let you pause and re-enact Legolas' archery moves if you want."

Tham sauntered back and pulled suede pants up his creamy, toned thighs. With the front lacings left untied he sat on the edge of the bed, his chest and abs flexing in the most delicious way. The mattress sunk under his weight and I tilted toward him. "Apologies, *neelan*, mayhap another night."

"Big date?"

He tugged at a couple wayward ebony spikes falling in front of my eyes. After a Tham session, my hair was usually unsalvageable. "Sort of. Julian said the package you helped me order from Victoria's Secrets arrived from the Modern Realm. I mentioned to some of the females that I would bring it to the village tonight."

"Ooooh, and you're hoping you get a chance to try some of it out?"

Tham waggled his brows and bent to kiss my cheek. I leaned forward to meet him, but winced when my back knotted. Tham eased me back against the pillows, his eyes narrowing. "Has Jade examined your back? It has been paining you for more than a week now."

"I'm fine."

He exhaled, a serious frown marring his hotness. "Mayhap a gentle rubdown with massage oil might ease your discomfort. I shall stay a while longer."

"Nah, you go. I can't deprive the Highborne females of their silk and satin experience. Besides, you haven't seen any good Highborne consort action in ages."

He chuckled, shrugged on his tunic and then scooped his knife sheath off the bedside table. After raising a bare foot onto the side of the bed, he tied the leather cord of his sheath around his thigh. "Do not worry on my account. The Haven action has been more than enlightening."

"So, have you decided your type?" I asked.

"My type?" The blue of his eyes lit up the way it always did when he was intrigued.

"Your favorite type of women. After a century of exile, with only fair skinned blonds to choose from, do you prefer them or brunettes, redheads, or raven-haired beauties?"

"Verily, a thorough study of the subject is underway but a preference is yet to be determined." Tham waggled his brow, capturing his long, blond waves and tying them back to reveal the pointed ears of his race. "Are you certain you are well, Lexi? I am pleased to stay if you need me."

Yes. "No. I'm fine. Really." I sat straighter and ignored the ache gripping my shoulder blades and gouging down my spine. "You go. Julian will be closing the Gatehouse soon and you want to be on the other side of the mirror when he does."

Tham strode into the bathroom, rifled through my medicine chest and came back with two tablets and a glass of water. The heavy-duty muscle relaxants were the ones I saved for the times Savage knocked the crap out of me in training sessions. As I reached up to accept them, he pulled back and waited until I gave him my full attention.

"Speak to Jade. Tell her you suffer, Lexi, or I shall be forced to break confidence for your own good."

I waved him away as I popped the tablets into my mouth. Tham was such a great guy. With a thumbs up from me, he nodded and the door *clicked* shut behind him. The battle I was waging with my composure crumbled.

Stronger than before, white-hot claws dug at the inside of my skin like an alien trying to break free. What the hell was wrong with me?

CHAPTER TWO

The night had been brutal but rested or not there was no way I could ditch my classes two days in a row. Reign was busy with the latest Scourge uprising yet somehow, he always knew what happened within the castle. If I bagged my duties again, he'd be on me like a shark on tuna. It went without saying . . . it sucked to be the tuna in that scenario.

"Yo, Lexi."

I scanned the ebbing sea of students behind me to see Nash's purple Mohawk cutting the air as he made his way up the hall. I backed against the stone of the castle and let the current of traffic flow by until he caught up. "Hey Nash, what's doin'?"

His winning smile crinkled the crescent, tribal tattoo encircling his eye. "I was at the Gatehouse this morning picking up some stuff for the Talon when a few of your deliveries came through. Going big for your b-day, eh?"

I nodded, and the two of us resumed the walk toward the weapons wing. "A leap-year baby only gets an actual birthday every four years. I like to celebrate."

"Well, Julian wasn't too thrilled about the boxes piling up in his space. He said if I saw you today, I should tell you to send some strong young students to pick them up."

I snorted at Nash's diplomacy. He was more than just an extraordinary graduate student and Talon squire. Since Mika got Samuel blown up and blinded six months ago, Nash had been promoted and was quickly becoming the best wizard the Talon had. "That's what Julian meant, but it probably sounded more like, 'My Gatehouse is not her personal warehouse. Tell my little sister to get her spoiled ass over here and get this party shit the fuck out of my way.'"

Nash laughed. "That sounds remarkably familiar."

"No problem, I'll send someone." We walked together, chatting about nothing in particular as we wound our way up the circular stairs to the third-floor landing. I drew a labored breath. The slow, steady ascension aggravated the muscles in my back.

"Lexi, you okay?"

Though I wasn't one to gripe about the aches and pains of being a warrior, I confessed that the pain in my back was just about crippling me.

He hesitated for a moment, then leaned down and whispered close to my ear. "I've got Haze if you need it."

A few of my fellow warriors smoked Golden Haze behind closed doors to take the edge off. Though it wasn't illegal, Talon Enforcers were held to high standards. Reign would flip. He'd actually kicked a few warriors off rotation for dosing too often.

"No thanks. I appreciate it, but I've really got to get to class." I gripped the banister and continued our ascent.

He bounced up the stairs beside me, keeping pace with no effort. "How will you get through two hours of advanced weapons training if you can't climb the stairs to get to the gym? Do you honestly think you can swing a flail right now?"

Gods, I should've pulled the covers over my head and stayed in bed.

"Come here." Nash grabbed my shoulder and steered me into the fifth year's co-ed bathroom. I got a handle on myself while one of

Jade's students finished washing up. After she left, Nash checked the stalls to ensure our privacy. "I'm not trying to coerce you, Lexi. Really, I'm not, but you look like roadkill. I want to help."

"I appreciate it, but I could get into a lot of trouble—"

He slipped his hand into his jacket and came out with a small package that looked like gum.

"What's that?"

"It's new . . . for those who don't smoke." He pulled out a few sticks of the Haze gum and handed them to me. "No one will know it's not a stick of gum. I'm just not sure how much you'd need. You're tiny, but I sit across from you at dinner. You have the metabolism of a barbarian."

"I don't know whether that should piss me off or not."

The three-minute chime sounded and without thinking any more about it, I unwrapped a stick of Haze and drove it in my mouth. Nash shoved the rest of the package into the pocket of my battle vest and— gods help me—it was done.

The day passed in a blissful golden blur of conversation, melee practice, and bacchanalia party preparation. I hadn't realized the oppressive grip my suffering had held me under, but with the pain lifted, I was in top form and ready for anything. I decided, after wadding in a third piece of groovy gum, that I'd name my first-born child Nash. It was catchy and I had a new-found love for that guy. I really did.

Sliding sideways past the boxes and bins stacked and blocking most of the main entrance hall of the Gatehouse, I hung my winter jacket on a hook and made my way inside to find Julian. Hopefully he was back to being the brother who didn't want to kill me.

"Yo bro," I called, turning the corner into the main control room. Three heads whirled around and not one of my siblings looked too thrilled that I had crashed their convo. I stopped short in the open doorway feeling like I'd just taken a blow to the gut. "What's this . . . a party and me the only one without an invite?"

Jade shook her head and her long burgundy locks danced against her chest. Funny thing about redheads, their blush always gave away when they lied. "Don't look so suspicious, Lexi, there's no conspiracy. Reign asked me to connect with the sea otter Finfolk off the coast of Alaska. You remember Storm right? The Native girl from the Hearthstone last spring? Well, she's running the clan now. Bruin and I just got back and were catching up with Julian on the Scourge front."

Bruin stood arms crossed, his turquoise stare solidly fixed on the monitor wall behind me. *No change there.*

My stomach tightened at the awkwardness choking the air. Stepping further into the room, I picked up the tablet Julian used to track deliveries and scrolled through the list. "I was told that some of my party supplies arrived."

"Some?" Julian scrubbed rough fingers over his skull-trimmed afro and scowled. "Is there more to come? You're five times over your yearly quota for Modern Realm deliveries and it's only February, Lexi. You've brought so much through the Athen's Gatehouse, I'm going to have to declare it a point of exposure risk."

"Yeah, right." I snorted. "No one's keeping tabs on deliveries made to an olive oil factory. Besides, I want my bacchanalia to be authentic. I need everything I ordered to make it special."

Julian shook his head, his mint-green gaze stern. "I get that you think so, but no party is worth risking realm safety."

"Well *sorry* if my birthday doesn't rank up there with Jade and Galan ordering half a baby supply warehouse or Bruin sending for everything Mika ever owned in Vancouver. I'll try to remember my place."

"Don't be petty, Lexi," Jade snapped. "We're worried about you."

I whirled, my mouth agape. "*Worried?* You've each been so busy excluding me from your lives I wouldn't have thought you'd have time to spare a thought for me."

Bruin growled and threw up his hands. "I told you it was useless. She's too selfish to hear anything we say."

"Selfish?" I spat. "Don't even pretend that you're mad about twinkle lights and statuary, Bear. I've apologized a thousand times for Mika. I've tried to make amends, but you and your mate won't even open the door for me."

"Stop apologizing and accept responsibility for it," he growled. "It was an accident you've said. You didn't mean it, you've said. Fuck, Lexi, actions have consequences. You hurt the people around you and don't even see it until they're bleeding and Jade has to patch them up."

I fought the urge to leave. It would only give him the satisfaction of saying I acted like a child. "Bruin, you know damned well I never meant to hurt her. Sometimes my strength gets away from me—especially if I'm provoked."

The growl of Bruin's bear vibrated through the room. "Are you telling me Mika taunted you into smashing her head into the marble tiles?"

"I didn't say that."

"Enough, you two." Julian stepped around his desk and pulled back on Bruin's shoulders. When he turned to me, his expression was pinched and stern. "We're worried about you, Lex. You're lashing out, flaking on training schedules, and skipping your classes. You're not yourself and haven't been for months."

Months? "I wasn't feeling well and missed *one* day's duties. One. You seem to forget that *I'm* the one picking up the slack at the Academy because Jade's busy puking every morning. And *I'm* the one at every early morning training session of the Highbornes because Bruin can't seem to dismount his mate long enough to—"

"Fuck, Lexi!" Julian placed his palms flat on Bruin's chest and planted his feet.

The growl that ripped from Bruin that time vibrated in my chest. The man would never hurt me, but the bonded Were animal in him was a truly scary thing. I eased back a few feet as his turquoise eyes flared gold. Jade took hold of Bruin's bicep and began to sing. Her enchanted melody wove an ethereal spell around Bruin until his bear calmed.

Julian glared. "What the hell is wrong with you?"

I turned on my heel. "Nothing. I'm just learning that the term 'family' is more subjective than I thought. Seems if you don't toe the line just right, you're as good as—"

Someone lunged behind me, caught my shoulder and whirled me around. Pressed against the wall, Bruin stared at me with deadly focus. He leaned close and sniffed. "You're on something."

Oh shit. I fought against his iron grip, trying to keep my cool. "What? So, you refuse to speak to me for six months and then accuse me of—"

"Blaze. Come check out her eyes." Bruin pushed harder to hold me in place as the room got a hell of a lot more claustrophobic. "I smell Haze."

I caught his jaw with an uppercut and twisted out of his grasp. "What I do stopped being your business when you cut me from your life. You want me gone? Consider me gone."

"No you don't." Julian reached across his desk and slammed his hand down. The hiss of the control room doors sealed the four of us in. "There something wrong here, Princess. You're angry, volatile and edgy. You're losing control of your temper and now you're using? We have the right to know what's going on."

Jade pushed between me and our brothers and grabbed my hand. The unwelcome warmth of her connection spread as she invaded my privacy.

I ripped out of her grasp. "Screw the intervention. Run to Reign if you want. Make up a dramatic story about how selfish, stupid Lexi went off the rails and became a doser. Then maybe *he'll* hate me too. Maybe he'll kick me out of Talon. Hell, why stop there, if you make it good, he might kick me out of your family altogether."

"Alexannia Grace," Jade snapped. "You are part of *our* family. Whatever is going on—"

"No." I shook my head, my eyes filling with liquid fury, "I was slow to get the memo, but it's clear I don't measure up to the standards of the group. You've got Galan and your babies now. Bruin's got his precious Mundie. Hell, even Julian's too busy for me since we moved to your mansion. Seven months and he still hasn't found an afternoon to spend wiring my sound system and Internet. He wired the rest of the house though, the Talon are all set up . . . hell, even the Dens have fiber connection so Mika can work over the web."

The words ripped from my chest as the three of them stared. I stepped over to the door and grabbed the handle. I looked tiny but they knew I had strength well beyond my size. "Let me out of here, Julian or I swear I'll rip the door from the fucking frame."

The hiss of the air lock was my signal to make tracks. I couldn't breathe. My ribs and chest ached almost as bad as my back did. Running from the Gatehouse, I followed the stone wall of Jade's compound and bolted for the forest.

Thoughts and emotions swirled in my head, disjointed images of misunderstanding and judgment. *Months?* Julian said they'd noticed I was off for months? Nobody said anything to me. Nobody even bothered to ask how I was.

A gust of February air slapped my face and bit at the tears freezing against my skin. A shiver wracked though me. Where was my jacket? *Damn.* Well, I wasn't going back to get it.

With my arms crossed over my chest, I ignored the sensation of icy shards tunneling into my skin and pushed into the forest. How dare they point fingers at me? I tromped around a rock formation. Sheltered from the scream of winter, I was enveloped in an almost deafening rush of quiet.

Everywhere hurt. My head. My heart. My back.

Why hadn't I gone to Jade about my pain? Tham had urged me enough times. Jade was a great healer.

I dropped to my knees at the edge of the small pond where Reign had found me years ago. He'd said that each one of his kids needed a place of our own. This was mine. Alone in my special sanctuary, my sobs wracked me in earnest.

I didn't cry. Ever. Usually.

I needed to go. The thought of leaving Haven made my throat tighten. Everything I was . . . everything I had become was tied to this mountain: daughter, sister, teacher, fighting instructor, Talon warrior.

..

Where could I go? My first memory was of Reign looking down on me in this forest when I was eight. He'd seemed so fearsome, but then he'd led me across the grounds and toward the Haven castle. *"No tears, Princess,"* he'd said. *"Everything's fine now. I got you."*

When my shins grew numb against the frozen ground, I rolled my weight to the side and leaned up against the trunk of a young birch tree. After lifting the neck of my shirt to cover my skin the best I could, I brought my knees up and wrapped my arms around them.

I'd been wearing a red pendant when he found me. I pulled it out from under my shirt and looked at it. It had grown too tight by my twelfth birthday so Reign had taken it and threaded a new chain. When I began fighting he replaced the delicate white gold links with a leather cord.

My fingers felt stiff, brushing over the polished carving. For sixteen years, I had stared at the piece of red jasper and tried to determine what it was. Some days I saw a flower, others a shamrock, shaped with four identical petals and a design repeated on each of them. Sometimes I thought they looked like curling waves, sometimes I was positive they were wings. Whatever they were, they always warmed me.

I ran my finger over the etched pattern and yawned. It had been so long since I'd had a solid night's sleep and exhaustion was dragging me down. I dropped my necklace back into my shirt and tucked my frozen fingers under my armpits.

Gods I was tired. Something niggled at the back of my weary mind about falling asleep in the cold. The thought was there . . . just beyond my grasp. I yawned and laid my head back against the tree, my heavy eyes falling closed.

I'd just rest for a minute. Just for a minute.

"Alexannia Grace . . . ." An ethereal voice spoke into my dreams and swept through my mind. "Alexannia Grace . . . open your eyes."

My eyes cracked open and I lifted my head. Still sitting in front of my small pond I watched the silver surface glow and give off a lighted mist. Gone was the frozen, ice-encrusted sheet, replaced by the shimmer of liquid gold. I blinked and rubbed at my frozen lashes.

"Alexannia Grace." A girl rose from beneath the ice. She appeared slowly, first a crown of long ebony hair, then graceful shoulders draped in a midnight blue gown and then a small, slender figure, stunning and graceful. I stared as she drew closer. It was as if she were climbing an unseen staircase below the surface.

I was dreaming. Had to be.

When only her ankles remained underwater I scrambled to my feet. She was my size and about my age. When she raised her face and looked at me straight on, I stepped back.

Definitely dreaming. Either that or I was looking into a mirror: amethyst eyes, ebony hair—hers long where mine was short and spiked—the resemblance was spooky.

She eyed me with the same interest. When our gazes locked, she nodded. "So, it's true. Well met, Princess, I am Freya Love, your sister."

"My sister?"

She nodded and held out a gloved hand. "The Queen sent me to bring you home, Princess. You have been absent from your royal life far too long. Your family awaits."

Whoa, Nash hadn't warned me there would be tripping on the downswing of a Haze ride. But after my fight at the Gatehouse I couldn't blame my subconscious for choosing an escape. I stepped to the edge of the pond and peered down by her feet. It just looked like the same dark surface of water it had always been. "And where would we be going?"

She giggled. "To Attalos of course, the home of your people, your birthplace."

The hair on my arms stood on end and I scanned the forest around me. Was this really happening or was it a dream? *Hypothermia.* That's why you weren't supposed to sleep in the cold. I looked back at where I had been napping against the tree, the snow indented from where I had been. Or was I still sleeping? Was I in some kind of interactive vision? I'd had visions where it was tough to separate what was real and what wasn't, but this. . ..

"There is no need for trepidation, blood of my blood. I mean only to return you to our people. The time of our sixth is upon us. We must prepare for the celebration."

"Our sixth?"

"Anniversary of our existence. It has been six year cycles since our beginning."

"Oh? Are you a leap year baby too?"

A strange look flashed behind her eyes but she nodded. "I am your twin, an Eligible as you are. All born of the Queen, on the forgotten day, are Eligibles."

"The Queen? So, I really am a Princess?"

"Of course. Do you know nothing of your heritage? Who was your mentor?"

I shook my head. Reign had arranged fighting mentors and the four of us had academic tutors, but as far as I knew, nobody knew anything about who I was or where I came from. "Am I some kind of a changeling?"

Frustration creased Freya's ebony brow and she studied me. "With the arrival of two, it seems our breeder hid one daughter and presented the other to the Queen. She only just learned of your existence and has sent for you. Do you know none of this?"

"No. I was adopted by a man named Maximus Reign. He never knew where I came from. Just found me abandoned and wandering in this forest when I was eight years old."

"Two," she said, then smoothed out her expression. "We do not accept the markings of time from the other realms. You were placed without the Queen's consent at the age of two."

"I was *placed* without a note or a memory to go on."

Freya's brow arched and her resemblance to me strengthened. "You truly have no knowledge of what is to come? Our celebration? What it means to be an Eligible?"

I shook my head. "Nope. Totally in the dark."

She seemed to find that amusing, but after few seconds of what I could only describe as gloating she held her hand out again. "Then, it truly is time to go. The hour of celebration approaches. Our family awaits."

Family? A real family? Not a cobbled together mess that shits on me the minute I make one little mistake? I brushed my hands over the goosebumps on my arms. My instincts said none of this sat right. That I needed to fall back. Bring her to Reign. Ask questions. Yeah, but apparently my instincts had been off—for months.

Unsure if I was dreaming, tripping, or if this was really happening, I considered leaving. I'd just said I needed time away. Jade and the others would probably think I went underground to cool off. I glanced at the golden mist floating in wisps around Freya's feet and snorted. I supposed this counted as going underground. Besides, if I was gone they might realize how much they'd taken me for granted. Maybe a little worrying would do them good.

"Sure," I said, stepping out to join her. "Let's go."

CHAPTER THREE

I expected the water to be cold, after all, it was mid-February and the pond had been frozen solid ten minutes before my princess sista emerged and did her Jesus lizard on the water impression. It wasn't cold though. It was like stepping into the hot springs. Soothing. Until my cold limbs began to thaw. Slivers of pain splintered across my skin and into my bones as my blood began to flow again.

Freya took my hand before we submerged entirely and for a fleeting moment I wondered if I really wanted to make my first appearance for my homecoming looking like a drowned rat. That thought was short lived. As I opened my mouth to say something she took a breath and went under. I followed.

Bizarre . . . as my head submerged at Haven it emerged into the warmth of a Mediterranean afternoon. Blue skies. Warm salty sea breeze. We rose out of a raised reflection pool in a city center. And I wasn't even wet.

The rush of ocean waves breaking filled my ears. I blinked and tried to absorb. I searched my surroundings to see where the sound was coming from.

The city rose around us expansive and almost Mundie futuristic. Metallic looking buildings with strong architectural arches and rising staircases carried my gaze over the empyreal landscape. The city wasn't composed of skyscrapers. Most of the structures didn't exceed five or six stories, but the hustle and gleam of the surroundings felt very metropolitan.

In the distance, a massive, bronze palace melded into the solid rock of the mountain beyond. With the afternoon light streaming in from above, spires and parapets shone like liquid caramel, reaching up to the bluest sky I'd ever seen.

I turned a slow three-sixty, my ears still thrumming with the rush and crash of water. Ocean waves crashed against an iridescent dome covering the entire city. I followed the line of shimmering silver, bronze and brass spires. Up and up, I followed the arc of an iridescent field. Amazing. It was like one of Jade's privacy bubbles, but it domed the entire city on a massive scale.

Freya and I were helped out of the wading pool by two uniformed guards wearing bronze, sleeveless breastplates, black Kevlar-looking pants and metal wrist cuffs. They each held a six-foot staff with runes running the length of the weapon. Without a word to either of us, they resumed their posts as soon as we descended the six steps into the bustle of the walkway below.

"Follow me," said Freya as she moved into the crowds.

Well-polished citizens draped in silken chitons and richly colored tunics made their way along glittering walkways and across wide, expansive courtyards.

I'd been invited to the most elaborate toga party ever.

I glanced back to the guards at the pool and others at the gates and bridge posts. Sleek, black armor, military stance, and a ranking system that could be indicated by the color banding the shoulder brackets of their chest pieces. My inner warrior nodded in approval.

After checking myself out, I nodded. Passable. My new Jimmy Choo boots were fab and I still had on my leathers, my long-sleeved Under Armour and battle-vest from my 5th period weapons class. I quickened my step to keep up with Freya as she crossed a maze of bridges and paths over and along a complex system of canals.

Water crafts hummed up and down the crisscrossing waterways. I couldn't hear if they were motorized over the sound of water crashing. "How can you stand the noise?" I shouted to Freya. "It's deafening."

Two women ahead of us jumped and turned.

"Then turn it down." Freya rolled her eyes. "In your head."

I stared at her for a moment and she rolled her eyes again. "It's as basic as it gets," she said. I followed her lips, thankful that lip reading was a mandatory surveillance study for the Talon. "For goddess sake, you're a water Fae."

I am? I laughed without humor as my ire rose. Good to know. Fine. If I was some lost descendent of one of the water Fae races I should be able to affect water, right. Hells, yeah. *Silence*, I thought. *Be quiet.* Nothing happened. *Enough.* Freya was fighting back a condescending smile, which just added fuel to the fire of my mood. *Turn. The. Fuck. Down.*

I huffed and turned away from my new-found sibling. Picturing the noise as static coming out of a stereo I reached for my mental volume control and turned down the dial.

"*Ha!*" I shouted as the rush quieted to a background buzz.

When I glanced back to Freya she frowned. She swept her straight, jet black hair over her shoulder and strode off again. "You'll stay at the Palace, of course, until after the celebration of our sixth. Then all Eligibles move to our new homes."

"Cool. What's—All of us? How many of us are there? And what are we eligible for? And what race of Fae are we, cause I've tried to figure out for years where I come from. I've researched them all. And if I'm staying at the Palace why are we going into the town?"

She sighed heavily and eyed me up and down. She fingered my battle vest and glared at my leathers. "You can hardly go before the Queen looking like this."

Freya's shoes *click-clacked* over another wide waterway that passed between a light gold office building and a chrome restaurant. With her skirts fisted in her hands, she booked it toward what looked like a busy part of the city. The gathering of her skirt exposed her feet and the gorgeous pair of midnight blue, open toed sling-backs she wore. Well, whatever her shortcomings in hospitality, she had good taste in footwear.

After a few more twists and turns down side streets and across storefronts, the street opened to a large courtyard. Bronze, metallic trees lined the streets on all four sides, bordering a wide, cement courtyard. From each of these fake 'trees', two or three shiny chrome, hula-hoop swings hung with teenagers perched and twirling in rotating circles. The reflection of the surrounding water pathways bounced off the hoops and glittered in sparkles around the courtyard giving everything a kind of happy-happy kaleidoscope feeling.

"Oh, my." Freya froze then double-timed it along the row of store-fronts. "Over here. Hurry."

A crowd had gathered in the courtyard, voices meshed in raised whispers. I scanned the group and my heart beat faster. I had always stood out because of my size, or lack of it, but here I fit right in. The men were slightly taller than the women, but everyone seemed to have features which either matched mine or accented them. Could this really be where I came from? Where I belonged?

"Would you hurry up?"

I jogged after my sister. "What's the crowd gathering for? What's doin?"

"Nothing you need worry about." Freya climbed the three steps to the entrance of a dressmaker's shop and knocked on the door. "Simply a worthless lawbreaker getting his due."

The door of the dress shop opened and a little man stepped into the doorway. His high-pitched trill cut through the hum of the bustling street. "Princess Love, come in, come in. A courtyard beheading is no place for you and your friend. Such nasty business. Come in."

"Beheading?" I cast a glance over my shoulder. From the store stoop I could see a dozen men in battle-gear standing on a raised platform at the far end of the courtyard. They were erecting what could only be . . . "A guillotine?"

The dressmaker winced, ushering us in to the elegant shop. "Nasty business. Nasty indeed."

After closing the iron door, the little man drew the window shades. I wasn't sure if he had inherited some dwarfism through genetics or if he was suffering from a physical condition. The man barely topped four foot and his legs were proportionately smaller than his upper body. His skin had the faintest green tint to it and his hair was a wiry mass of white standing on end. It gave him the appearance of a summer dandelion gone to seed.

"Who have we here?" He hobbled in a quick circle around me. "Obviously an Eligible. That cannot be mistaken. No. But who? Who indeed. I know all the Princesses—" His eyes lit as his mouth fell open. "You're the one. You are her. The missing. . . Oh, my. Oh, my, my."

Amused by the total befuddlement of this odd, scattered man, I offered my hand. "I am Alexannia Grace."

As the dressmaker gasped, Freya grabbed my wrist and pushed my hand away. "Eligibles do not touch the common." She turned to the man, who was dabbing his wrinkled brow with a swatch of bunched up linen. "Stop sniveling, Stitch. She doesn't know her place. She never had a mentor."

"No mentor?" His eyes softened with an unmistakable sympathy. "How awful for you, Princess. To be taken from your home and not have a mentor."

"I'm sorry." I said, rubbing my temples. "I didn't mean to upset everyone."

Stitch waved my words away and tucked his hanky away "Shall we find you something to wear that exemplifies Grace as the virtue it is? You did say you were the Princess of Grace, yes?"

I caught Freya's nod and repeated it. "Ah . . . yes, that's right. Grace."

Apparently, my second name was the virtue I represented and the Princess of Grace should be decked from toe to ear lobs in lavender. A lavender chiton with a smooth lavender rope twined around my waist and a lavender choker. I adjusted the gown where it gathered over my left shoulder. That, at least was good. If I needed to draw a weapon, I wanted my right arm free. I checked out the look from every angle, pivoting in the mirrored room Stitch and I were in.

It wasn't hideous. Actually, far from it.

And other than giving me a hard time about strapping my thigh sheath under my dress and the fact that I preferred boots to the shoes he insisted I wear, Stitch had been decent about trying to not make me too much of a Faery creampuff. He was right though, I loved the brushed velvet platform pumps.

"Do you have a gown ready for your Sixth-day celebration?" Stitch asked.

"Yeah, a Vera Wang strapless—" I sighed. That dress was hanging in the Haven castle awaiting the bacchanalia ball that was scheduled to take place in six days. Not that anyone in my family seemed all that enthusiastic about it. I bit my lip and shook my head. At least here, my birthday was an event to be celebrated. "I have a beautiful dress in the other realm. Do you think I could send for it?"

Stitch shook his wispy, white head, looking mildly affronted. "I'm afraid not, Princess. A few years back Attalos went through a bad time. The city was sealed off from the other realms and the nobles forbade further import from the two realms. Attalos builds on its own foundation now."

"Oh . . . I see."

"Don't let that sadden you, Princess, I have long finished the preparations for the other Eligibles and will dedicate my undivided attention to creating something spectacular for you. If you wish, of course? I would never overstep."

As he pulled out the fabric swatches again and started to fidget and pat, I shook my head. "No. I'd love to see what you come up with. Should I come back for a fitting tomorrow?"

He lowered his eyes and wrung his hanky in weathered but nimble hands. "Could you give me two moonrises? I must send for a few things from the middle rings. I do apologize."

"The middle rings?"

Stitch dabbed his forehead with his fabric hanky again. "My apologies, Princess. Attalos is laid out with the palace and water lands serving as the nucleus of our world and then the other Faery elemental lands expand in great rings. Next to water is earth, then wind and the outer ring is fire. It rests against the far edges of the cupola shield. I will have to get the permits to import what I need from earth and wind, but I am sure the result will be well worth it."

"No worries. Two moonrises it is." After Stitch and I exited our little funhouse of mirrors, I joined Freya where she'd propped herself on the counter by the door. She was peeking outside from behind the shade, obviously unamused by our little Project Runway.

I patted the pockets of my leathers as I folded them and slipped them into a woven bag I'd been given. "How should I pay you for my gown?"

Freya let out a horrified squeak.

Stitch shrugged. "I am in lifelong servitude, Princess. All I have is yours to take. There is no cost to you or anyone of the royal line."

To take? Before I could respond, Freya grabbed my wrist.

"We have more important issues to address." Freya pushed the door open and dragged me out behind her. "We'll never get back before the Queen retires if we don't get going."

I barely snatched up the bag with my Haven clothes before she yanked me out the shop door. "Thank you, Stitch," I called over my shoulder. "I appreciate your help."

Freya stopped as if she'd hit an invisible barrier and whirled, her lips flapping a mile a minute. It took me a second to turn down the sound of the ocean again, but I got the gist of her rant. "—servitude, for goddess sake. You are an Eligible. Why don't you get that?"

"He is a man who spent the better part of the past two hours with his shop closed so he could dress me. A quick thanks is the least I can offer him, especially since he won't get paid. And since we're on the subject, how is that right?"

Freya rolled her eyes and I had to stop myself from smacking her. That was getting real old, real fast. "What does it matter? He's in—"

"—servitude. Yeah, I got that." With my temper raising I felt the tension snap in the air of the courtyard around us. My instincts kicked into high gear and I reached for my knife. Right. Damn. I hated being light on steel. I glanced into my bag to ensure my battle-vest weapons were within reach.

Freya cast me a dirty look before turning a saccharine sweet smile toward an officer moving to join us amongst the now dense and unsettled crowd. "Master Constable Estes."

"Princess Love." The officer bowed as he stopped before us. Standing more built than any other man in the crowd, Estes reminded me of the warriors of home. Thick, dark hair pulled back in a queue, charming smile and biceps the size of my head. He wore a guard uniform, like the others, but his chest plate was brass instead of bronze and he wore a full, indigo cape instead of the colored banding strips across his shoulder brackets.

"What are you ladies doing here unattended?" Without waiting for our reply, he raised a long, gold whistle to his lips and after two short peeps and one long, two more soldiers cut through the throng of the crowd to join us. "Return the Princesses to the Palace. I don't trust this mob and I wouldn't want anything unforeseen to happen."

Mob? It looked like a whole lotta normal people worked up about a guy getting his head lopped off. "Actually, I'd like to see what's going on."

"That isn't possible, Princess. This is a military matter."

I lifted my wrist to the Master Constable and called my brand. As the enchanted ink of Talon's signature golden hawk prickled onto my skin his eyes widened. "I am a Talon warrior, a military enforcer in all realms. Don't let the gown and heels fool you, Master Estes."

I'm not sure the officer knew what to make of me, but he made a valiant effort to smile. "Be that as it may, I don't think that under the circumstances, that is such a—"

"I can decide for myself, thanks." My gaze shifted back over the crowd. The shrill call of Estes' whistle seemed to have drawn the attention of more than the two soldiers. I was stunned at how many people were throwing thinly veiled scowls our way. "Who is the man being taken onto the block and what exactly is his crime?"

Estes looked at me, then to Freya.

"Excuse me." I waved my hand between them and snapped my fingers. "I asked you the question. Not her. Now tell me, who is the lawbreaker sentenced to die?"

Estes narrowed a dark gaze on me and I saw the warrior within him rise. Despite his air of refined civility, the man didn't like being on the receiving end of an order. "He is a betrayer of the Queen, Princess, and before you ask, he has confessed and has accepted his sentence. This is a fully sanctioned execution. No need to concern yourself."

Over the heads of the crowd I checked out the bronze stage. It glistened in the descending sun, casting copper light up the stone wall it backed against. A man with disheveled brown hair was led across the raised platform to the guillotine. By the slow shuffle of their procession and the awkward gait of the prisoner, his feet must have been bound at the ankles. He wore what once had been an elegant tunic, now ripped and stained with blood. Apparently, other forms of penance had already been exacted from him.

With the guillotine's blade and mouton rising toward the late afternoon sky, a pompous man, wearing a long red coat and a golden sash, strode to the front of the stage. No matter the land or realm, there was no mistaking preening politicians.

Raising a scroll before him, the man read aloud, "Balor, fourth generation breeder to the Queen, barer of Eligibles, has been charged with the following crimes: concealing the birth of an Eligible from the Queen, unlawfully rearing said Eligible for two cycles, accessing the portal pool without permit, traveling beyond the boundaries of Attalos without permit . . ."

The crowd buzzed with a cacophony of gasps and chatter as the orator continued.

My stomach twisted, my mind numb. Was he saying . . .

The prisoner shuffled to the front of the stage heavily favoring his left leg. Battered purple and blue, he straightened to his full height. The hum of the crowd fell silent as he cleared his throat. "I, Balor, seven-time breeder to the Queen of Attalos, confess to all charges and make no apology. The child left in the Realm of the Fair was placed with a host family of my choosing for her own good. Neither she nor her caregiver knew of my deception, actions, or intentions and should not be held responsible."

The man with the sash grabbed a fistful of Balor's hair and yanked his bowed head up to face the crowd. "You see, he confesses and shows not a *kotyle* of remorse. And how did you breach the City safeguards and enter the Realm of the Fair undetected—"

That's my father.

The world spun as the pounding of water crashed inside my head once more. I tried to Flash up to the stage, but my power didn't come. Grabbing shoulders, I squeezed past bodies, forcing my way through the blurred and swirling crowd. The words from the stage were swallowed by the buzz of my own blood thundering in my ears. With my legs and arms heavy as I continued my struggle, it was like swimming with lead limbs to an ever-distant horizon.

"—and you swear no one helped you open the portal pond. You had no aid or accomplice in your actions?"

He smiled then, and I could see what a handsome man he was beneath the violence of his situation. "I do so swear."

The politician scoffed. "A confessed betrayer of our Majesty's grace and a righteous kill for us here today."

"No," I gasped, unable to find my voice. Listing to the side, I grabbed another woman, still well back from the stage and tried to straighten. "Stop this."

With Balor's admission complete, two uniformed soldiers walked him around the back of the structure and laid him along the bench. *I'll never make it.* Balor's hands and legs were strapped down. His head rested in the bottom lunette. They lowered the top piece to encircle his neck.

I'm not sure if he heard my screams or sensed me somehow, but before the blade fell he found me amongst the crowd. The sheer joy that stirred in his soft eyes shattered me to my depths. His irises were violet, like mine, his nose a bit bigger, but the same shape. "Alexannia," I heard in my head as if a memory unlocked, "my sweet daughter."

The violent keening of metal cut through my scream and the world fell away.

CHAPTER FOUR

"*E*asy Princess. Take a couple deep breaths."

I tried to open my eyes, but my eyelids wouldn't obey. Instead, I lay still, letting the deep male voice calm the chaos in my mind. Almost without thinking about it, the rush of water inside my head dialed down to white noise. I breathed through my nose, the spice of the man's cologne and the sweetness of fresh coffee filling the room.

My stomach rolled. "Where . . . am I?"

"You fainted," someone huffed. "Right in front of two hundred people."

My mind pieced together the past few hours, my sibling's judgment, passing through the portal pond, coming to Attalos . . . my lost past.

"A little compassion, Princess," the man said, as two warm fingers pressed against the inside of my wrist. "To discover the man who bred you at the moment of his execution would shock anyone."

The hollow thud Balor's head made when it landed in the catch-basket triggered a violent writhing in my belly. A cold sweat broke over my skin and I rolled to the side.

Freya squealed. "Oh, that's disgusting. Do get up, so we can get out of here." Skirts rustled and she flitted to the other side of the room.

I blinked, my head hanging forward, my watery eyes locked on a pair of stylish charcoal dress shoes splattered with taco nachos extra jalapeno. Oh gods, I'd puked on the shoes of a total stranger. Steeling my insides, I forced myself to sit up and . . . *holy gods*.

Highbornes notwithstanding, this guy in grey slacks and a crisp white shirt was hotness personified. Not a pretty-boy. He was all hard, masculine lines and strong features. His sure grip secured my shoulders and held me over the edge of the settee. "How are you then, Princess. Better?"

He righted my position, propping me against the backrest of the gold velveteen seat and squatted down beside me. "Can I get you a drink?"

I accepted the handkerchief he offered and wiped my eyes and mouth. "Yes, thank you. Something strong. Sorry about your shoes."

He chuckled and stepped away. "I've suffered worse indignities. Don't worry about that."

A clink of bottle kissing glass rang out and then a tumbler with amber liquid pressed into my palm. Whiskey burned its way down my esophagus and warmed my insides as I tipped my head back. "Again," I said, holding up the empty glass to my host with the loose brown waves. "And thanks."

"Not a problem." he topped me up and set the bottle on the dainty side table.

"Where are we?"

"One of the Queen's townhouses," he said. "It was close when you collapsed and I have a key. Master Constable Estes has gone to fetch you a carriage. He should be back any time."

I glanced to the front window of the parlor. It was full dark now, the swirling pink sky of the afternoon killing gone and forgotten. I ran a shaky hand down my leg until I found the nylon hilt of my Guardian, sheathed to my thigh beneath lavender silk. I had no intention of plunging it, though I would muster the strength if needed. My double-edged blade functioned more like a messed-up security blanket.

"And you are?" I tipped back the last of the whiskey.

"Rowan—"

"The carriage is here." Freya whirled over, grabbed me by the elbow and dragged me half staggering off the settee. Before I could think to object, we were across the foyer and through the door. Unsteady as I was, I had visions of tripping down the steps and taking a header right into the large circular fountain in the center of the posh courtyard. Thankfully, I managed to avoid joining life-sized bronzes of the Fates and escaped at least one humiliation for the evening.

"*Love*, is it, Princess?" Rowan's silky timbre had me glancing over my shoulder. The guy leaned casually on the jamb of the townhouse doorway and crossed his feet at the ankles like he was posing for a GQ cover. "Well, it certainly wasn't Compassion, was it? Pleasant evening, Princess Grace. I hope you feel better."

"Lexi," I said, lifting my arm to return his wave. "Please, call me Lexi."

The carriage was more covered Jet Ski than Cinderella's coach. The Master Constable propped a steadying, black boot on the resin edge and helped Freya and then me inside. His ebony gaze was intense, his touch too familiar yet polite.

I ducked under the tasseled cloth canopy and sat in the molded leather seats as the vessel pitched and righted itself. I was numb. My head sloshed as our transport swung into the canal proper.

Everything around me seemed foreign. Had I really been here before? Had I walked these streets as a little girl? Why couldn't I remember my childhood? Even now that I was learning about my past, I had no recollection of the time before Reign took me in at Haven.

Reign. My stomach rolled again and I gritted my teeth. I wanted my dad more at that moment than I ever had. But he wasn't my dad. My dad was that nice man who just—I cut off that thought and covered my mouth with the handkerchief fisted in my hand. I hadn't realized I still had it, but was thankful. It carried Rowan's cologne on it and I focused on that sexy-spice until the fall-apart threatening to overtake me knew enough to stand down.

"Would you like to be dropped at the main entrance or the private residences?"

Freya looked me over and huffed. "Are you serious? I can't introduce her to the Queen looking like she's going to vomit on her. Take us to the residence."

"As you wish, Princess."

I drew a deep breath of warm sea night and sighed. "Does it really matter what I look like? After twenty-four years, wouldn't she want to see me regardless? I'm her daughter."

Freya laughed and shook her head. "No. You're her offspring."

The carriage lurched back as we sped between two manned guard towers and neared the castle. The metal walls of the royal residence looked slick and foreboding against the gleam of the mountain stone. Moonlight spilled through the dome above, illuminating a natural phosphorescence of the stone and causing it to glitter like the tunnels of Dragon's Peak.

Gods, it seemed like a lifetime had passed since Castian sent Jade and me to release the Highbornes from exile. What would they be doing now? Had they realized I was missing?

The canal widened and we merged with the arching waterway that encircled the front of the bronze palace. And again with the black armored guards. "What's with all the military force? Are there security issues I should know about, Estes?"

"Don't be stupid," Freya said. "Really. Who raised you?"

My fists clenched, aching to strike. "A great man and fearsome warrior—Maximus Reign."

Freya looked at me like I was clueless for answering. Obviously, she wouldn't give two shits about who raised me unless it benefited her somehow.

Master Constable Estes, however, cast me a knowing look and my heart ached. Maybe even in this hidden realm, my father's name meant something. He was a legend in the Realm of the Fair. A legend.

And I just walked away from him and everything he'd ever done for me.

"Finally." Freya said as our carriage rocked to a stop. She stood and gathered the skirt of her gown. With the Master Constable's arm at her elbow she stepped out of the boat and under the canopy of the covered dock.

I followed her lead, a little less coordinated because my head was spinning and I was fighting another trip into hurlsville after our water travels, but I think I pulled it off. "Thank you, Master Constable."

He let go of my arm and smiled. "You are most welcome. And Princess, I am sorry your evening turned out as it did. It was . . . unfortunate . . . what happened."

Unfortunate. I straightened my skirts and joined Freya at the residence entrance, my mind and body at war. The little girl in me wanted to ball up like a kitten and cry, but the warrior in me wanted blood. I needed to stab someone. Kick someone's ass. Give me a Scourge raid to attack or a training session with Savage and I could work some of this off.

How could I have lost two fathers in one day?

CHAPTER FIVE

"Forgive me, Princess. I didn't mean to wake you."

I focused a sleepy gaze at the servant girl placing a tray on the dresser, a candle lighting her way. Last night I'd dropped like a rock the moment Freya left, but when images of guillotines and disappointed siblings morphed into agonizing wails and screams for justice I woke and couldn't face dreaming again. "I wasn't sleeping."

"I am Elani. Clothes have been provided in your dressing room. If you have need of anything else, it would be my pleasure to serve you." The little waif bowed, the golden light of her candle illuminating her as she ducked out in the hall without another word. She reminded me a little of Aust's mom, always skirting the shadows of Jade's home, invisible as she delivered a tray of food.

I pushed away all thoughts of Haven and sat up, stretching out some of the night's kinks. Without a window in the suite, there was no way to gauge the time. The only thing I knew was that I couldn't lie around any longer. The glorious Golden Haze had worn off, my back was aching, my nerves were thrumming, and my head was spinning. If I didn't get moving, I might actually peel my skin off my bones.

I would meet my mother today. My mother the queen.

My stomach knotted, the muscles still sore from last night. I revisited Freya's disgust as I puked on the Queen's royal hardwood and laughed to myself. I think she got more than she had bargained for yesterday.

Poor Princess Love.

Princess. I sighed. I'd always loved it when Reign called me Princess. It made me feel special. Choosing it as my *nom de guerre* when I became Talon had been natural too. At Haven and with all my friends, I was *Princess*. Somehow yesterday that changed. Being called Princess here was almost a slap to the face. From the looks of the people in the city crowd, I had a feeling the last thing I wanted was to be one of their Princesses.

As my feet hit the plush carpet, I leaned over and clicked on a lamp. Maybe Freya was the exception. Maybe the other Princesses were nice, normal girls. They would be my half-sisters not my twin, but that was still good, still a family connection. I scanned the gold-leafed, silk strewn room looking for my bag of clothes. There was no sign of it.

I hadn't been carrying anything when Freya dragged me out of the townhouse. I bet my stuff was either still there or lost in the courtyard somewhere. *Damn.* My Jimmy Choo boots were in that bag. *Shit.* Iadon made me that battle-vest and I'd be damned if someone else would palm my blades.

With new purpose, I walked the mile to my dressing room and opened the double, leaded glass doors. Lavender assaulted both my nostrils and my vision. Wonderful. My life had a theme. Ignoring the invasion on my olfactory glands, I took a lookie-loo in the two dozen drawers built into the wall. Lace, silk, tulle, chenille, more lace . . .

Gods doesn't anyone workout here?

I grabbed the lavender silk robe from the hanging bar and smiled as I shrugged it on over my black, leopard print underwear. For now, the matching bra was lost with the rest of my clothes. After tying the robe closed I checked to make sure it was long enough to cover the tip of my dagger. Just in case I tugged my thigh sheath up my leg a little higher.

Heading out the door I thought, maybe I should—

A hand gripped my shoulder.

I reacted before I could think. "Oh, shit, sorry."

Dropping to my knees on the marble tiles, I inspected the kid sprawled outside my door. He wore a brown uniform, different from the soldiers I'd seen yesterday, with a leather sleeveless vest instead of the brass or bronze. Younger than me, probably eighteen or nineteen max, he looked as new as a mint condition nickel. Cute kid, sandy blond with pale sage green skin. He was probably cuter before the split lip.

"Sorry buddy, you scared me. What the hell are you doing sneaking up on people?"

"Uh . . ." He shook his head, blinking shiny moss-green eyes. "Guarding your door?"

I heaved the poor guy to his feet and handed him his weapon. Not the six-foot staff I'd seen in the city, but more like a rune-covered nightstick. "I think I won round one."

He looked like he was deciding whether to be pissed or amused. I was glad when he chose the latter. "Right you are, Princess." He stretched his jaw and probed his swelling lip with long fingers. His eyes widened at my robe and took an immediate survey of the crystal and bronze light fixture on the ceiling. "Forgive me. I . . . uh, please don't report me."

"Report you? For what?" I shoved my girlie parts back into my robe and tightened the sash. "For scaring the crap outta me or copping a look at my rack?"

The moan that echoed in the corridor was almost as cute as the blotchy scarlet blush covering his cheeks and neck.

I laughed. "No harm done. Not much to look at anyway. What's your name?"

"Chamber Guard 11."

I snorted. "Catchy. I take it your mother had a long and painful delivery? Marked from the start, eh? Beaten as a child?"

He chuckled, still studiously surveying the lighting. "Well, no. My given name is Terran."

"Cool. Well, Terran, since first blood has been drawn, I consider us friends. I need a favor."

He looked at me, a determined smile forming. "What do you have need of, Princess?"

"Okay, two favors. One, call me Lexi. I'm sick of all this pompous Princess shit. Two, I need me some workout clothes." Terran's eyes widened. Maybe he was a bit slow or maybe I'd cracked his egg a little harder than I thought. "You know, yoga pants, spandex, something for morning workouts. I'd give my left nut for some Lulu Lemon."

He choked, sputtering until he took a few deep inhales. When he had regained his composure, he gestured down the hall. "I'm sure we can find something in the training wing."

Maneuvering the maze of corridors, we eventually made our way to the training wing. Terran led me to a stack of clothes that reminded me of martial arts gis. Pressed and arranged by size, I picked the smallest one I could find. The drawstring took care of the waist sizing and I cut a foot off the length of the pants and sleeves to complete the tailoring adjustments.

After sheathing my knife, I left Terran standing guard outside the men's locker room and freshened up. My entire world had flipped on its ass in the past twenty-four hours. I didn't think an early-morning moment with some hair gel and mouthwash was too much to ask.

Talon warriors trained to compartmentalize pain and confusion. With the warm water of my wipe down bringing me back to center, clarity returned and my determination to find answers focused.

It left me Jonesing for a little hand to hand.

"Why isn't there a ladies change room?" I asked Terran as he led us out through the staff wing toward the side lawn. "Is that some kind of a male dominance, macho bullshit?"

He chuckled. "Are you always like this, Princess?"

"Like what?"

"Uh . . . head down and horns raised?"

I smiled, liking that analogy. "Call me Lexi . . . and yes."

"Well." He jogged ahead and opened the door for a couple women pushing a linen cart. They froze when they saw me and bowed their heads before shuffling off. "You'll find women here—women of status, I mean—aren't quite as . . . lively as you. They would never instigate sweating, let alone risk the possibility of bruising skin or mussing hair."

"Oh, how feminine." I stuck out my tongue.

He laughed and opened another door. This one led out the far end of the palace to the outside world. After checking if the way was clear the two of us darted for the bronze, metallic wall on the far side of an open-air patio. Terran nodded to the guard posted at the gate. We didn't seem to garner much interest.

By my experience, guards were more attentive when people were breaking into a palace rather than out. When we made it to the shadows behind the wall Terran relaxed again. I glanced back the way we'd come. Because of the height of the wall, I couldn't see anything beyond the upper spires and the points where it met the mountain behind.

While I played within my mind, lowering the volume of the ocean hitting the protective field, Terran led us down and around what felt like a labyrinth of utility paths and over the first of the three moats that Estes had told me emulated the city's rings. The barrier wall edging the one nearest the palace was that same bronze metal I'd seen a dozen times already.

As we walked, I ran a hand over the smooth, sculpted designs etched into the wall, surprised to feel energy surge under my palm. "Cool. What is this made of?"

Terran cast a glance at me rubbing the wall and stopped. "That's orichalcum. It's our primary alloy. We use it for building, coins, lady's trinkets—"

"Weapons?"

Terran shrugged. "Usually not, though I have heard one of the city smiths is forging it strong enough to make a blade. Usually though, it's too pliable."

"And why does it pulse like that when you touch it?"

"Beg your pardon?" He arched a sandy blond brow. "Pulse how?"

I dried my palm against my pants and placed it flat against the metal wall again. The same sensation of electrical current wriggled through my hand and up my arm. "I don't know. It tingles. Like it's got an active component somehow."

Terran placed his hand beside mine and shook his head. "I've never heard of that. Maybe it likes you and is welcoming you home."

I laughed and followed him around the gentle arc of the moat's dividing wall. A rhythmic feminine sigh was coming from somewhere up ahead. It was obvious by the pitch and gasp that someone else was out enjoying the early-dawn seclusion of the staff areas. Terran and I froze as male panting joined the chorus of coitus.

"Oh, Princess," the man said, "how you intrigue me."

Cue more of the feminine giggles.

Doubling back the way we came, we hustled down another side path, leaving the dawn lovers to their fun.

"Forgive me," Terran said, clearing his throat. He kept a solid gaze on the path in front of us. "A poor first impression of life at the palace."

I snorted. "Please, that was the most like home I've felt since I got here. My sister, Jade, married a Highborne Elf. He and his family all prefer to get their grind on in the glory of nature. Tripping into backyard sex is almost a daily occurrence. Voyeurism is unavoidable where I live."

Not for the first time since Freya found me at the pond, I found myself missing Tham. We had fooled around under the moonlight dozens of times ourselves. Not that Terran needed to know that. I wished I'd sent Tham a text or something before I left. Even with everyone angry at me, Tham would understand why I had wanted to come here. Wouldn't he?

Yes. Yes, he would. This was my chance to find out who I was. He would get it. If he were here, he would have snuggled in beside me last night and let me cry, scream and fall apart. Then, like the true friend he was, he would've dusted me off and kicked me in the ass to keep going.

"May I ask you something?" Terran asked, pausing before an opening to another path.

"Sure, shoot."

"Did you really not know who you are all this time?"

"Nope. The big reveal yesterday came right outta the blue. I still need the deets about this whole Eligible thing and how that Balor man was my breeder and gave birth to me. I've never heard of men bearing children before, but hey if I can avoid pushing out a mini-me, that rocks. I like my boobs right where they are and my vagina can crack walnuts.

When Terran could breathe again, we continued.

"And the other realms? What are they really like? The portals were barred before I was born. I've always had a fascination with the forbidden."

I shrugged. "I'd imagine it's not that different from here: good guys versus bad and all the life, love and laughter in between."

Terran nodded. "But the Modern World, the vehicles, their sense of abandon, their vernacular—it's amazing."

"You're crazy. The best thing about the Modern Realm is shopping. Hands down." I thought about the party supplies I'd imported for my Bacchanalia, things I might not get to use now. Was Julian right? Had it been selfish to want to have an amazing birthday? Had I really risked exposure?

As we continued to stroll, Terran and I fell into an easy step. "Was it terrible, Princess? Being raised in the Realm of the Fair? Everyone seems so horrified that you were taken from Attalos, but I think it must have been thrilling."

We turned a corner and headed toward the sheer wall of the mountain attached to the back of the palace. I ran my fingers along the arcing design of the orichalcum wall and sighed. "It's bizarre really. I mean, obviously, I love my family and my life, but I never quite fit. I don't think you really can when you don't know who you are."

I looked down at myself and laughed. "I'm obviously not human. I'm short, stronger than almost any man and have an unquenchable almost obsessive thirst for all the good stuff in life: fighting, drinking and fucking."

Terran choked again and I pounded him on the back.

"So, I knew what I wasn't, but it didn't matter to anyone I cared about what or who I was. They accepted me. Lexi, daughter, sister, friend, fighter or teacher, it didn't matter."

The look on my siblings' faces last night triggered a tightening in my gut. Well, I thought they'd accepted me.

"What is it that you teach?" Terran asked.

"Strategic assault, weapons mastery, anything to do with kicking someone's ass. Likely nothing anyone here would approve of."

Terran frowned. "No, but it just might keep you alive."

CHAPTER SIX

"*A*live? What the hell does that mean?" I jogged behind Terran as he rounded the corner and we found ourselves in a green, grassy clearing surrounded by an orchard of fruit trees. Across the way, a dozen of those black, Kevlar guards faced off, working on close-combat grabs and running through striking weapons and entrenching tools. *Yee-haw.*

Terran gave me a look and I nodded. We'd finish our conversation later.

Tightening up his youthful lope, Terran straightened his back and squared his shoulders. The commanding officer of the group was barking direction as we strode up behind him. Hierarchy in the military saves lives, I knew and respected that, so instead of bounding in and joining the fun like I wanted to do, I played nice and observed until we were addressed.

Standing barefoot on the soft, carpet-like grass I realized, this was the first real greenery I'd seen since I got here. Bronze metal walls and stone floors had a remarkably soothing effect on me, but the cool, strength of green things reminded me of Haven.

When the commander's attention shifted, he looked at me for a long moment, quite expressionless. "What is this?"

"Constable Tasso, Sir," Terran said, staring straight ahead. "The Princess of Grace has asked to observe your men in training. She is new to our City and has heard of the skills of our Queen's mighty Strati soldiers."

"And why does she wear indoor training gear?"

Terran blinked but showed no emotion. "Having arrived late last evening, she has yet to be fitted. The wardrobe provided her was not to her liking and it was too early in the day to rouse her sisters in search of something appropriate."

So . . . Terran wasn't slow after all. The commander's scowl softened, but his beady eyes didn't leave me for a second. He wasn't the first man to feel threatened by me.

"I'm sorry for interrupting your session," I said, offering what I hoped was a genuine smile.

The scowl returned. "If you wish to observe, do so. Settle yourself out of the way and don't disrupt training any further. Princess or not, there is no place for the mounds and valleys of a female in the field of war. I don't care who you—"

"Constable *Tasso*," a voice boomed behind us and squelched the rebuttal about to spew from between my clenched teeth.

The three of us turned to the harsh glare of Master Constable Estes. With his shoulders stretched to his full height and his brow deeply creased, his dark features raised the hair on my skin. "You are addressing an *Eligible!*"

"Apologies, Master Constable."

Estes joined our little group, his gaze sweeping over my garb. "Princess Grace is an important guest of the Queen's and will be awarded the highest courtesy you and your men have to offer. If she wants an extra guard you will provide it. If she wants a dance partner you will clear the floor and start the music. And if she simply needs directions to the grand dining room you will escort her through the palace and pull the damn chair out for her. Is that clear?"

"Perfectly, Sir."

Estes frowned, still looking piqued. "Take a shuttle to bridge two-sixteen. There are reports of violence and thievery along the outer ring."

"Two-sixteen is in the Badlands of the fire ring, sir."

Estes arched a brow. "And?"

Tasso shifted his weight from one foot to the other. "That's tier one work. I'll send one of the duty soldiers—"

Estes looked almost amused as he leaned closer. When he spoke, his voice was calm and controlled. It crept across my skin like shade beneath the passing sun. "I said nothing of deploying duty soldiers. You are relieved of your duties here. Now go."

Tasso didn't argue. He lowered his gaze and turned to go.

Though the scene was really none of my business, the tension was electric, much too entertaining to turn away from. As he stepped past me, Tasso's eyes fixed on mine, dark coals in the bright morning light. 'You did this' they said, and, 'I won't forget it'.

That's fine. Neither will I.

When the fiery orange of Tasso's cape disappeared out of the clearing, Estes pulled Terran to the side and spoke to him privately. The Master Constable didn't seem to be angry and though Terran was standing at attention a good distance away, his responses remained straight forward. Yes sir. No sir.

"Princess?" Estes said as they rejoined us. "Chamber Guard 11 assures me the two of you have gotten on well enough this morning. Do you share his opinion on that?"

I caught Terran's wide gaze and smiled. "Yeah, I do."

"Very well. I'm assigning him as your personal guard." Estes held up his hand as I made to speak and shook his head. "Indulge me. Your return is the talk of the city. It would lessen my worry if a palace duty soldier was with you. This is no time for an Eligible to be alone."

"All right." I tilted my head toward the five soldiers in black, glaring at me from where Tasso had been holding their training session. "So, what's up with them?"

Estes lifted an ebony brow. "Your guard said you were looking for a dawn workout." He gestured to the stiff-lipped group. "I offered for you to join these men."

That piqued my interest and I took a closer look. Physically they were conditioned, thickly muscled through arms, shoulders and thighs. They held themselves with confidence and seemed comfortable within their frames. Young, but strong.

"There are two types of soldiers in Attalos," Estes said. "The duty soldiers and the Queen's guard, which we call Strati. The Strati are the city's strongest and most promising warriors. With the rising conflicts flaring from the outer ring, the Queen is strengthening her forces. I'd like to see how they fare against a warrior from outside the realm"

I eyed the five and my heart quickened its pace. They were out to make me suffer. "Cool . . . but I have to warn you, with the Alice in Wonderland turn my life has taken I'm going to be tough on them. I need the exertion."

"Then enjoy your workout." Estes gestured for the Strati to close in. "See if they possess the mettle to become more than they are. I believe the trainings here have left them lacking in some areas. The nobles refuse to listen. They think it foolish to restructure a military system that has been in place for millennia."

I eyed the men. They were obviously insulted by our conversation and the order to spar with a woman in front of a high-ranking commanding officer.

Ooooh fun. "All right. I'll see what they've got."

Estes bent at the waist and stepped back. "Begin at your pleasure."

A guttural growl came from the one on my right. "Permission to speak freely, Princess?"

"Of course. Always."

"There's not much to you. Ydorus and I will snap you like a glass doll. You should run along back to your quarters and play hair and dress-up. We don't wish for you to get hurt."

"Yeah," another one chimed in. "You have much to learn from the other Eligibles."

I snorted. "Ah, that's sweet, but when I can't sleep I get cranky and when I'm cranky, I really should crack a few heads before I'm put under pressure or I tend to go off. I'm supposed to meet the Queen for lunch. Wouldn't want to cause a scene now, would I?"

"Enough talk," a soldier in the back said, his gaze narrowing on me. "If she needs a lesson on what roles are fit for women in Attalos, I have no problem teaching her."

I snorted again. "You're not my type either, hon, but my father taught me it was rude to point out a man's short-comings. It makes him bristle."

"Bristle, eh? Well, Princess, if you swear not to go crying straight to the courts saying that we abused you, and you're sure you won't reconsider . . . ready yourself for battle."

Yee-haw.

~

A good while later, with my mind finally settled and my body aching for all the right reasons, I accepted the canteen from Estes and joined him and Terran under the shaded umbrella of one of the clearing's date-plum trees.

"Well?" Estes asked, watching the last two soldiers I'd faced off with. Their comrades had hauled their asses upright and were currently in different stages of regrouping their manhood. "What do you think?"

"They're decent fighters." I gulped down three large swallows of sun-warmed water. It was stale but wet. I gulped down a bit more. "They're too rigid in technique. It makes them slow on adaptation. Maybe because I'm a woman they underestimated me. Maybe not."

Estes nodded. "Thank you, Princess. If you find yourself in need of another workout and wish to continue working with the Queen's men, that can be arranged."

Terran's unfinished warning still niggled in my head. "I'm not sure what my days will be like yet, but I'll think about it." I scanned the crowd of bruised egos, reluctant respect, and all out fury. "Nicely done, guys. Don't let your pride take a hit because I'm a woman. Like you said, I'm not from around here. Besides, you gave me quite a workout."

One of them huffed, his lips pursed. "Don't patronize us, Princess. You aren't even winded."

"Next time. If you'd like a rematch I can show you where you faltered." The daggered looks were nothing I hadn't seen a hundred times before.

"Who taught you to fight, Princess?" one asked.

"My father." My stomach knotted and a pang of betrayal flipped in my gut. The kind-eyed man in the courtyard had been my father too, yet I knew nothing about him. "I was raised by a warrior named Maximus Reign."

Estes adjusted his breast plate when he stood and joined us. "You men would know him as the Reign of Terror. Those legends of the unstoppable warrior from the Realm of the Fair have been whispered as bedtime stories for decades."

Eyes widened and jaws dropped slack. It warmed me that Reign's reputation had touched this secluded corner of the Realm of the Fair. Made me feel less cut off from him.

Terran and I turned back toward the palace. "If you want a rematch, boys," I called over my shoulder. "I'm sure the Master Constable knows how to contact me. Or not. Your choice."

CHAPTER SEVEN

"You move like lightning." Back in my suite, Terran showed me how to open the vanity mirror in the dressing cabinet and then took up a formal position standing just inside my door. "I've never seen anything like it. And your sister, Jade, is a warrior too?"

"Mhmm." I'd finished my bath and was trying to get my spikes to stand up with the slimy paste that passed as hair gel in this city. "She's different though. I'm speed and strength, Jade has powers. She can call on the strength of the gods."

"Truth or tease?"

I giggled. Terran seemed to catch on to sarcasm rather quickly, but still couldn't tell when I was using it or not. "Truth. She was adopted by Reign, like me, but her biological father is Castian Latheron, God of Fae gods."

"And you know him?"

"Castian? Yeah, I know him." I flicked my way through the forest of eye pencils standing at attention and found a green that would accent the purple of my eyes. Terran stared across the room at me, his face screwed up like he didn't believe me. "Truth, I swear. I know him. When I get this all figured out and contact my Haven family, you can ask Jade."

Terran sat up straighter. "Contact your other family? How will you do that?"

I shrugged and pushed my lips out. I found a great mango lip-gloss in my welcome basket. "Once I get my clothes back, I'll call them on my phone. Between my genius brother Julian and Castian's godly mojo, Talon tech works in any realm."

Terran rubbed his palm over his mouth, looking concerned. Moving directly behind me he bent down to speak close to my ear. "You must be careful. You shouldn't—"

"Oooo there she is." A chorus of giggles and chatter invaded my suite. It was hard to determine how many Princesses had descended upon me since they had obviously just popped out of their genie bottles and all of them dressed and spoke exactly the same.

"Princess Grace," one of the harem said, "these are Princesses Charity, Faith, Hope, Mercy, Peace, Purity. . ." The list went on as elegant fingers and curtsying maidens identified themselves one by one. I scanned the crowd, the vapid smiles, the flowing skirts and the ringlets bouncing against blushed cheeks. Besides them all having the same amethyst eye color as me, I couldn't see any indication that these were my peeps. I mean . . . *really*?

It took about two seconds before they noticed I was still in my robe and started scrounging in my closet, picking out what I should wear to be presented to the Queen.

"Princess Love told us all about you not having a mentor." Insert a chorus of identically pity-filled gasps. "And that you weren't even raised as a royal?"

In that moment, I had never been so glad that Reign had raised me in my life. Thank the gods, or the Fates, or Balor or whoever connived to have me raised differently than these women. They were staring at me. I'd missed something and they were waiting for a response.

Shit.

"Of course she does, Princess Zeal," Terran said, accepting a violet scarf from the outstretched hands of one of the blond ones. "Princess

Grace was just saying how she loved the contrast of violet next to her eyes. How thoughtful of you all."

I nodded and reached out for the embroidered scarf Terran was holding. "Yes. Thanks. It's beautiful." I flashed Terran an adoring smile until a familiar sensation heated my spine.

Oh, no. *Not now.*

With as much calm as I could fake, I grabbed Terran's wrist and shot him an urgent look. His gaze met mine and his eyes widened. My irises would be almost completely violet by now. *Shit, I should have given him a head's up on this. Just once could I leave my freak-defect out of things?*

Terran discreetly sat me back into my make-up chair and ushered the crowd out of my bathroom and toward the door. "All right ladies, Princess Grace needs to gather her composure before meeting the Queen. It's a very exciting time and she needs to . . ."

From one instant to the next my consciousness transported from my suite inside the palace into a windowless room, dimly lit by the glow of pillar candles. Blue smoke rose up from a wide stone hearth to coil beneath blackened beams and what appeared to be an earthen ceiling. The sinister cloud roiled above the head of a sixty-something brunette with a hot-pink racing stripe in her hair. She tipped her head back with a glass bottle propped between red wine lips.

I sniffed cautiously. Beyond the tang of incense and the earthy musk of moss, the heady bite of alcohol filled my head. I stepped further into the shop.

The woman lowered the bottle and swallowed. Ahh, cherry brandy . . . and by the kick and burn that hit the back of my throat, it was quality stuff. I swallowed reflexively and moved toward the long wooden counter that ran the length of the room. When I got close, she clutched her hand shut and stiffened. With narrowed eyes, black in the dim cast of the candle's glow, she swept a suspicious glare around the room.

Cool. Could she see me? No, she stared right through me into the glow of the candles beyond. After a shake of her head she took another swig and really focused on making some deposits into her mindless buzz account.

Why was I here? Usually visions showed me something important, something that needed to be stopped or interrupted: a Scourge raid on an unsuspecting village, an exiled race about to be reinstated . . . or occasionally where I left my cell phone. From time to time I got a voyeur's look into the personal lives of the people I was close to. Sometimes real personal, but hey, I had no control. The Fates showed me what they showed me and I had no choice but to sit back and enjoy it—no matter how naked people got.

I stepped over to the sideboard on the opposite wall and snooped: candles, herbs, essential oils, charms and potions.

Wing of bat and eye of newt.

After downing the majority of her liquid relief, the numbing blanket began to settle over my bones. It did nothing to ease my mind, but interactive boozing was an unexpected perk and the tension in my muscles and bones eased. When a clock in the distance struck noon, the woman got to her feet, took a quick balance check and then brushed back the tangle of chestnut and fuchsia hair that fell behind her shoulders.

Abandoning the near-empty bottle for a freshie, she blew out the candles and scooped soil from the dirt floor with her boot to smother the fire. Straightening, she reached for the edge of a glass fronted cabinet and I expected her to pick out some kind of sleep remedy or hangover cure. She didn't. The entire cabinet pivoted from the wall.

Behind that neat lineup of bottles, herbs and potions was a hidden door. Before I could get close enough to follow her, she slipped through the opening and pulled the cabinet to right itself against the wall.

"All right, Terran, here she comes."

I followed the soothing timbre of two male voices. As they whispered, warm fingers brushed against my brow and pressed against my neck. I hated to wake up. There was an inverse relationship between the clarity of my mind and the distance between my head and the floor. When I came back from my little trips to vision-landia my head spun and I wouldn't have the strength or the capacity to sit up.

"Lexi." Terran's voice was much higher pitched than usual. "Lexi wake up. Please Princess. Wake up."

I pried at my eyes but the best I got was a weak-ass flutter before they closed again. Yep, the centrifuge had started and my brains were scrambling in a cyclone of the dizzies.

"Lexi?" The second voice was much deeper, richer. "Try to open your eyes again, Princess. Come on. Your guard heart will surely fail if you don't come around soon."

Poor Terran. I didn't want him to stroke out. I tried to lift my hand but it weighed a thousand pounds. Did I manage to flex my fingers? I must have because someone clasped my palm. I tried again to open my eyes.

"Hello again. Welcome back." It was the looker with the loose brown curls. No. In the buttery light of the gold-leafed sconces there was quite a bit of copper in his hair. Nice.

I blinked fast and swallowed hard. *Gods, please don't let me puke on him again.* A low moan escaped my chest before I could stop it. I breathed deep. There it was . . . that delicious scent he had. Male spice blended with clean masculine sweat and coal smoke.

Mmm, you smell delicious.

He raised a brow and chuckled.

Shit. Did I say that out loud?

"Now Princess, would you like to sit up?" My head bobbed heavily on my shoulders as he sat me up. When I listed to the side he slid behind me, wrapped a solid arm across my collarbone and pulled me against his chest. Warmth leached from his chest to my back and everywhere else his body made contact with mine. "Better?"

I nodded. "Chocolate."

"You'd like chocolate?"

I nodded again.

"I'll be back," Terran said and disappeared in a blur.

With my eyes closed and my head cradled under Rowan's jaw I let the world spin in whatever vortex it wanted to. After what could have been hours, but was probably only a few minutes, the worst had passed. I forced myself to give up my happy place and sit up.

"This is becoming a bad habit," I muttered.

"Or a good one," he smiled. It was genuine and lit his hazel eyes. "I've always had a bit of a white knight complex. Swooning damsels are my specialty."

"Dream on. I'm no one's damsel. You just happened to be—" I looked around my suite and then back at him sitting on my plush gold rug. "What are you doing here?"

"You passed out."

"No. Not in my suite. What are you doing in the palace?"

"I was checking on one of the other Eligibles. Seems she had a nasty run in with one of her sisters and a hot iron. First degree burns to her forehead and ear."

"Really? And they called for you?"

He narrowed his eyes. The hesitation was subtle, but after years with the Talon, I heard the lie before the words were spoken. "Seems so."

"Don't they have medical staff within the palace?"

He leaned forward until we were almost nose to nose. "One would hope, though I do specialize in burns. Dangerous things, straightening irons."

The air crackled between us. "If I was intending to do damage to someone, I'd use daggers."

A smooth brow arched as his features softened. "Right, I forgot. I brought you something." Rowan launched to his feet in one graceful motion and strode out of my ensuite. He returned a few seconds later holding the cloth bag Stitch had given me to hold my belongings. "Peace offering. You rushed out of the townhouse so fast, you forgot them."

Dragged out, was more like it. "Thank you."

Rowan handed me the bag and took a step back. "It's all there, I assure you," he said, as I had a quick look, "leather pants, boots, a well-armored vest . . . oh, and my personal favorite." He reached into the bag and fished out my black leopard print bra.

I snatched it from his hands and stuffed it into the depths of the bag. "You went through my stuff?"

He shrugged, unrepentant. "I was curious about the mysterious 'missing Eligible'. The whole city is talking."

"I honestly don't care."

He laughed. "Most of the Princesses—no, all of them—would die to be the talk of the city."

"Yeah, well, I'm not much like the other Princesses if that giggling display of skirts and estrogen was any example." With an assessing gaze, he held his hand out to help me up. Ignoring the offer, I got to my feet and moved to the living area of my suite. Those bright hazel eyes continued to scrutinize me to the point of thoroughly checking me out.

I pulled out my battle-vest and shrugged it on over the figure conforming robe.

The corners of Rowan's mouth twitched. "Better?"

Clutching the two hilts sheathed over my navel, I drew both daggers. I flipped and turned the weapons in my palms like a bored kid with two pencils. "Better," I said and slid the blades home.

"Interesting look." Terran kicked the door closed behind him and strode to my side. After a quick once over, he handed me a big-as-your-head wedge of chocolate cake. "Are you well? You scared the stuffing out of me."

I snorted, choking on the cake I'd just shoveled into my mouth. "Stuffing? Oh, man we gotta work on your warrior vocab."

Terran's smile was short lived before he grew serious. "Are you, Lexi? Well?"

I swallowed the chocolate ambrosia in my mouth and licked my lips. "Sure. Happens all the time. No biggie."

"No biggie?" Terran hissed, his arms now animated and flailing in the air between us. "I thought I'd failed you on my first day as your personal guard. I thought you were poisoned . . . or dying. I didn't know whether to call the palace medics or the guards or—"

I set the cake on the sofa table and gave Terran a hug. "Breathe, my man. I've heard it's freaky to watch, but really, I'm fine. You didn't sound the alarm, did you?"

He shook his head.

"Good. I'd like to keep my business to myself if you don't mind. Besides, Doc Rowan was house-calling it anyway. What's one more Princess train wreck."

Rowan retrieved the plate and placed the cake back into my hand. "I'd hardly call you a train wreck, Princess. And if chocolate helps with the aftermath of your seizures, eat more. Doctor's orders."

I took another mountain of a bite and considered setting Rowan straight. Should I tell him it was a vision and not a form of some kind of epileptic shake-rattle-and-roll? Did I really need him to know about my inner freak? No. I'd tell Terran later when we were alone. Maybe the two of us could figure out what I'd seen after—

"What time is it?" I shoved my plate at Terran and checked the digital panel on the wall beside my bed. "Shit. I'm late to meet the Queen."

I tore toward the dressing room then remembered my bag. Racing back, I grabbed my bra from the bottom and sent Rowan a warning glare as he started to snicker. "Not one word, Doc. I can cut a man's balls off eight different ways and I'm not above doing it."

The bastard just laughed harder.

CHAPTER EIGHT

My bare feet squeaked on the polished marble as I skidded to a halt outside the Queen's receiving room. *Damn.* I was really late. "Well, my first meeting with my biological egg donor is off to a roaring start."

"Don't panic," Terran whispered, passing me my shoes and offering a hand to steady me as I slipped them on. "Just remember what I said. Try to conform to their ideals. Or at least appear to. Nobles are a backstabbing, dangerous group."

The Strati guards standing sentinel on either side of the massive doors pretended not to notice my hiked-up skirt while I slipped into the shoes Stitch had sold . . . well, given me yesterday. When I was buckled and smoothed and had caught my breath, Terran gave me a hand signal I equated to thumbs up and I nodded. Each guard took hold of a long curlicue door handle that resembled an ocean wave and, before I could change my mind, I was gliding across the gleaming, bronze floor toward a couple dozen dapper citizens.

The room wasn't so different from the main receiving room at Haven castle. The long rectangular space was bordered by an arching colonnade on both sides which drew the attention of visitors up a grand four-step staircase to the throne. The opulence of it all reminded me of the ballroom I recently converted for my Bacchanalia.

I pushed away thoughts of what was behind me and raised my chin. I was late. I needed to be present now in mind as well as body. Maybe 'better late than never' translated into this world and I would be forgiven. I met the cold emerald green stare of the Queen and flinched.

Then again, maybe not.

A classic beauty, Hollywood-leading-lady gorgeous, from the elegance of her high cheekbones to her flawless olive skin to her sleek, feminine lines. She stood as I approached, her glossy raven hair falling dagger straight to her hips. Every male in the room stood a little straighter. Descending the stairs, her scarlet silk gown flowed and shimmered in the light of the crystal chandeliers.

"Good of you to join us." The *finally* was silent, but understood. Gods, her voice was amazing and the instant after she spoke, every trace of hostility vanished.

I bowed and lowered my head. "I'm so sorry I'm late. I meant no disrespect to you or your court." I scanned the faces of the close to thirty courtiers dressed to the nines, all of them scowling down at me. All, that is, except one smart-assed onlooker with loose brown curls who scooted into the back of the pack.

What is he doing here?

"Don't mention it." The Queen cooed. "I was told you fell momentarily ill?"

Without her smile and the hint of gentleness in her voice her words could have seemed harsh. Instead, what she said almost came off as concern.

"Momentarily," I said, shooting Rowan the sweetest, dirty look I could manage. He stayed stoically straight faced, but his eyes sparkled with amusement. Bastard. "I'm better now and I apologize for keeping everyone waiting."

The Queen nodded and grasped my wrist, her touch cool and firm.

Without a word, she led me past the crowd of royal admirers and through another set of double doors, to a dining room. Crystal glittered, reflecting the day's light beaming through stained glass windows. The table was set with sparkling silver cutlery, bronze chargers and gold vases overflowing with enough flowers to choke a horse.

Flowing straight toward a massive gilded chair at the head of the table she released her grip. Nettles pinged and tingled into my hand as the blood began to circulate again.

"An introduction before your homecoming luncheon begins." The Queen scanned the crowd and caught the gaze of one of the men in the shadows and half-hidden behind other members of the court.

At first glance, he seemed a few years older than me with short dark hair and a stride which reminded me of what Jade and I called the Highborne prowl. Yep. When a man looked at you a certain way and strode with loose limbs of a jungle cat and confidence in his hips, there was nothing you could do but curl up and be his prey. And this guy had that. In spades.

"Alexannia Grace, birthed of the late breeder, Balor," she paused mid-sentence, looking down to smooth the waist of her gown where it clung to her perfect figure. "May I present Lir-Zale, son of the seventh house, and your betrothed."

At that moment, the world became a blur of WTF. "I'm sorry, my wha—"

The dark-haired Mc-dreamy kissed both my cheeks and whispered something about how lovely I was.

I pulled back, a whole lotta oh-no-you-don't on the tip of my tongue.

Servants appeared in every direction with champagne flutes of sparkling blue liquid. The crowd gathered and before I could put the brakes on the celebration, Zale and I were swept into toasts and congratulations then seated across from each other at the right and left hand of the Queen.

"And so, as is customary," the old priest-guy next to me said as the luncheon droned on, "the hand of the Eligible goes to a son of one of the Noble Houses. It was set in the stars the night you were born and now that you've returned to Attalos, you will be wed."

I gave up picking at my lunch and took another long swallow of blue drink.

It was hard to argue with a priest. Probably, the reason he'd been chosen to sit next to me to explain this. Good strategy. I'd dreamed about having a mother my whole life but there was no way in hells I was marrying some guy just because my birthday was five days away and she wanted me to. I needed to speak to her alone . . . to explain that this arrangement was crazy. Marriage didn't happen like this where I came from . . . but this *was* where I came from.

I upended my blue cocktail and set the empty glass back onto the silk tablecloth.

The priest patted my hand. He seemed harmless despite his nose being broken too many times to ever be straight and his fingers, which curled as if they too had been broken but hadn't healed properly.

"Wow," I said for what must've been the eleventy-millionth time. "But—"

"There are no buts in tradition, Princess," he said, topping my glass with a sympathetic smile. "The laws of Attalos are absolute. All Eligibles must wed by their sixth celebration and yours is within the week. Thank the goddess Lir-Zale has been gracious enough to forgo the term of courting for the sake of time."

"For Her Highness, it is my pleasure," Zale said, bowing his head from across the table.

My mother patted the back of his hand where it lay on the golden silk. He was deliciously charming, but the thought of marrying the guy parked a Volkswagen squarely on my chest.

"Now," he said, flashing me a conspiratorial wink, "if I might steal away my soon-to-be-bride, we have much to learn about each other."

"Of course." The Queen raised her hand and gestured that we were dismissed.

Zale strode down the length of the table and back up again on her side. I wondered why he didn't just pass behind the Queen's chair but then thought maybe that was a no-no. When he arrived at my side, he held out his hand. "Shall we, Princess?"

Somehow, I got my feet under me and stood. The dozen or more men at the table stood and bowed their heads. What was I supposed to do? Who the hell knew? I placed my napkin on my chair and curtsied. "Your majesty, gentlemen, ladies."

When the clink and murmur of the royal luncheon faded behind us, I chanced a glance at my companion. He stood out in a well-groomed, polished sort of way. For some reason, I thought about Rowan. He was a looker too, but not as pretty. Rowan had a more chiseled 'been-there-lived-through-it' energy that showed in the clench of his jaw and the depths of his gaze.

"So that's what all the *Eligible* stuff has been about? I'm eligible to get married?" The two of us walked along the side grounds of the palace. Terran followed just behind us, walking with a boy who accompanied Zale. The kid was a skinny little rake of a thing with a mop of ginger hair. "That seems a little anti-climactic. I was thinking it was going to be some sort of Hunger Games competition where we had to prove ourselves worthy. Maybe fight to the death to be named the top daughter. A real 'there can be only one' moment."

Zale's eyes widened, but quickly regained his air of perfection. "It is a betrothal. The Queen claims no daughter. Eligibles are merely offspring, nothing more."

I managed not to curse out loud, though my gut clenched. I'd waited years to find my parents and now my mother was no more than a genetic donor who had my father executed and was pimping me off to one of her noble followers.

I'm not sure what my expression showed—anger and confusion at being denied after finally finding my mother, defiance of the whole death-do-you-part scenario being forced on me—but Zale smiled as if he understood. His dimples showed and reminded me of Tham.

Damn, how I ached to talk to Tham.

We continued to walk in the awkward silence of strangers until finally he took my hand and squeezed. "I realize this must be a shock for you. A mentor would have prepared you on what it means to be the wife of a noble. The realm is in the midst of chaos. We must ensure the continuation of the strength of our race."

"Continuation? Like kids?"

"Savages from the outer rings have been targeting the inner city. It is incumbent on the nine houses to ensure the well-being of all Attalos' citizens. It's about more than children. We promote the image of well-being to the common. We host fine parties, sponsor sporting tournaments, make ourselves visible in the city center. We safeguard the image of normalcy."

"Sorry to disappoint you, domesticity is no strength of mine."

"No matter. There will be plenty of time after our union to settle into your role. Besides, you will have staff and your sister wives to help you acclimate."

Staff? Well, okay, that sounds— "What? What the hell is a sister wife?"

Zale lifted my hand to his lips. *Awkward.* He had soft, well-manicured hands. Exactly the kind of hands you'd expect from a nobleman. "You are an intelligent woman, Grace, attractive too—despite the cut of your hair and your girlish form. I'm certain you will rise to be head-wife before long. You already intrigue me beyond the others."

I tried to slide my hand out of his, but he squeezed tighter. My first instinct was to drop him right there on the manicured lawn, but I thought better of it. The past twenty-four hours had been a shitstorm of emotions. I didn't understand the rules of this game yet, but I wasn't ready to quit and go home.

My chest tightened as I remembered Bruin saying those exact words to me back in August. He and Mika had just been branded as mates and she was resisting him. I couldn't stand the hurt in his big turquoise eyes and was damned if I'd give her a polite pass on it like everyone else.

Bruin told me Mika was new to the game and I couldn't kick her out before she had a chance to learn the rules.

I didn't get it then. Yeah, well, I guess the Fates were having a good laugh now. Yuck it up, bitches.

Zale leaned closer. "This is the way we have rebuilt the houses of the nobles for almost three decades. The laws of Attalos are absolute. Besides, it could be worse. Couldn't it? I'm not a tyrant or an ogre. I have all my teeth and the men in my family keep their hair."

Yes. It certainly could be worse. I forced what I hoped was a convincing smile and relaxed my hand in his. "And just how many wives do you have?"

He nodded to the guards opening the gate for us and we exited the palace grounds. The afternoon sun warmed the chill that had set over me as we strolled toward the city center.

"Currently two," he said as if the women were luxury cars parked in his garage. "Temperance was my first. She and I were wed eight years ago when I was twenty-one. Then Chastity joined us on the last cycle. You'll like her. She has a bit of the same defiant quality I see in you. Likes to hide my keys to get a rise out of me."

My minded buzzed as Zale painted the bizarre picture of his marital ménage. "So, now I'll be added in as the third wheel?" *Hells no.* Not how I pictured my happily-ever-after. And no offence to Chastity and her kinder-klepto routine, but he'd never seen defiant like I was about to show him.

"Yes. You'll be the third and your twin sister Love will be the fourth. Your unexpected return to the fold caused quite a stir in the allocation of brides. Idikos, son of the second house is not even four cycles and wasn't intended to be a husband until one more cycle had passed. They weren't sure where to place you, but I assured them that I would welcome both you and your sister as one."

I'm a twofer. Fucking Fates.

My mind-buzz caused the tides in my gut to churn. By the time we arrived at the next gate, I was seriously considering ducking into the metal shrubs to vomit. Stepping over the bridge, we walked along the orichalcum wall as Terran and I had early this morning. I raised my free hand and skimmed the surface. Like before, energy surged into my arm, tingled through my bloodstream and unexpectedly calmed the eels flipping in my stomach.

Zale scanned the bronze spires and glass walls of the cityscape as if deciding where to head next. "Since you had no mentor, you must be overwhelmed with questions. How about we spend the afternoon together and you can learn a bit about where you come from."

As much as I wanted to punch Zale in his precious pie-hole and scream, instead, I nodded, craving information about my heritage more. "I'm not sure one afternoon will cover it."

"I'm all yours. First question."

"Can I step down as an Eligible? Refuse this?"

Zale actually had the gall to look hurt. "Refuse? We're trying to rebuild our noble houses. Being an Eligible is a position of the highest honor in Attalos."

"Yeah . . . so, can I? Refuse?"

Zale's lips pursed tight. "You cannot. If you aren't wed by your sixth anniversary in five days' time, you will be executed as a betrayer of the Queen's will."

My hand skimmed down the purple silk of my gown and found the bump of my knife hilt sheathed just beneath the fabric. "Then maybe I should consider this whole thing a wash and go home. I'm sure my father is frantic and is tearing apart the realm searching for me. Maybe I should just go."

Zale searched my expression with a focus I didn't understand. "I hadn't envisioned you would give up without learning the answers to questions which have surely plagued your entire life."

As we walked on in silence, I glanced over my shoulder to make sure Terran and Zale's servant boy were still cool. When our gazes met, Terran's gaze lacked any sign of his natural spark. His expression remained guarded and cool.

"Attalos is a floating realm," Zale said bringing my attention back to him. "It travels unseen by members of both realms. We are a private race of Fae who chose to distance ourselves from others in the dark times of persecution."

"And I'm Water Fae? That's what Freya said."

"Yes. All Eligibles have been engineered to be Water for almost seven cycles—since a civil uprising cost many lives. Water are known for their intelligence and leadership. Unlike the savages attacking and stealing from the outer rings."

"The citizens of other elements? They were behind the unrest?" He nodded and we turned to follow a wide canal toward the metropolis of the city. I checked over my shoulder. Terran nodded, looking calmer.

"When I was a young boy, Fire Fae tried to overthrow the Queen. They demanded Her Majesty stand down."

"Had they ever been violent before?"

He shook his head. "There was a terrible battle, but when they failed to overthrow the Queen they went after the nine houses of nobles. It was a terrifying time. My father locked Mother and I away in a hidden cabinet behind the library bookshelf. It was dark and we were stranded for days, hungry and frightened."

"And what happened?"

"The very structure of our race is governed by the nine houses. With many of them killed, there was a restructuring of the affinities. Fire Fae were sent to the outermost ring, Wind and Earth the next two in that order and Water kept control of the city."

"And your father?"

"Killed and praised as a hero of a terrible time."

"And all this happened when?"

"A few years before you would have been born."

"So, the Queen began rebuilding the noble houses by prostituting her offspring to the sons of the nine houses of Water Fae?"

Zale cast a frantic glance around us. "How could you say such a thing? Our Queen is a righteous and proud woman. Everything she does, she does for the benefit of our people."

Uh-huh. "And if they stand against her they get their heads chopped off. Very democratic."

Zale squeezed my fingers until I felt the bones grind together. "I don't know how it is where you come from, Princess, but here in

Attalos women know respect and obedience. You'll learn soon enough to bite that forked tongue of yours or it will be removed."

I back-handed Zale across the face and freed my hand with little trouble. Terran was at my side in an instant and I slid my hands down my fancy dress. "We're through here, Terran. Lir-Zale, you can scratch my name off the invitations. I'll pass on the nuptial servitude. Thanks anyway."

CHAPTER NINE

"Can you believe that asshat?" I stomped through the streets, mindless of where I went or who I bowled over as I went. "I mean really, can you see me married to that smarmy beefcake batting my lashes and kneeling before him? Hells no." No way would I kneel for him as a supplicant or as a woman.

"Lexi," Terran said, jogging to keep up with my rant. "Please, Princess, cool. People are taking note. Your words are treasonous. Please."

"Terran." I pointed my finger into his chest. "I have never been anyone's doormat and I'm not going to *chill*. If that woman wants to sit on her throne and refuse me as her daughter, then why should I care? There are some major flaws in the hierarchy of Attalos and I'm not going to get railroaded into a fucked-up marriage to some pretty-boy yes-man just because mommy dearest says so. Screw. That."

I heard the intake of breath around me and realized that I did, indeed, have an audience. Terran and I were standing in the merchants' square with wide-eyed amazement surrounding us on all sides. My mind tried to recap what my mouth had just been spewing and I winced.

Getting my head chopped off is not on my 'to-do' list for today.

My apology was on my lips when a woman in an apron stepped off the stoop of the bakery and stretched out a dainty, flour-dusted hand. Her blue, velvety wings stretched to their full span as she snapped her fingers. Not sure what I was expecting, but as the sharp snap, snap, snap, continued and gained strength, I just stared. In a matter of seconds, a chorus of snaps rose up and filled the square.

I scanned the faces of the crowd and caught a flash of fuchsia. On the far side of the merchant area, the woman from my vision turned away and melted into the crowd.

Ignoring Terran's protests I rucked up my skirt and swept across the stone courtyard and around the corner. Trying to catch a glimpse of the drunken brunette I'd seen not three hours ago, I hustled through the narrow stone streets, the click of my heels tapping out my hurried pace.

"Where is she?" I asked Terran, searching up and down the alleys and doorways as I ran.

"Who, Princess?" Terran asked behind me.

"The woman from my vision." When his expression blanked out, I remembered he still thought I collapsed with some kind of seizure. As we made our way back and forth, weaving along the water-bordered streets, I gave him the Cliffs Notes version of my visions and what I had seen.

"And you saw this woman just now? In the square?"

"Clear as day." I came to the end of a street and headed around the corner, searching the faces of people we passed. No one looked famil-iar. Crestfallen, I dropped the fabric of my dress and let it flow to my feet. "Damn. I lost her."

Standing with my hands on my hips I took stock of our surround-ings. I recognized the fountain from the night before and strode closer to the bronze statue of the Fates. Last night was a blur, but I distinctly remembered stumbling past that fountain on the way to the royal carriage. I oriented myself, glancing from the dock where Estes had met us with the launch and tracing my path back along the row of neo-classical townhouses on my left.

For the briefest moment, I wondered which one Rowan had taken me to. Was it his? No. He'd said that it was one of the Queen's townhouses, he just had a key.

"Terran? Why does the Queen have townhouses? The palace is big enough to house half the city. Who uses them?"

Terran's gaze roamed down the long line of crisp architecture set against the blue sky. "Military Commanders, breeders, some of the sons of the noble houses—citizens who are important to the Queen—"

"Whoa," I raised my hand and Terran stopped mid-sentence. "Breeders? Did my father live in one of these? Do you know where Balor lived?"

"Not which one, exactly, but the breeder's homes are farther down. The Queen saves the view of the fountain and waterway for her more important guests. Breeders are across from the market shops."

At my insistence, Terran led me further down the row and around the bend. He was right, the farther we walked from the fountain, the dirtier and more crowded the streets became. This retail sector certainly wasn't like the market square where Freya had taken me shopping, and it was a far cry from the scenic view of the waterway and the fountain back in the courtyard.

"If I had to guess, I'd say Breeder Balor lived in that house there."

I followed Terran's pointed finger to a postage-stamp yard and the plain row house beyond. The front door was open and four duty soldiers slugged large totes out of the gated yard. One by one, they carried their loads out into the street and loaded them on a hovering wagon. When they set the trunks on the platform, the cart adjusted to the load and leveled out.

"She's seizing his belongings."

Terran scrubbed his palm over his mouth and nodded. "It would seem so."

I closed the short distance as quickly as I could. If they took everything, I might never know who my birth father was. Could the Fates be so vicious as to let me find him just to strip every ounce of hope away from me? *Yes. Yes, they could.*

"Get it all. Got it?" a familiar voice barked from inside, "Every trace of the traitor is to be wiped from the city."

Joy, twice in one day. Lucky me.

Constable Tasso darkened the doorway. Something about the way he stared at me made my skin crawl. "We meet again. Princess. Grace, wasn't it?"

The way he smiled at me, I'd lay money that he had a voodoo doll of me tucked away somewhere with pins sticking out of my eyes and a tuft of stuffing bursting from the slice across my throat.

"Why are you doing here?" I wanted to sound tight when I spoke, but emotion leaked out and my voice shook with fury. If they had their way, I'd have no chance to look through my father's things. "Master Constable Estes ordered you—"

"Estes does not outrank the Queen," he snapped. "Official palace business, this."

"Packing the things of a dead man. Super impressive."

Tasso's eyes narrowed. "The Queen *herself* called upon me to—"

I raised my hand and watched another soldier pass with a full armload. "The Queen, *herself*, eh? Well, good for you. You can climb up my mother's asshole if you wish but I have no interest in following you."

Constable Tasso lunged across the little yard and was in my face before I blinked. The rank stench of stale garlic washed warm over my face and my fingers inched the fabric of my skirt up my calf. He obviously thought his size was of benefit to him, but with my agility, I could palm and plunge my knife faster than this asshole could cry for help.

Come on douchebag. Make your move.

As far up in my grille as Tasso was, I heard the gentle vibration as something in his breast pocket buzzed. With a glare at me, he retrieved a small electronic tablet, flipped up the cover and stared at the little screen. His face softened, displaying the smug look of a spoiled child with a secret. Tasso clicked his communicator shut and signaled for the men to finish up.

"Off to lick my mother's boots?"

"Actually, I *am* called to serve the Queen. This errand is not an obligation of duty, though. This I will do simply for the personal satisfaction of watching the aftermath." Tasso's lips twisted in a smile as his gaze danced over me. Before I could figure out what he was up to, his men finished loading the last of my father's belongings and off they strode, my father's life boxed and forgotten.

"That guy is bad news, Terran. I've known a lot of evil in my life and that man is dangerously unbalanced." I drew a deep breath and tried to calm my Spidey-senses.

"I'm not sure what his wreckage is," Terran said, watching the back of the wagon disappear around the bend.

I had to laugh. "Damage, Terran. You don't know what his damage is."

Terran recaptured a wisp of blond bangs that had escaped his queue in our run and resumed the order of his military look. It didn't suit him nearly as much as the floppy bangs. When he gestured to the door, I followed him up the walk toward the now empty townhouse. "I don't know what you expect to find now. Duty soldiers are trained to be thorough."

The faded cream on cream walls and modest tile floors spoke of a simple life forgotten. Forgotten. Is this where I lived? I walked through the empty space, pushing at the resistance of my own mind. Gods, why couldn't I remember any of this?

The furnishings had obviously been skeletal to begin with but with the Tasso-troupe finished their fine-tooth-combing, nothing personal or even decorative remained. "What? Did they think leaving a picture on the wall might leak some traitorous secret?"

Terran stepped into an adjoining room and I moved behind the plain, brown settee in the living area. I tried to imagine that battered man from the courtyard living here in better days. I couldn't picture it. That man had life in his eyes and this place had no sense of personality. It was sterile and sad. My heart sank knowing, without even looking, that the rest of the townhouse would be the same.

"Why do you think he did it?"

Terran tilted his head. "Who? Balor?"

I moved to the rectangular window at the front of the house and glanced out at the shops across the way. "Being a breeder is a bit of a big deal, right? So why risk defying the Queen to keep me, just to turn around and give me away?"

A small boy, probably ten or eleven years old, carried a package out of one of the shops across the street. He had the same mint green skin that Stitch and Terran had and I wondered if that was an identifier of an Earth *Attalosean . . . Attalosi?*

Standing too long in one position had me stretching my back from side to side. There was no help for the ache that was now my constant companion. I knew almost nothing about my life, and standing in this empty townhouse wouldn't change that. "Forget it Terran. Let's go. We're not—"

The creak of a floorboard in the back of the house had me reaching under my skirt and drawing steel. Terran heard it too and jogged to my side, his nightstick out and humming. He must have activated something within the baton, because the rune designs that covered its surface glowed white against the black cylinder. With quick hands, he signaled for me to stay put while he moved toward the back hall.

Yeah. He had a lot to learn if he thought that would work. *Gods, what I wouldn't give to be wearing my leather gear instead of floor-length silk and heels.*

Faint footsteps had us aimed at a partially closed door at the back of the house. I eased the door open. The blinds were raised and mid-afternoon light filled the space.

"Come out," I said, ready and steady. "Don't do anything stupid. We're armed." The shadow of movement passed behind the open crack of the door and I adjusted my grip.

"Armed, Gracie girl? I guess his plan worked then."

It took a second for the words to sink in, but when my mind caught up, the woman from my vision stood directly in front of me. She looked different—focused, angry, drunker—though there was no question it was the same woman I'd seen.

"Now stand still." She reached forward and for some reason, I did as I was told. Her finger touched my forehead and a tingle seeped into my skull and stung my eyes. "Give it a minute."

Standing face to face, forgotten images flickered at the edge of my mind. Teasing. Flirting with my consciousness like a clouded dream in the waking hours. I knew her. I studied her more closely. What appeared to be dark brown hair in the shadows of her haunted hollow was actually a deep auburn laced with the silver-grey of rising age.

Fire Fae. *How did I know that?*

"Who are you?" I lowered the point of my blade to rest against my thigh.

"I am Sera."

"And how did you get in here? Surely Tasso and his men didn't let you in."

The coy smile that spread across her features softened her appearance. "No. I waited until those bastards left. I want to speak with you. Alone." Her cold stare raked over Terran and I stepped between them.

The woman shrugged. "The Queen has spies everywhere, Princess. Not a word in front of your soldier friend."

It went against my every instinct not to defend Terran, but I needed answers and what she said was true. I'd only known him since I woke up this morning. The woman was important. The Fates were manipulative bitches, but what I saw in my visions always meant something.

I cast an apologetic glace to Terran. "Hang back so we can have some girl talk time."

It was surprising, in the short time of knowing one another, how well the two of us could have a silent conversation of looks and head shakes. It reminded me of how Galan and Nyssa knew exactly what was going on in the other's head without a word spoken.

After a heated argument of furrowed brows and tense glares, Terran had expressed just how much he disagreed with stepping back and leaving me alone, and I had reminded him I could take care of myself.

Terran threw his hands up and eased back to the far wall. It warmed my heart, how he kept his weapon ready and his mossy-green stare locked on our Fire-Fae visitor. Sweet.

"Now then," I said, stepping closer to the woman, "what do you have to tell me?"

The woman turned and without a word pivoted back into the bedroom. Crossing the room, she ducked into the closet and disappeared behind the sliding door.

I followed, dagger ready, peering inside the dark space to where a hidden panel in the floor lay exposed. A run of twenty or so steep steps led below and as I started to descend, Terran's hand caught my shoulder.

"It's all right," I assured him. "Wait here. If I'm not back in half an hour, come find me."

I didn't wait for his response but heard the jumbled attempt at modern world cursing as I left the bedroom behind. I giggled to myself. I'd have to help him with that.

At the bottom of the stairs, an earthen tunnel lit with multi-colored firelight stretched outward. Flames danced from six strange stoneware bowls fastened to the wood supports of an underground passageway.

"Giving you up nearly killed him. You should know that." The voice of the woman drew me farther down the length of the tunnel toward two framed doorways opposite one another. "The Queen's breeding program is meant to wipe out any lingering Earth, Wind and Fire genes in the noble families. Balor was Water as far back as time. His genetics are . . . were the strongest I've ever seen."

I followed the voice and stepped over the packed-earth threshold through the doorway on my right. The fire in the sconces increased the lighting, illuminating a charming, comfortably decorated underground studio apartment. It was homey, from the soft white-washed walls to the oversized sofas, to the iron bed in the back. "He loved you very much."

"You knew him well." It wasn't a question. Bits and pieces of memories fluttered together in my mind. My gaze swept over the mementos of a life shared: pictures, candles burned low, books, a child's quilted throw framed on the wall over the small table. "I remember this." I stroked the velvet symbol embroidered in the center panel. "This was mine."

The look of disillusioned loss I'd seen in my vision returned. "Years ago, it was." She took a picture frame down from the top of a bookshelf and held it out to me.

"You spent time with us. You played with me."

"Sort of. Balor always turned my visits into a game but they were much more important."

I eased closer and accepted the picture she offered. In the framed photo, I stared into the same kind eyes I'd seen last night on that horrible stage. What it would have been like to get here a week ago . . . a month . . . what about a year?

"I've lost my chance to know him. I came back to find my family and now all I have is this Breeder-Eligible-sister-wife crap. It's really fucked up, if you ask me."

She nodded and ran her fingers along the back of the cushy, white club chair.

"And that is the crux of everything you are, child." She fingered my hair and eyed me top to bottom. "Everything we made you."

A smile softened her expression as her gaze focused on something beyond the windowless room we were in. "He walked into my apothecary in the outer ring shortly after the fortnight of conception six cycles past. He knew he carried twins and had it all worked out, how he would present one child and keep the second, hide her from the corruption of the nobility, groom her to value justice and diversity."

"So why come to you?"

"My family's reputation for magic is know in some of the oldest circles of citizens. Balor wanted my help to protect the elemental diversity that makes Attalos unique."

Sera moved toward the open door and gestured me to follow. "When the Queen declared that all Breeders be pure-blood Water Fae, Breeders of all other elements were slain. She boasts of purifying the race for the longevity of all."

"How very Aryan of her."

Sera lifted the latch on the door across the hall and stepped into the same apothecary shop I'd seen this morning. "Your father believed otherwise and hired me to equip you with what you would need to unite all four elements of the citizenry."

"Equip me how?"

CHAPTER TEN

"What happened down there?" Terran asked for the fifth time in as many minutes. His long, loping strides kept up with mine even though I was pretty much bolting through the grittier areas of Attalos market shops. "Did that woman do something to you? Are you hurt?"

"Do I *look* hurt, Terran?" I whirled on him, fighting the urge to slap him. It wasn't his fault. I knew that. I did. It wasn't his fault that I was some kind of Franken-Faery, but really. "Can I have a minute to myself without you nagging? What Sera told me is my business. My life. Do you mind?"

The edge in my voice astonished even me.

The warmth leached out of Terran's expression. "Forgive me, Princess, I overstepped." With that, Terran fell behind me, straightened his stride, and assumed a soldier persona.

Shit. I really could be a bitch at times, but could a girl catch her breath between one catastrophe and another? We walked on, the afternoon waning into evening. The blue sky above and beyond the iridescent field glittered in brilliant gold and fuchsia swirls.

Red sky at night, sailors delight. *Yeah right.*

The scent of coal smoke mixing with the salty sea air had me searching for an exhaust chimney. The *k'tang, k'tang* of hammer falling upon metal echoed from a distance. "Terran, there's a blacksmith shop around here. Do you know where?"

The reservation in his normally warm gaze stole my breath. "Yes, Princess, follow me if you will."

"Terran, wait . . . Terran, stop." I jogged behind him, but his long legs propelled him along the streets, around one corner and the next. Straight backed and stiff shouldered, he didn't turn nor give me the chance to apologize.

"There." He pointed, then clasped his hands behind his back and stood at attention.

He'd led us to another of those futuristic bronze buildings with sweeping arcs and ornate scrollwork details. The one-story structure had huge wall panels folded back on three of the four sides. It gave the impression of an open-air building. The exhaust from the forge vented straight up from the chimney in the center of the building and out the hole in the roof. It rose in a swirl of charcoal smoke toward, but not nearly high enough to reach, the arch of the dome above.

As we closed the distance, I checked out the solid back wall. Covered in cut stone, it was cluttered with forge tools and a stunning array of custom weapons. There was something indescribably sexy about the sharp edges, spikes and barbs of new weapons. Having never been swung or struck, the line of the metal and the slice of the cutting edge remained perfectly unmarred.

With the walls open, the scorching heat crept along the paved street and met us like a cloying blanket. The forger, his back to us, set down his hammer, rose from his stool and stepped away from the flames. Pulling on the tie of the heavy leather apron he wore, he stripped off the protective layer and then his shirt. As he strode to the workbench on the back wall, he wiped his skin with the balled-up fabric.

Oh. Wow. The muscles on his back glistened and pulled as he retrieved a bottle and uncorked the neck. His shoulders and lats were thick in all the right places and tapered to a glorious ass cradled in a tight pair of jeans. At the small of his back, a silver buckle fastened the worn pair of leather chaps that protected his legs from flaring embers.

Heaven.

I swallowed hard as he tipped the bottle back and drank deep. Firelight danced along the smooth surface of the glass bottle and he turned to lean against the bench. My eyes were glued to the sweat-glistening definition of his abs. They plunged me into chiaroscuro bliss and the way his jeans hung low on his hips . . . *yummm.*

"Slumming it, Princess?" The low, velvet amusement in the voice snapped me out of my haze.

I abandoned the sightseeing sexpedition and met Rowan's smug stare. His gaze stayed locked on mine, the intensity of those shadowed hazels warming me inside and out. I prayed to Castian and his dim-witted nieces that it was dark enough to hide the flush of my cheeks as I straightened. "I . . . uh, what are you doing?"

"Being ogled?"

I stepped toward the forge and examined the billet he'd been working on. He was in the beginning stages of tapering the edges. Without touching the glowing metal, I let my hand hover above it and traced its length. The tingling in my palm climbed over my skin as it had twice already today. "You're using orichalcum for the flexibility within the core?"

"You know smithing?"

"A bit. Mostly I know swords. And I teach Spathology."

His mouth lifted in a crooked smile. "An Attalosean Eligible who thinks beyond the color of her nails and gown? Who could have guessed."

I pulled my hand from the singeing heat and stepped back. Sweat glistened on my own forehead and my lavender gown was starting to cling. "I've been misjudged before and, no doubt, will be again. I thought you were a doctor."

"Surgeon, actually. You could say I work with blades of all sizes." My skepticism must have shown because he cast me an impatient glance.

"Did you study medicine in the Modern Realm?"

Rowan kicked up his chin a notch. "Believe it or not, Attalos has a strong and modern infrastructure of its own. Whatever the shortcomings of our government, everyone, including the Noble Council and the Queen, work to ensure Attalos thrives."

"Considering the Nobles and Queen think arranged marriages and systematically eliminating cultural diversity is a good thing . . . well, friends can disagree."

A look of hostility crossed his face. "Don't flatter yourself, Princess. We're not friends."

His tone stung. The truth of those words was as solid as the scowl etched on Terran's face. Bruin always said we worked better in a pack than as lone wolves, but apparently, no one in Attalos wanted to join my pack.

"My mistake." I eyed the showcase of weapons hanging on the stone wall. "I'll leave you to your work."

I turned to leave and almost tripped over a child. The boy looked up at me with the darkest pair of eyes I'd ever seen. Maybe it was my sense of isolation or maybe the effect of the firelight on his dirty little face, but Zale's servant boy had the haunted look of someone who'd lived through far too much. And he couldn't have been more than eight years old.

"Hello again," I said, accepting the note he handed me. "What's this?"

The child plunged his hands deep into his torn pockets.

"The boy doesn't speak, Princess." Terran growled. "He can hear. He just can't speak."

"Oh," I said, my voice catching. "Well, don't let that slow you down, hon. I have a friend who can't speak either. He's the fiercest warrior I've ever fought with, other than my father. No one messes with Savage. Voice or not, he's a respected warrior and many of us would die for him in battle."

"Truth or tease?" Terran moved forward, starting to thaw in the heat.

"Truth, I swear." The little guy listened intently, a million questions swirling in his eyes. "Would you like to hear stories about Savage some time?" A mass of matted, ginger hair bounced as he nodded. "Good. Then let's do that."

Before I could say any more, he nudged my hand and pointed at the letter.

"Oh, right, and what's your name, buddy?"

His round little face blanked out as his coal black eyes filled with anxiety. I looked up to Terran. "What did I say?"

"He hasn't got a name. He's a fire orphan and indentured servant. He probably was born into it. Many Fire were taken as slaves after the uprising."

"What?" No wonder the poor bugger looked lost and alone in the world. I knew what that felt like. I'd be damned if I let this boy feel tossed away and unwanted. "Well, everyone needs a name. I'll give you one . . . if that's all right."

The surprise in those dark eyes made my chest tighten. "Coal. I'd call you Coal. You're a Fire Faery and your eyes are dark black. Do you like it? I'll think of something else—"

He shook his head, his tiny hand patting his chest and then pointing to his eyes.

"You like it?"

He nodded.

"Okay then, Coal, let's see what you brought me?" I angled the linen letterhead toward the light of the fire and smiled. Jade was the one born with the Rosetta Stone embedded in her cranium. I was the one who copied off her tests. Yet, since Sera had touched my forehead, memories of Balor and my childhood had started coming back.

I could read Attalosean. *Freaky.*

Princess Grace

Her Majesty requests your immediate presence in her private study. Your refusal regarding your allocation to be my bride has been deemed an unfortunate miscommunication due to a lack of understanding of Attalosean tradition.

In anticipation of a new understanding between the three of us, she has arranged for a gift of betrothal which she believes will clarify any further miscommunication.

> *Yours in affection,*
> *Lir-Zale*
> *Son of the seventh house.*

I snorted and tossed the letter into the fire. "Yeah, like a crystal punch bowl is going to convince me to marry that polygamist worm." Coal stared up at me, his eyes far too glossy in the firelight. "Gods, I'm sorry, Coal. I shouldn't say rude things about your master."

He shook his head, picked up my hand and after a sequence of frustrating charades, I finally understood. "You want me to marry him? Why on earth would I do that?"

He looked thoroughly deflated and pointed first from himself to me and back to himself.

"Married or not, I'm your friend, honey. And one thing you should know about me is that I'm a very loyal and trustworthy friend. We don't need your master's permission for that. Now, I suppose we should go and get this over with."

"You're out of your depths, Princess," Rowan scoffed. The copper in his brown hair caught the glow of the fire as he shook his head. "You spit in the face of the Queen's plans and expect to just get it over with? That's naivety talking."

I pushed my chin out and straightened. "What do you care? You just finished saying we're not friends."

Rowan scrubbed his palm across the stubble of his five o'clock shadow. "You underestimate the lengths the Queen will go to ensure control over her city. If you flounce your independence, she will squash you." The vehemence in his voice had me dumbfounded.

"What did I do to piss you off? I've been nothing but—"

He stepped away from the back bench and stalked forward. "You stood in a crowd of disgruntled citizens and declared opposition to the Queen. Attalos isn't a democracy. Rumors fly to her like traitorous little birds."

"And this is your business, how?"

Coming around the forge, with his shirt off and his lithe body moving in angry strides, his movement was better than a strip show. "Look," he said, his voice lowered. "The Queen rules with fear and with violence. Your recklessness is going to get you, or those around you, killed."

"I'm not reckless. I'm honest." My thoughts stopped being logical the moment all that rippled, tawny flesh was close enough to touch, or nip, or lick. He smelled like sweated-out male and didn't that make my heart beat faster. "Besides, as much as I appreciate you high-lighting everything I'm doing wrong, I've had enough of that. Fingers pointing. Judgement. Disappointment. That dance card is full."

I stepped back and opened my hand to the side. Coal slipped his little fingers against my palm and my pounding heart warmed. He might be tiny, but that gesture of trust was huge in this hostile world. Zale might think he owned me like he owned this boy, the Queen might think she owned this city, but neither of them knew me. "Thanks for the warning, Doc. I'll take it under advisement. And just as an FYI . . . I don't *flounce*. I fight."

CHAPTER ELEVEN

With my purple heels dangling from one hand and Coal clutching the other, the three of us strode through the gold-gilded hallways, past the sculptures and art, and eventually found ourselves outside the Queen's private meeting chamber.

"Coal, stay in the hall with Terran, 'kay? I promise, as soon as I'm done with the Queen we'll find Zale and see if we can figure out some way to improve your situation." With a look of mature resignation, Coal released my hand and went to stand next to Terran. It was bizarre how the mere loss of that fragile contact left me feeling bereft.

After slipping my feet back into my shoes and getting a reluctant nod from Terran, I signaled to the two soldiers standing guard. The double iron doors moved the air in silent warning as the room beyond opened to me. The Queen sat perched behind an antique, neo-classical-looking desk. The carvings and details of the Parthenon relic were repeated in the backrest of her throne and in the fireplace mantle. The room itself was refreshingly simple by comparison, with walls hung in ivory damask.

"Well," said a male voice from the corner behind me. "Are you always this petulant or was that worthless little *kopros* too stupid to find you?"

I whirled to where Zale stood, arms crossed, in the corner and then glanced to the open doors. Coal blanched at his master's words. "I was deep in the market shops. I'm sure Coal found me as quickly as possible."

"Coal? You named the little *chit?*"

"Hey, don't call him names!"

A cruel smile curled across his pretty face. "Why Princess, you've taken a liking to my pet."

"*He* is a sweet boy and *you* are nothing but a bullying ass with a title."

Zale moved faster than I gave him credit for. Dazzled by his fury, I almost didn't duck his hand fast enough to avoid the slap to my face. Almost.

Straightening, I smiled at his confusion. What? Did my 'sister wives' just let him go slap-happy on them?

A moment after I righted myself, Coal raced to my rescue. Fast as I was, I wasn't fast enough to stop the backhand which struck Coal and knocked him sliding across the polished floor.

"You stupid, worthless, *scorch*," Zale growled, stalking toward the boy's crumpled frame. "I am your master, not her—" As he hauled back to hoof a balled-up boy, I swung in a roundhouse and kicked his thigh with all my weight

The bastard spun off balance, but came back at me within seconds. His eyes grew as wide as gold-rimmed dinner plates when face-to-face with my Guardian blade. I leveled the tip of the knife at his sternum and stepped to block his path. "You and I need to straighten out a few things. First . . . I am *soooo* not yours. Second . . . you strike that boy again and you and I are going to have more than irreconcilable differences. You feel me?"

Coal shuffled behind me and buried his face into my lower back. With his little arms wrapped tight around my waist, I was torn. My mobility with him and the floor-length dress was compromised, but having a solid hold on him ensured Zale didn't have an opening.

"Enough," the Queen said. She waved her hand, her eyes glossed over as if the whole scene bored her to napping. I hadn't noticed the dark circles under her eyes at lunch, but she looked exhausted. I looked closer. The emerald green of her eyes was now closer to the moss green of Terran's.

"Lir-Zale," she said, her voice quiet as a whisper, her finger stroking the handle of a letter opener on her desk. "As a token of goodwill for your nuptials, I suggest you allow your boy servant to become the property of your betrothed. They have formed a union and Princess Grace needs people she cares for in this time of transition. This would demonstrate your willingness to compromise in order to gain her trust."

Compliance was more likely, but I didn't argue.

Zale's Mc'dreamy charm evaporated completely at the proposition of letting me have my way. I held my breath, waiting for either his answer or his head to explode. With white knuckled fists, Zale backed himself into the corner he had been standing in earlier. "Of course, Majesty, thy will be done, my lady."

After adjusting my position to include Zale in my periphery, I turned to the Queen and slid Coal around to my front. I didn't look down. Busting into a Cheshire grin wouldn't be prudent, and despite what my siblings thought, I did think before I spoke. *Sometimes.*

The elephant in the room was the fact that she thought there would be a wedding. Teaching strategic thinking for the past five years had the hairs on my nape up. For her to still believe that, she must be delusional or planning something.

And I didn't peg her for delusional.

"Thank you, Majesty." I filled my voice with as much gratitude as I could muster. "I apologize if I kept you waiting. Coal must have searched half the city by the time he found me. I was exploring, getting to know where I came from."

"Yes, I heard all about that. Which brings us to my nuptial gift." Her eyes cleared considerably, lit with a sudden satisfaction. "Take your new-found pet and return to your suite. I have arranged a delivery—an incentive, shall we say—toward a new attitude on your marriage."

With a hesitant nod, I tightened my grip on Coal and the two of us turned on our heels. We hit the hallway and Terran took up my left flank. Walking as quickly as I could through the maze of opulent corridors, I fought the urge to break into a trot. When we'd put some distance between us and the Queen's private study, I couldn't stand the silence any longer.

"That was too easy," I whispered, releasing Coal from my side to take his hand.

"She is a formidable woman, Lexi. You did well not to challenge her."

"I am not marrying that smarmy dick. I'll take Coal and run first."

"You'd leave us?" Hurt laced his voice. "You've seen the discord and rising conflict. Would leave your people and go?"

"I wouldn't abandon you. As a Talon Enforcer, I can do more with my fellow warriors standing with me than I can alone. Coal could be safely tucked away at Haven while we did something to improve the situation here."

Terran shook his head. "May I speak frankly without incurring your wrath again?"

I stopped outside the carved door of my suite and turned to face him. Attalosean men would be short in other realms, but even so they stood a solid foot taller than the females. At my four-foot-six I had to look up to meet his cautious gaze. "Yes. You can. I'm sorry I snapped at you earlier. It's been a mind-fuck of a day." My words still hung in the air when I thought of Coal and my tendency to follow Reign's vernacular. "Sorry, hon. I'll work on the swearing. My bad."

Coal's smile grew wider. I doubted anything would have bothered him at that moment. Gods he was adorable. I kissed his little hand and turned back to Terran. "Let me have it."

He leaned down to whisper directly in my ear. "I realize you are far more experienced in these matters than I, but I think you're grossly oversimplifying. The Queen gets what she wants . . . at any cost. Always."

With Coal looking at me like I'd just hung the moon, I had to disagree. Whatever the reason for her giving me custody of the boy, I had come out on top on this one. "Try not to worry, Terran. We'll all keep our eyes open. We won't get cocky and we'll see what the winds blow our way. Okay?"

Terran sighed and offered me a reluctant nod. "Okay."

"Now," I said, wrapping my arm around Coal's fragile little shoulder and continuing to the door. "Let's celebrate."

As Terran opened the door for us and I hit the lights, my moment of happiness transformed into slow-motion horror.

I couldn't grasp it. The blood was unreal. It spattered the alabaster cream of my entrance wall. Pooled thick over the perfectly polished floor. Like a disjointed sound bite, I heard Terran curse and the hiss of my breath.

"*THAM!* Oh gods, Tham!"

My mind fritzed. I knelt next to the bloody heap on the floor. The metallic tang of blood slammed me. I gagged. Shards of icy sliced through my muscles, tore through my sinew and bones and shredded my insides.

Unfolding his mangled body, I pressed slick fingers against his throat and wrist. Too much blood. I couldn't tell if there was a pulse. I smeared my hand across my dress and tried again. Tears stung my eyes. His body was twisted and broken. *He can't possibly be alive.*

"She killed you . . . because of me."

Terran said something and vanished into the hall.

My mind fritzed again. Without feeling my limbs, I tore away Tham's shirt. There was so much blood. He was shredded, leaking life from a hundred holes . . . impossible to stop. "Jade. I need Jade."

I stumbled to my feet, slipped on the floor and cracked down on my knee. I ripped my shoes off and scrambled for the sofa. "My phone . . . where . . ." The bag with my clothes had been rifled. My battle vest was there, but my weapons were gone. I grabbed it and searched the pockets as I sank back to Tham.

"It's gone." Tears spilled like hot rivers down my icy skin. "They took my phone." The scream that pealed from deep in my chest was inhuman. I fell across Tham's chest sobbing, the grief closing my lungs.

With my cheek on Tham's chest, I stared down his mutilated body. I laced his icy, trembling fingers with mine. Trembling? I reared up.

"Tham? Are you with me? Come on, Hotness, show me you're alive."

I searched his sallow expression. There was the slightest movement of his eyes behind his purple, swollen lids. My heart pumped triple time and the thrum of blood thundered in my ears. "Tham, baby, wake up." I gathered his cheeks in my hands and leaned close. *"Tham."*

His eyes flickered, opening behind the swelling in contorted angles. I cried out, brushing back his beautiful flaxen hair, matted and soaked with blood. "Thank the gods."

Rowan dropped to Tham's other side.

"What? How are you . . ."

Tham didn't even glance at Rowan, his clear blue stare stuck on me.

"You'll be fine now," I choked. "Rowan's a fabulous surgeon. Just hold on."

Tham tightened his fingers and clenched his teeth. "Liar."

His face blurred before me. "No. You *will* be fine. You're way too important to die like this. Rowan, tell him."

Rowan pressed Tham's neck for his pulse again, his hands dripping scarlet. Why wasn't he sewing him up or wrapping the cuts . . . or something. I searched Rowan's face, waiting to catch some glint of hope shining in his eyes. There was none.

He pursed his lips tight and caught Tham's gaze. His voice was soothing and steady. "Is there anything I can do for you . . . to make this easier for you?"

Tham blinked fast but his tears brimmed and flowed. "Take care of her. She seems tough . . . but . . . she's far too tenderhearted." Tham's voice cracked and his eyes shut.

Rowan stepped away.

I caught the warmth of Tham's tears on my finger and eased down beside him. "Tham, don't go. Don't leave me. Please. There's so much

happening here. I need you. You're the only one who loves me uncon-
ditionally."

Tham fought to swallow and coughed blood. "Promise me, *neelan*."

"Anything." I raised our joined hands and kissed his knuckles.
"Anything you want."

He choked again and I wiped the bloody spittle from his mouth.
"Treat life as an occasion. Rise to it . . . no matter what anyone thinks."

My tears broke my dam of restraint and streamed from my cheeks
onto his. "I love you, Hotness."

"You too, my little one . . . you too."

And then, he died.

CHAPTER TWELVE

barely noticed when Rowan and Terran joined me in the bathroom of my suite. Drawing the thick cloth down the ridges of Tham's ribs, I watched scarlet streams swirl in the bathwater and strengthen the pink sea around him. "Tham wouldn't want to pass unto the Fade all battered and bloody."

Rowan had done what he could with stitches and then he and Terran had helped me get him into the bath. The spa treatment hadn't hidden the bruises that blotched his usually smooth, Highborne skin, but at least he looked a little like Tham again.

"Highborne Elves have rituals," I mumbled to whoever was listening. "I need a mourning band. A wide black choker embroidered with Castian's symbols for love, hope and strength. Could we ask someone to make one for me?"

Terran nodded and moved toward the door.

"Have him make a few," Rowan said, kneeling across the tub from me. "We'll mourn with you, if that's permitted?"

I tried to draw breath. "It's a shame you didn't get to meet Coal, Hotness." I whispered against the tip of his perfectly peaked ear. I raised the small pitcher of warm water and rinsed his hair. "He's a great little guy and I know how excited you were about being an uncle."

My heart felt like it shattered inside my chest. Jade's twins would never know their uncle. The tears started again in earnest. "Oh, gods, what are we going to do without you?"

I clutched the cloth and wiped his cheek with slow, gentle stokes. "Galan will be lost . . . What can I . . . How do I tell him you were killed because of me?"

Rowan took the cloth from my hand. "You never meant for this to happen." He lifted my chin to look at him. "Take a minute and step into the shower. I'll finish here. When Terran gets back, we'll all take your friend to the second ring."

"Second ring?"

"The Earth ring. It's the only place with forested areas in Attalos. You want his pyre in a wooded area, right?"

I nodded, my chest too tight to speak. Tham's pyre . . . I couldn't think about that. "How did she know to hurt Tham?"

"She likely had spies tracking you long before Love was sent to bring you home."

He pulled three puffy towels from the cabinet beside the tub and laid them on the marble floor. "Rumor of a missing Eligible started circulating a week or more before you got here. Knowing the Queen, she had somebody watching you before she made her move."

I tried to recall the past two weeks. Tham and I had taken morning runs together with the wolves. He'd walked me to and from my classes at the castle a few times. We'd gotten completely shit-faced at the Hearthstone on Valentine's Day. My chest tightened. Tham had dressed up like a cheesy Cupid and carried around a bow and a quiver full of long-stemmed roses giving them to all the females. Jade and Galan had been there too. Who else? Aust and Bree . . . Iadon, Nyssa, Ella . . .

Oh gods. They're all in danger.

"Lexi?" Rowan's voice brought me back to the palace bathroom. He was sliding his metal tablet thing back into his front pocket. I hadn't even heard it buzz. "Take a moment to yourself. Master Constable Estes has arranged a launch."

Life from that point tumbled forward, blurred like the haze of thick, cold fog. It buzzed in my mind, chilled my bones and pressed on my chest until I thought I would suffocate.

After standing numb under the falling water for who knows how long, that young servant girl came in to help me dress. I refused to wear anything from the palace and instead, pulled on my leathers, my Under Armour and my empty battle vest. Funny, for the first time in two days I looked like myself but had never felt less like myself in my life.

Who the hell was I?

Rowan and Terran dressed Tham in a silver tunic and ivory pants, and after I fixed his hair the way he wore it, we laid his body on a hovering gurney. Rowan pressed a series of buttons at the foot of the gurney and two clear walls arced out of the side rails. With Tham sealed under a glass dome, we transported him to the launch waiting for us at the back of the residences.

I realized during the trip to the second ring that, at some point, Rowan, Terran and Coal had changed their clothing. Rowan wore a beautiful peacock blue coat with silver rope details and Terran was in a formal warrior's uniform. They'd even washed Coal up and found him a clean shirt. It hung loose on him, but made him look very grown up. In the pre-dawn light of what promised to be a long, horrible day, I pulled Coal into my lap and kissed the top of his freshly washed hair.

After who knows how long, Estes steered the launch beside the dock and two Strati stepped onto the lush treed shoreline and secured the boat. This area of Attalos was nothing like the metallic glamour of the inner ring. The Earth ring reminded me of the Highborne valley. The ground was covered in a blanket of pale green moss and the multitude of bushes and trees bore huge yields of red, gold and green fruit.

Estes sidled up the bank with Terran. The two of them stepped into the small clearing and met an older man waiting under a huge tree hanging heavy with blossoms. Terran embraced the man and I saw the resemblance between the two. After a short while, they parted and turned our way.

"Everything all right on this end?" Rowan asked.

Terran nodded. "My pater has everything arranged."

"Your father?" I mumbled.

"Yes, Princess," Terran said, helping me onto the simple wooden dock. "This is my home. Let me introduce to you to Demos, my father." I shook hands with Demos and then Terran introduced him to Rowan and Coal. When we were all standing within the clearing, Rowan activated the hovering ability of the coffin and transported Tham's body up the bank.

Breathe in.

Breathe out.

Terran caught the look on my face and slipped a hand under my elbow. "There is no place more beautiful for your friend to find his final rest, than the crest of our family plantation. We have orchards on the low ground and acres of forested land overlooking it."

My eyes stung as my vision grew wavy. *Don't you dare start again.* I blinked quickly and swallowed hard. "Thank you, Terran."

Terran kissed my hand before tucking it into the crook of his elbow and leading us away.

The sun broke across the line of the horizon just before our somber group climbed to the crest of a treed orchard. Terran was right. With the sunrise blazing fuchsia across the Mediterranean blue sky and the green trees flowing in the salty breeze, I couldn't imagine any place more beautiful. When we paused, Terran waited, a hopeful gleam in his eyes.

"It's perfect," I choked.

The pyre had been built to my ramblings and when the soldiers raised Tham's body into place, he looked like a perfect sleeping beauty in his glass coffin resting atop an altar. I prayed for the millionth time that this was all a trick of the Queen, that maybe he would wake up.

"Castian, please let him wake up. Don't let this happen. Don't let Tham be dead. He's our family. He's Jade's family. He's an innocent."

Castian didn't interfere in the lives of his charges. I knew that. He lived by a code; the members of the Fae Pantheon never influenced the lives of the realms. The only time he stepped in was when one of the gods or goddesses was taking unfair advantage and screwing with us.

As each second passed, the crack in my heart widened. "If I had listened . . . if I hadn't been so cocky—"

"Lexi, don't," Rowan said. "Nothing about this can be undone. Don't go there." He stepped forward and pulled strips of black fabric from his side pocket. "Are these all right?"

I touched the black, velvety choker and traced the silver symbols. My hands were shaking like flies' wings. "Perfect. Will you put it on me, please?"

When the four of us had our mourning bands in place I accepted the torch.

The world crackled and snapped as the kindling caught and the fire grew in strength. The air whooshed, flames rising in a wall of gold and orange, reaching toward the transparent dome far above the land. Shifting colors flickered, the oppressive heat slapping my face and stirring my hair. The moisture blurring my vision lessened the sting of smoke as the silhouette of Tham's body, dark against the brilliance of fire, was engulfed.

I was barely aware of my words as we watched the flames grow, my mind a whorl of images and moments. "Highbornes believe in celebrating the life as the dead pass Behind the Veil. They recount stories of joy and laughter so the spirit of their friend can take those emotions with them."

I did my best. I chuckled as I retold my adventures with Tham over the past eight months.

The clean ones anyway.

Tham, dressing up as Legolas for Samhain and charming a crowd of women until a cat-fight broke out over who was going home with him. Tham, running naked through the first snowfall, then diving into the waters of the hot spring caves. Tham, breaking up an argument at the Hearthstone and then proceeding to get smashingly drunk with the two who almost leveled the place. How could one man have such a gift to live life and have it taken away?

That was it, wasn't it? Tham was heart and laughter, love and acceptance. He lived every moment with the strength of a warrior and the passion of a lover devouring you. His spirit burned brighter than any star in the night sky, but he was too good to last.

Tham had become my best friend. Jade, Bruin and Julian would always mean the world to me, but they were my siblings. They expected things of me. They pushed at me. Tham was . . . *Tham.* Loving, inspiring, fun. I would miss him every day of my life.

Fighting the quiver of my lip, I did as Tham would want and discarded the guilt weighing on me. For the first time in hours, my throat let oxygen pass. I cried my last tears and wiped my cheeks. "Goodbye, Hotness. I will miss you forever. Safe travels."

Turning away from the smoldering, charred remains I tried to draw breath into leaden lungs. "Terran, could we possibly impose and go to your home for a bit? I'd like a little time before we head back."

CHAPTER THIRTEEN

It was the rich scent of vegetables roasting in garlic that woke me from the dead. The curtains were closed in the pale-yellow guest room, but I could see by the softened glow peeking around the edges that the day was waning. Thankfully, my nap had stopped the surreal scattering of my brain. My vision was clearer, my ears had stopped ringing and my inner centrifuge had slowed to an uneasy swirl. I tried to breathe past the mid-sized sedan parked on my chest.

Nope. Not quite yet.

My stomach rumbled long and loud and I forced myself out of bed. I didn't dare look in the mirror as I shuffled to the door. The last thing I wanted was to look at myself. I may never be able to look at myself again.

Down in Terran's family kitchen, Rowan stood at the side counter pouring a cup of coffee while Terran's mother, Gaia, bustled around between the counter and the stovetop situated on the wide island across from it.

"Where's Coal?" I asked, searching the corners of the room as I entered.

Rowan clattered the coffee pot against his mug. He cursed beneath his breath and I grabbed a cloth to mop up the spill.

"Sorry. Are you burnt?"

He shook his head, the copper highlights in hair catching the light as it flowed. He poured his coffee and set the pot back onto its hot-pad. "Terran and his father took Coal to the barn to introduce him to the livestock. The poor little bugger's never been outside the first ring. Agriculture is a marvel to him."

Rowan poured me a cup of coffee and gestured to the cream pitcher and sweetener. I nodded, waiting behind one of six hand-hewn chairs nestled around the long, wooden table.

He handed me a mug. "How are you holding up, Princess?"

"Honestly, not great." I barely got the words out before my throat began to close again. I pushed past it, focusing on the warm brown scruff shadowing his chiseled jaw. With the growth of a long day, the thin white line of a scar was revealed just under his right cheekbone. "I've taken up your whole day. I'm likely keeping you from something."

"We're fine. Estes returned to the palace to cover for us and sent the launch back. He said as long as we returned with his men by this evening's guard rotation he could keep your business your own. He's going to find out who did this, Lexi. He wanted you to know that."

I hadn't thought much about that, but yes, as soon as my mind was steady, I'd track down the coward who did this and gut the fucker. The fingers of my free hand caressed the hilt of my knife where it lay, sheathed against my thigh. My chest eased a bit with that thought, though the pain just seemed to relocate into my back.

"Is there anything I can do?"

I could use a hug. "I . . . uh, I'm really hungry actually." I sipped at the caffeine ambrosia and joined Terran's mom by the stove. "That smells amazing. What is it?"

"Zucchini friers and stuffed peppers, tomatoes and eggplant." She turned and bobbed her head then spun back to the stovetop and continued flipping the friers. "If that pleases you, Princess. If not, I could—"

"No. That sounds delicious."

Gaia's shoulders relaxed. "I made all of Terran's favorites. It's been so long since he's had leave to come home. It's wonderful to have him here, if only for . . ." Gaia turned, spatula in hand, her smile failing. "Forgive me. How thoughtless to be glad for anything right now."

I shook my head. "Don't apologize. Tham would be the first one to celebrate you spending time with your son. He loved families. He grew up alone and rejoiced in the little moments with as much enthusiasm as the momentous ones."

"He sounds like a wonderful man."

I nodded, pointing to the pastry spirals set out on a plate to cool. "May I?" With her motherly insistence, I picked one up and bit into it. The flavor burst into my mouth and my insides inched toward feeling alive again. There was no helping it. I wolfed down three of them before I could stop. "I don't think I've eaten anything since lunch yesterday. Gods, this is good."

Terran's mom beamed and curtsied. "What an honor it is to have you in our home."

I waved away her formality and accepted the platter to take over to the table.

"Eat," she said. "There are plenty more for when the men return from the barnyard. Are you feeling any better?"

"I feel like a limp sock being thrown around in a dryer, actually."

Rowan slid a golden frier onto a small plate and blew on his fingers. "I remember what that's like. When I found out my parents had been killed it was the same." He winced and for a second I thought it was because he'd burned his fingers. "Sorry, you don't need to hear about that."

I took a long sip of coffee and let the warmth of it slide down the back of my throat. "That's okay. What happened to your parents?"

"The Queen." He set his plate down next to his coffee and pulled out a chair for me. "Sit. You look like you're going to drop over."

"I'm fine."

He grabbed my shoulders, plunked me down and then sat next to me. "Doctor's orders."

"Do you manhandle all your patients?"

His mouth twitched at the corners. "Just the difficult ones. Now eat."

I bit back the urge to crack him one in the face and took another swig of my coffee. "You really get off on being a bully, don't you?"

"It's what I live for." He edged my plate closer. Ignoring my scowl, he bit into his frier and sat back. "I was in my final segment of medical training when they were killed. It had been five full cycles since the Queen started her campaign to strengthen the noble houses and segregate the races into the four rings. Things weren't great in Attalos, but the hostile times seemed to be behind us. Otherwise, I never would have left the city."

"So, what happened?"

"My little sister hit puberty." That seemed innocuous enough, but by the way Rowan's brow pulled together it was obviously not. "My parents were both Water Fae and carried those traits, as did my sister and I. But if there's going to be a shift in an Attalosean's dominant gene it happens during puberty or because of an incredibly stressful event."

"And hers was puberty?"

He nodded. "My mother's mother hailed from the Fire colony outside Tavas. She married my grandfather when they were quite young and moved into the city to find work. Both my mother and her sister were born there and inherited Water traits."

"With my father water-blooded back through generations, they never thought Elani would be any different."

My mouth dropped open. "Elani? Not the little—"

Rowan nodded. "Yes, your servant girl is my sister. She's four cycles younger than I am, but we're very close." He took a long drink of his coffee. "When puberty hit, her hair changed color. The Queen charged my parents with deceiving the Noble Council. They were accused of falsely registering an offspring as Water and conspiring to conceal her fire gene. They killed my parents and seized Elani as an example to the citizenry."

"Did they come after you?"

The look of devastation that flashed across his face sent a chill up my spine. He pushed his plate away, his pastry hardly touched. "Not to capture. The Queen made sure I was worth more to her free and disgraced."

"How so?"

After another drink of his coffee, Rowan stared into the half-empty mug. "My family name was traipsed through the gutters of Attalos, my parents murdered, our home vandalized and our standing in the community tarnished."

"Can you rebuild?"

"I intended to. I reacted much like you when you first got here. I stormed into the Nobles' Council and demanded justice. When those cowards wouldn't even consider helping me, I went to the palace and tried to reclaim Elani myself."

"What happened?"

The muscles in his jaw flexed. "The Queen had me restrained while Elani was stripped and raped by her Strati guards in front of me. She was only a child and I didn't know how to free her."

"Don't think about it. We'll go back to the palace and we'll get her out."

"And do what, run? Where? The Queen has spies everywhere. If they catch us it'll only make things worse."

"Then we'll go back to Haven. I live in a mountain sanctuary. You'll be safe."

"That's all well and good assuming you can get her out of the palace, which is unlikely. Then we need to get access to the portal pond, which will sound the general alarm. Then you have to make it so the Queen's personal Strati don't come after us, which will never happen."

"It could—"

"*Then*, we'd have to forget about how all the citizens of Attalos still suffer in a life of violence and iron rule while we're hiding, tucked away on a mountain where we don't know anyone."

"Well, it's better than being raped or not standing up for yourself."

His body went rigid as his expression hardened. The legs of his chair scraped against the tile floor as he pushed away from the table. We were alone in the kitchen. Terran's mother had left us during the telling of Rowan's story.

"There's nothing to be gained by running," he growled. "Trust me, I've thought of nothing else for ages. Every time that bitch touches—"

"What?" I was out of my chair and squaring off before I thought better of it.

"Nothing."

"Every time the Queen touches what? Who? Rowan, what aren't you telling me?"

"Princess? You okay?" Terran asked from the hall.

I whirled around to the doorway of the kitchen. Terran, Coal and Terran's parents looked like they had stepped into a den of feeding lions and desperately wanted to back away.

"Yes," Rowan said regaining some attempt at composure. "Forgive me for raising my voice in your home. You and your parents have been most gracious hosts. If you'll excuse me."

"Where are you going?" I shouted after Rowan. Holding my hand up for Terran and Coal to stay put, I followed him outside and along the front of the house. His stride was long and I had to jog to stay at his side. "What don't you want to tell me? What else is there?"

"Leave it alone."

I snorted. "Yeah, like that's going to happen."

"Then leave *me* alone." Strong fingers strangled my upper arms as he seized me up and shook me so hard my teeth rattled. "Go back to your sanctuary and grieve your boyfriend. Forget about Attalos and our tormented city. *Just go.*"

My blood pulsed in my veins, his anger affecting the both of us. "I'm not going anywhere until I find out who killed Tham and figure out how to fix whatever is broken in Attalos. Like it or not you're stuck with me."

"I *don't* like it," Rowan shouted in my face, looming over me until his nose was an inch from mine. His breath was warm, his eyes flashing with flecks of gold and green. "Why couldn't you be as vapid as the rest of them? Why do you have to be so . . ."

"So, what?" I snapped, twisting in his vise grip.

"So, *you*."

Before I could register the shift in his mood, he yanked me forward and captured my lips. His kiss was fierce and hot, hungry and possessive. His tongue raided my mouth as his hands released my arms and pulled me against the solid wall of his chest.

Never in my life had I tasted anything like him. Passion and dark spice tingled in my mouth and seared through my bloodstream. He tightened his fist in the back of my hair, his desperation lighting a fuse inside me. It sizzled through every nerve and had my body aching. For the first time in days, the pain of anger and disappointment abated, replaced with something even more powerful. Gods, the man could kiss.

His tongue fought with mine as my hands explored his honed, rippled muscles. A low moan escaped my throat as every hormone in my body fired at once. Eyes closed, I breathed in the scent of his skin mixed with a faded trace of his cologne.

When he spun us to the side of the house and pinned me against the stone surface, I thought our bodies might ignite. There was fire in this man and more than just in his DNA. As his free hand slid under my shirt, my hands found the back of his slacks. I rucked up the tail of his dress shirt and set my finger loose across the smooth, muscled plane of his back.

His hips rocked forward, those linen pants doing nothing to soften his erection against my stomach. A shudder of need tore through me.

It was more than wanting to vanquish the guilt and anger. It was more than trying to refill some of the emptiness of losing Tham. I wanted Rowan. I wanted him on top of me, pressing me into the cool, hard ground. I wanted to writhe, skin-on-skin, have my way with all this lean, toned muscle. No interruptions. No inhibitions. I wanted the two of us to lose our minds until both of us were sweaty, sated and spent.

His kiss left my lips and seared a trail across my jaw to my neck. His thumb stroked and teased my nipple as his thigh parted my legs.

"*Yes.*"

"*No!*" Rowan growled and pulled away. Shaking his head, he ran both his hands through his tousled bronze hair "Gods, what's wrong with me . . . I, uh . . . that was . . ."

"Fantastic?" I traced my fingers over my swollen, still tingling lips.

A devilish smile pulled at his mouth as he sucked air into his lungs. "I was going to say it was a mistake."

"Why?"

The look he flashed me was so hilarious I had to laugh.

"Have you forgotten your impending marriage to Zale at your sixth anniversary celebration? That's in four days."

I sank back, using the wall of the house to hold me up. "Never gonna happen. I say we go back to the palace, get your sister and head to the outer ring until we have a plan. You must have family there somewhere. What about that Tavas place your grandma came from?"

"I can't, Lexi." Rowan turned his back to me and let his head drop back. "You don't know how badly I wish I could, but you just don't understand."

"Then make me understand."

Rowan's shoulders tensed and when he turned, a wave of emotion crashed over his rugged features, anger, pain, regret. "If I tell you, you'll never look at me the same way again."

I swallowed. What could be so terrible that he thought it would forever taint my opinion of him? I didn't say a word, I just stood there and waited.

"It's stupid to keep it from you. The whole city knows."

"Knows what?"

Rowan dropped his gaze to the palm of his hand and scratched at nothing. He swallowed and seemed to brace himself. "To ensure that my family's humiliation is not forgotten the Queen has made me her whore. It's public knowledge that I'm her filthy play-thing. If I refuse, the Strati take it out on Elani."

The tangle of emotions on his face choked at my throat.

"I'm sorry I kissed you. I had no right." Rowan's body was so tense he looked like he might break out of his own skin.

My mind whirled with a fury I'd never known before. Pushing

away from the wall of the house, I paced and tried to form the words to make this right. The woman was horrible. She had to be stopped.

I thought about what Sera told me in the apothecary room beneath my father's townhouse. She and Balor had given me every advantage they could . . . to ensure I grew up with what I needed—

"I see how angry you are," Rowan said, turning toward the direction of the waterway. "I hope you can forgive me."

I moved directly in front of him and blocked his path. "I *am* angry. I'm furious, but not at you. I'm furious for what you and your sister and Coal and everyone has gone through under this psycho-bitch's rule. I'm furious that she had Tham, the sweetest, funniest man I've ever known, killed for no reason other than to show me that she could. And I'm furious that you thought so little of me that you expected to be judged for something that's been taken out of your control."

"You don't condemn me for it?"

"For *what?* Enduring? Surviving? Sacrificing yourself to save your sister?" I ran my hand down the scruff of his stubbled jaw and grabbed hold of his face. "Nothing has changed. I don't judge my friends . . . *ever.* You're still the same hot Doc who moonlights as a swordsmith and can out-kiss an incubus demon on the make."

I waggled my brow and flashed him a smile. "And I know that firsthand, by the way."

Rowan exhaled hard and exhaled. "Who are you Alexannia Grace?"

"I'm a friend. I'm hot tempered, impulsive, headstrong . . . but loyal."

He leaned forward and kissed my forehead. "I'm not used to anyone standing with me."

"Well, get used to it. We'll figure this out." I drew a deep breath and was reminded that dinner was waiting. "But first we eat."

CHAPTER FOURTEEN

"Matera, enough. She's full." Terran shrugged in apology as his mother slid a third piece of her decadent fruit flan onto my plate. "She's going to explode if you don't stop."

"Nonsense, it's so refreshing to see a woman not afraid to eat. The skeletal girls you used to bring home were like little twigs. I was always afraid a strong breeze would crest the cliff edge and snap one of them in half."

"Stop it," Terran snorted, "they weren't that bad."

Terran's mother raised a brow and set the platter down in front of me. When I caught her gaze, she tilted her head toward Terran and mouthed, *'Yes they were.'*

"I saw that, Matera."

I laughed and pushed away my plate. "No. He's right, Gaia, I really am stuffed. It was delicious, but I couldn't eat one more bite." Gaia bowed her head, visibly crestfallen and I looked at all the food still sitting on platters. "But I'm not sure where I'll be staying when we get back to Attalos. Would it be terribly rude of me to ask for a care package for later?" Well, that fixed things. Terran flashed me a smile as his mother began buzzing around gathering plates.

Rowan swung his head around, an unattractive crease between his eyes. "What do you mean you don't know where you're staying? You're returning to the palace. The Queen will—"

"The Queen can kiss my rockin' white ass. I'm not going back there."

Demos choked, his after-dinner drink spritzing amber down the front of his tunic.

Terran clapped his hand on his father's back as the man's face blotched pink. "I warned you she had a wicked tongue, Pater. She's not like the others."

"No." He coughed again. "That's why she's eating from my hearth. I wouldn't spare a withered prune on any of those other Noble females."

Rowan scowled deeper. "The Queen will be expecting you back. Don't push her, Lexi."

"I'm not," I said, and I meant it. "Not even the Queen—narcissist that she is—would believe I would just lie down, marry Zale and accept her killing my best friend. She'll expect a period of resistance."

"And you're willing to bet on that?" he snapped.

I stood and pressed my palms flat on the table. "I teach strategic thinking for a living, Rowan. So, yes, I am."

"And if you're wrong?" He strode behind Terran's chair and glanced to the floor where Coal was playing with the family dog. "The Queen doesn't do things out of the goodness of her shriveled, black heart. There's a reason for everything."

"I get that." Coal's goofy grin ripped my heart in two as the scruffy mutt licked every inch of his dinner-splattered face. The Queen gave me custody of Coal as leverage, a weakness she could exploit to her own advantage. Or so she thought. "Do you honestly think after what happened to Tham I would let—"

An electrical charge crackled in the air.

Instinct kicked in hard and fast. In a blink, I was airborne; my blade unsheathed my focus on the little boy playing on the floor. I vaulted over the table and landed in a crouch. My Guardian sliced through the space between me and the golden mist solidifying in front of us.

No one would hurt my boy ever again.

"Lexi?" The brunette with iridescent skin fidgeted with her long braid. It took a moment to rein in the urge to kill. She shuffled back a few steps, her gaze wide, her ice blue gown swirling like smoke around her feet. "Lexi, it's me."

I sheathed my blade and straightened, my chest still pounding like a war-drum. "Shit, Zo, you scared the crap out of me. What are you doing here?"

Her ethereal expression fell as her eyes brimmed far too glossy. "I was tending to the tapestries. Is it true? Did someone kill Tham?"

The tears in her eyes threatened to trigger mine, but there was no way I was going there. Abruptly, I rammed a mental stopper in that bottle, trapping the grief and regret for another time. My next steps were simple. Stay focused. Search out the bastard who dared to kill someone I loved. Make them pay.

The tug at my belt loop brought my attention back to the room. No one was moving . . . or breathing. Right, these people weren't accustomed to a goddess manifesting in the kitchen. Coal's alarm was clear. Terran's parents looked like they might faint. And Terran and Rowan looked from me to each other and shook their heads.

"Um . . . sorry everyone. This is Zophia. She's one of the four Fae Fates. Keeper of Lives in Progress."

Zophia curtsied low, her arm flowing out to the side with a grace that only a Fae goddess could manage. "I apologize for intruding uninvited, Sir. I shouldn't be here at all. My only defense was my state of distraught. It's just, Tham . . . I needed to know for certain."

I swallowed. "It is true. He died early this morning. Was it your sisters?"

Zophia shook her head. "No. I checked each of their Fate pools before I questioned them myself. Whatever happened to Tham was not of the Fates, it was the free will of someone within the realms."

"I figured as much."

Zophia wiped the tears from her cheeks and sighed. "Tham was so dear to so many."

"Unbelievable," Rowan said, a flash of annoyance darkening his features.

"You can say that again." Terran stepped around the table pointing. "Did you see her flip over the table? I'm supposed to be *her* personal guard. The woman scares me. She truly does."

"Zo," I said, ignoring the peanut gallery. "Tell me what you saw in the pools. Tham had no blood family and no wife, so I'm claiming the Right of Vengeance. Whoever killed him is marked for death. Just point me in the right direction."

Zophia bit her lip, her tears falling in a steady stream. They sparkled as they rolled down her cheeks and solidified as they fell to the tile floor. *Plink. Plink.* So, it was true. The Fates really did cry diamonds. Well, Zo did. I was quite sure her three bitch sisters didn't give a shit about anything or anyone enough to shed an enchanted tear.

"If I could help you, I would. You know I would."

"Don't give me any crap about not getting involved, Zo. You're involved. Jade's involved. I'm involved. Tham's death doesn't fall into one of Castian's loopholes about the Pantheon staying out of it."

"I am afraid it does. If anyone Behind the Veil found out I was here it would be bad enough, but if I help you—"

"No one will find out."

Zophia glanced at the five other people in the room and then back at me.

"Okay, so I can't promise that, but I'll defend you. I'll talk to Castian. I'll make him see."

Zophia accepted the handkerchief Gaia offered her and closed her eyes. "No one makes Castian see anything. You know that."

"But you're his favorite niece, surely he wouldn't—"

"And he's the God of gods, Lexi. It's not just him. If anyone found out, they could demand I be exiled from Behind the Veil. What choice would he have? Laws are laws."

I stopped my inner warrior from flying into a rage.

It wasn't fair to ask her to risk her entire existence just to make my life easier. I could find out who was responsible for Tham's death and

I could do it alone. It would take me longer, but I didn't have any travel plans until after I killed every last maggot in the manure pile. "Fine, I see that. Still . . . could you do one thing for me?"

"If I can, I most certainly will."

"If Jade and Galan don't already realize Tham is missing, they will soon. Could you tell them what you can about what happened? Tell them I'm sorry . . . and that I was with him when he died and that I did right by him. He was cremated in a beautiful wooded area and I recognized all the Highborne traditions I knew so he could be at rest in The After."

Zophia's head bowed. "I shall."

I blinked fast and swallowed, trying to speak past the lump in my throat. "And tell them I won't be back until I've avenged him. And that I love them. And not to worry."

She sighed and took my hand. "It shall be done."

"Oh, and most importantly, tell Julian and Reign that Haven was compromised. There was probably someone watching me for weeks before this all started. Tell them to guard Jade and the others. I don't want anyone else killed because of me."

"I shall take care of it," she said.

The moment her hands clasped mine I felt the vision coming. As Zophia dissolved into a golden mist, my eyes began to dilate. "Terran . . . I, uh"

"I see, Princess."

Slender arms led me to the living room sofa. The sounds in the room echoed and whooshed in my ears as the images began to form.

"It's okay, Coal," Terran said. "She's all right. The vision will pass in a few . . .

Sitting on the back bench of the launch with Coal's head resting in my lap, I searched the faces of the Strati soldiers in the front of the boat escorting us back to the inner City of Attalos. The three men who had ambushed, beaten and kidnapped Tham were not among them. I'd seen each of his attackers clearly in the vision Zo had given me and committed their faces to memory. In truth, I couldn't get the vile images out of my head.

And although you couldn't *unknow* something once you knew it, I had everything I needed to avenge Tham. His attackers had gone through the pond portal and found him on the forest path on his morning run. They had him from the moment their commander showed him one of the knives from my battle vest. Savage had forged the blade and Galan had custom fitted the hilt to my palm. Tham recognized it immediately.

They told him I was in trouble and he needed to come. Tham insisted on calling it in to Julian and that's when things got violent. The only satisfying part was that the leader of the death squad was someone I was only too happy to put down.

"Constable Tasso?" Terran whispered close to my ear. "You're certain?"

I nodded. Dull pain throbbed from the back of my neck to the small of my back. I stroked my fingers through Coal's hair and stretched my neck from side to side. Rowan scrubbed his hand across his jaw and continued to scowl at me. If I didn't have a child sleeping on me, I would've cold-cocked him by now. "What's with the glare?"

"You're going after them."

"With everything I've got." I tilted my head toward the soldiers at the front of the launch and lowered my voice. "This is what I do, Rowan. Don't try to protect me. I'm not that kind of girl."

"I'm not expecting you to forget and make nice," he growled, "but you're not invincible. Taking up arms against the Queen and her men *is* going to get you killed."

Maybe. "It beats the alternative."

"Oh? And what's that?"

"Hook up with Zale to affect change within the Nobles' Council and be sister wife number three. What do you think I'd have to do to climb up those ranks and have a voice?"

Rowan blanched.

"You don't like that equation any more than I do."

"And how do you get out of a public ceremony being held in four days. The laws are clear. If you don't follow through, you're derelict in your duties as an Eligible. You'll be executed."

"Laws-schmaws," I snapped. "My father always said, "In any situation you can either be the hammer or the anvil." Let me give you a hint, Doc. I'll *never* be the anvil."

Rowan gritted his teeth and sank back against his seat. "You're impossible."

"Welcome to the new world . . . where women fight and have brains and everything."

"I haven't lived under a damn rock, Lexi. I've had my share of strong women."

Well didn't that just bite me in the ass? Yep, that pretty much did it for the convo. By the time the launch docked in the market district of Attalos, the moon was a glowing white orb directly overhead. Other than a tiny part of the curve that looked like it had been shaved off, it was a perfect sphere of light. By tomorrow night it would be full.

Two of our military escorts stepped onto the dock and secured the lines. One of the men reached down and took Coal from my arms while the other offered his hand to guide my exit against the pitch and yaw of the boat.

When we were ready and steady, the soldier holding my hand released me. "The others will take Lir-Rowan to the palace and return the launch. Ydorus and I will see you and your guard safely to your destination, Princess."

The voice of the soldier had me taking a closer look at him and his friend. The two had matching olive skin along with dark, military cut hair and brown eyes. I'd met them before. They were part of the squad Estes had let me spar with in my exercise session in the palace orchard. "I'm sorry, I didn't recognize you boys earlier."

"Understandable, considering the day's events. We're, sorry you lost your friend like that, Princess. It wasn't right . . . what happened to him. We've all been through it and it's just not right."

I nodded, but couldn't go down that road. "Eury, isn't it? How's the rib from the yesterday?"

"I am well, Princess." Eury rubbed his side with a smirk. "Where are you headed? We should get you off the streets quickly. There are no secrets in Attalos and with what happened to your friend . . ."

"I was thinking I could go back to Balor's townhouse. It's been cleaned out and—"

"She's going to my family home," Rowan muttered. From the shadows of the canopied launch he extended a silver key card. He kept his face well back of the moonlight, so I couldn't see him. I could, however, still hear the tension in his voice. "I'll have the garden gate unlocked. Go in through the back. No one has lived there since my parents were killed except our housemaster. It should be safe enough to hide her away for a few days."

"Understood." Eury accepted the key and slipped it into his pocket.

"That's a terrible idea," I said, raising my hand. "You can't risk your sister or your honor any more than you have."

Rowan leaned forward. In the pale light of the moon, his complexion had drained of its usual golden tone. It could have been a trick of the silver moonlight or it could have been something else entirely. "I'm tired of being the anvil, Lexi—so desperately tired. And besides, she might already know. I was called to appear at the palace a half hour ago."

My stomach knotted at the thought. Did my mother know Rowan helped with Tham or was she randy and looking to hit the horizontal? Between one heartbeat and the next, my insides were consumed by a surge of hatred. "I should go too. If it's me she wants, Elani might already be in danger."

"You stay out of sight. I'll feel out the Queen and see what she knows."

Feel her *out* or feel her *up*? Fighting back the urge to chain Rowan to the nearest tree, I reminded myself I had no right to the fury burning through my blood, no right to forbid him going into her den of depravity. It took all my inner strength not to scream as vile, unwanted images flooded through my mind. My mother's lips touching his . . . his calloused, strong hands touching—

"Lexi." Rowan stared at me like I'd just punched him in the stomach. "Don't."

I swallowed the bile burning the lining of my throat and forced my expression to relax. Registering the pain in my right hand, I realized I was choking the life out of my knife. On a deep exhale, I slid the gleaming blade into its sheath and pried my fingers off the hilt one by one.

Annnnd there we go. I'm calm. S'all good.

"Fine. Go," I said, thankful that my voice held steady. "But don't plan any trips down suicide alley, Doc. If you're in a jam, protect you and yours. If it comes down to Elani or me, I can take care of myself, she can't."

Cue crickets in the background.

Rowan cursed, his face going grim. "You say that, like you actually believe I could throw you to the sharks."

"I'm telling you to. I mean it. If it comes down to a choice, choose her."

CHAPTER FIFTEEN

"You are a phenom, little man." I patted Coal's head as his smile lit as bright as the iridescent field arching above. The kid was a natural at weaving through the night unseen. I tried not to think of how he'd grown to be so proficient on the streets but because of his mad skills, we'd skirted through the market center, past the canals of the commercial districts, and into a residential sector without coming across a single soul.

My only concern was that he might not know where Rowan's house was because we'd passed the modest two-bedroom row houses, we'd skipped around the larger detached homes with the fenced front yards and now we were into the estate section of Attalos.

"Are we sure we know where we're at?" I asked. "Cause we're not in Kansas anymore."

"Of course not, Princess," Terran said with a sideways glance. "We're in Attalos."

"No, I . . ." I waved away his confusion and let Coal tug me alongside a tall, metal retaining wall. The thing must have risen a solid twenty feet from the ground. The Orichalcum vibrated into my palm as my fingers skimmed the smooth surface.

I'd never been anything close to a tree hugger, but found it strange that in a city this size there weren't any green areas. Within the first ring of Attalos there were courtyards, fountains, metal walls and canals. No trees lined the streets, no shrubs or flowerbeds landscaped the lawns.

With my mind wandering and my feet trudging along on autopilot, I almost knocked Coal flying when he stopped right in front of me. I caught him as he flew forward and righted him. "Sorry, buddy. What's up?"

Ydorus, Eury, and Terran took up the rear more gracefully.

I scanned the street. We were standing in shadow of a—

"Holy shit. Is it a house or a mausoleum?" I stared open mouthed at a stone mansion that looked to be the much-older-yet-slightly-smaller-brother of Jade's mansion. Except this one wasn't poofed here by Castian, God of gods. Men had slugged these chunks of rock here and built this sucker one hernia at a time.

"Do you think there's a hunchback in that bell tower?" I asked, staring up—way up. It was magnificent, tall windows reflecting the glow of the moon's light, and ornate wrought iron balcony railings guarding the black alcoves behind them. High above, three stories, maybe four, the roofline followed undulating turrets, more windows, more balconies and a bunch of wide stone chimneys. "Did Rowan's parents own a fricken quarry?"

"No," Terran said, accepting the key card from Eury. He slid it through the security box and a loud clack echoed into the quiet night. "They own the fifth sector of the city and all its wares. Now, with his parents dead, Rowan does."

"What?" My mouth hung open as someone pressed a firm hand on my back and pushed me through the open gate. "I thought he . . . he's a swordsmith and a doctor."

The backyard was completely enclosed and the security wall reached high enough we were guaranteed our privacy. Ydorus secured the gate behind us. "He is, Princess, but his birthright is that of the son of the fifth house."

"Rowan's a Noble?"

Terran shrugged, guiding us around a dry fountain in the center of a courtyard. I imagined the last time the peaceful sounds of falling water filled this area would have been when Rowan's parents still lived here with Elani.

"I'm not sure how it works now that his family is shamed," Terran muttered. "The Laws are absolute. Rowan's rights—"

The brilliance of the light cutting from the house across our group had us blinking and shading our eyes. Coal tucked tight to my side.

"Princess Grace?" The whispered voice came from an ebony silhouette blocking the open doorway. It was impossible to make out any features against the light of the backdrop, but the slender frame of the man seemed relaxed and unassuming. "Master Rowan told me to expect you. Please, come out of the night air."

"Ydorus, would you mind?" I raised my chin toward the open door and waited for our escort to take point. Eury stayed behind us and we drew our weapons and moved as one. I tucked Coal behind my back and smiled at the tug of his fingers lacing though my belt loop "Stay close little man."

The lush décor of the living room stood in direct contrast to the drab façade of the house exterior. Rose-colored stucco walls set off the sapphire, ruby and emerald décor which spilled across the over-stuffed sofas, thick draperies and broad swaths of buttermilk marble.

A genuine warmth oozed from the scattered array of family photos to the books and possessions piled haphazardly on surfaces around the room. The family Rowan lost.

"If it pleases you, Princess," the old guy said. "Let us begin your welcome in the front atrium and greet you properly." He scooted down a candlelit hallway with more spring than I would have thought possible. Eury took one last look into the moon-washed courtyard, then locked the back door and we hustled to catch up.

I could see why Rowan's butler wanted to begin in the main foyer the moment we arrived. The wall of the three-story atrium was a back-lit, tiered, glass fountain. Water trickled and splashed down the textured contours, falling from the top floor to pool into the tropical grotto below. Lit from beneath the champagne surface, schools of multi-colored fish lazed and swam in and amongst a rainbow of anemone.

"Welcome to the home of Lir-Rowan, of the Fifth house. I am Jonash and anything you need is my pleasure to provide. Shall I give you a tour of the manse?"

I didn't want to burst the old guy's bubble, but I was d-o-n-e —*done*. "I'm thinking: booze, bath and then bed."

His lips tightened. "I shall have Leta draw you a bath, Princess. Would you like something to eat first?"

I shook my head and glanced to where the stairs disappeared. "No thanks. I'll be good 'till morning." Jonash milled his long, slender hands. What was it about the people of Attalos and their weird preoccupation with feeding me?

I cast a glance over to Ydorus and Eury. "My escorts haven't eaten. Could I ask for something for them?"

"Of course, Princess." He bowed deep at the waist. "If you'll give me a moment, gentlemen, I'll show Princess Grace to her room and be down to tend to your needs directly."

"We'd rather escort the Princess—"

"Thanks boys," I said raising a hand, "but I'm beat. Terran will see me up. You two should take off and get some rest. And thanks for everything."

"If it's all the same, Princess. We'd prefer to secure the house."

I cast a glance at the mansion sprawling in all directions, three stories above and more below to be sure. I tilted my head back, scanning all the way up to the third floor. I was much too tired to argue. "We're only here a few days. You might not get done."

The two soldiers chuckled, but after Ydorus checked the locks on the front door he and Eury marched off through the dimly lit wing on the right.

With lead legs, I shuffled toward the stairs while Jonash bounced up the steps in the lead. "I will show you to your rooms and then bring up a tray in the event you change your mind about the food."

"Sounds great."

The four of us trudged up the plush runner covering the hardwood stairs all the way to the third floor. The landing sported a wide window seat and a floor to ceiling bookshelf chocked full of spines standing at attention. Jonash was practically skipping down the left corridor while Terran, Coal and I struggled to keep up.

"How long have you been with Rowan and his family?" I asked, only to slow the man to a less obscene pace.

"Oh, my ancestors have served the Nobles of the Fifth house since the time of separation." He paused next to an alcove with a nude marble statue of a Fae god.

Oh, please, let it not be Castian. The last thing I needed was to go to sleep with erotic images of Jade's father in my head. I tried not to look, but was drawn to satisfy my curiosity. Thankfully it wasn't Castian. It looked more like his brother Dane.

Coal noticed me eyeing the statue and giggled.

Yes. Naked was funny to an eight-year-old.

"Here you are, Princess." Jonash said from a short way down the hall. "I'm certain you'll be comfortable here and the two rooms across the hall have been readied for your guests."

Coal's eyes flared and I squeezed his hand.

Terran eyed the door across the hall and I realized that both Coal and I had taken naps, while he had been going full tilt since yesterday. "Terran, go. Get some sleep. We'll meet in the garden at dawn for training."

If I'd had the energy, I would have laughed at Terran's expression. As it was, I just shoved his shoulder and pushed him into the room. "Go. That's an order."

He yawned. "See you at the crevice of dawn."

I laughed. "Crack, Terran. See you at the *crack* of dawn. And Terran?" He stopped and met my gaze. "Thank you. For Tham, and taking us to your home and . . . yeah, well, today."

He eased the door closed. "Sleep well, Princess."

CHAPTER SIXTEEN

The moment the dream morphed into something sinister, I was aware. One of the more peculiar side effects of being a conduit for visions was having a body and mind acutely attuned when reality collided with what would be considered by normal people as *other*.

Running through the Haven forest with Tham at my side and the wolves at our heels, I could almost breathe again. With every fiber of my being, I clung to the fruitless hope that this was reality and yesterday had been the nightmare. Even as we ran, chuckling about stupid everyday drama from the Academy, the Talon, and of course our collective family, I knew in the pit of my gut it wasn't real.

The shadow edging into my dream, however, was. Subtle at first, it was a rumble in the distance. A feather brushing the synapses of my mind. A prodding finger testing the waters. I gave no indication I was aware of the intrusion, entranced by the joy of spending time, however imagined, with Tham.

The shadow edged further. My heart raced in my ears, thundering like hooves against packed earth.

What was it? Or rather . . . who?

I leapt over a large rock and grappled Tham right before we

turned the bend toward the main path. The two of us toppled toward the brush. He rolled mid-air, at the last minute pulling me against him to absorb the blow of the forest floor. Laughing, the two of us crashed in a tangle of legs and elbows and giggles.

Breathing deep, I relished the scent of him—suede, outdoors and Elven male.

The entity pushed further.

No longer just the sense of someone probing my subconscious mind, the slither of an icy awareness snaked through my skull, down my nape and into my chest.

Tham sat up, his brow pulled tight, the deep furrow between his blue eyes a rare sight. "You need to go, *neelan*. It's not safe for you here."

The warrior's voice in my mind agreed. I had lingered long enough in fantasy.

Telling myself to wake up, I tried to open my eyes. They wouldn't open. Whatever it was . . . whoever was inching inside of me had taken hold. I fought against my insides.

No, no, no. This was wrong. Way wrong.

Tham leaned over me, shaking my shoulders. "Wake up, Lexi. Fight."

My teeth clacked together as Tham shook me harder.

"Go, Lexi. Open your eyes. You must go."

The slither of icy evil grew as it spread. My vision dimmed, a damp fog covering my mind. I couldn't breathe, suffocating on the frigid cold as it leached through my lungs into my arms . . . my legs . . . my—

My hands came up as I launched off the bed and landed in a crouch. Wide black eyes fixed on me from a bed the size of a football field. The room was mostly dark, the only light coming from the soft illumination escaping the adjoining bathroom. I sucked oxygen into my heaving lungs. The room was secure. Just me and Coal, sawin' logs in the guest suite of Rowan's mansion.

"It's okay, buddy," I breathed. In. Out. "Just a bad dream." I forced myself to straighten, my hands shaking like leaves in a hurricane. I tugged down the front of my shirt and pressed it flat. "Just a bad dream."

I crawled back under the covers and opened my arms for Coal to cuddle in. Chilled to the marrow, I gave thanks to have my own personal space heater bunking with me. Did all Fire Faery run hot? A few minutes with Coal snuggled against me and my quakes started to settle. After a minute, he pulled back and looked at me. I could read the frustration in his face. He had something to say, but couldn't get it out there.

"Am I all right?" I asked, taking a guess.

He nodded.

"Yeah. Fine. You? Sorry. I didn't mean to scare you."

He shook his head, his shaggy ginger hair standing up in every direction like cockerel tails. He still wanted to say something. His lips pressed into a scowl and he growled low in his throat. I propped him up on the pillows and thought about what it must be like to not be able to express myself. No sarcasm. No venting. No way to laugh or yell or tell a joke.

"Do you remember I mentioned my friend, Savage?"

After the confusion drained from his expression, he held his hands wide, then reached high over his head and scowled.

"Yeah, the big, scary warrior who can't speak."

He pointed to his mouth and throat, and then shrugged.

"I'm not sure why, exactly. He's never shared his personal deets and no one has balls big enough to ask."

He smiled at the mention of *balls* and I rolled my eyes. "Well, he always wears a spiked dog collar or bandana tied around his throat, but once, after a particularly ugly battle, my sister, Jade, had to take it off so she could heal his neck."

Coal's eyebrows disappeared under a fringe of bangs.

"He had a terrible scar from here . . . all the way over to here." I dragged my fingers across the velvet pile of my mourning band from one side of my throat to the other. "It was a nasty wound. Hamburger. It looked like someone ripped his voice box right out."

Coal bit on his bottom lip, his gaze locked on mine.

"The reason I brought it up is that when we're on a mission we need to be able to communicate. The Scourge—that's our enemy—well, they love to ambush, so a lot of what we do is sneaking around. We communicate what we see and what's coming at us without using our voices. It doesn't even matter that Savage can't speak."

Coal propped himself onto a spindly arm and rested his head in his palm.

"So, when we're on a mission, we use hand signals. Some are from something the Modern Realm calls sign language and some we adapted ourselves. I was wondering if that might be something you'd want to learn?"

Cue the bright-eyed head bobbing.

"It'll be confusing at first, but if we practice, you'll be able to tell me exactly what you're thinking." The hug was all I needed to wipe the last of my unease away. I set him back on his pillow and held up my hands so they caught the light from the bathroom. "Cool. So, here's an easy one."

Lying half buried in the rolling plains of an overstuffed duvet and navy satin sheets, I watched Coal's tiny chest rise and fall, slow and deep. Up. Down. Up. After learning dozens of signs, his eyes had grown so heavy I told him to close them. Two seconds later, he was gone. Now, lost in what I hoped was a kinder world, he was free to be a kid. I, myself, after my last brush with dreamland, might never sleep again.

The crevice of dawn—I think Terran had something with that one —came an hour or so after Coal drifted back to sleep. I'd told him not to panic if he woke up and I was gone. I'd be in the garden working out. After assuring him that he and I were a team now, he relaxed but still made me promise I wouldn't go anywhere beyond the grounds without him.

I slid out of bed with my plan. Shower. Dress. Back garden.

Except—once I was face-to-face with the stone tile and shiny bathroom fixtures I had no idea how to make the shower work. The mechanics of the nozzles and drain were different from the palace. No matter what I tried, no water came.

Okay, so work out, then shower.

I fingered through the basket of toiletries Jonash had provided and did my best impression of ready for my day. Not for the first time I wondered about Rowan. How had it gone with the Queen? Did he come back here last night or stay at the swordsmith shop? Terran said he'd lived there since his family was destroyed. Or, maybe he was still at the palace.

My empty stomach wriggled. Gods that would be seven hours with her. Seven hours of Rowan being her plaything. Against my will, I wondered what a session with Mommy Dearest would entail.

I shook my head. Maybe that's not how things had gone down at all. We were playing a very dangerous game, he and I. If the Queen knew Rowan wasn't towing the line, Elani would pay the price as Tham had.

A burst of heated fury burned through my veins. What was going on here?

I thought about what the Queen's end game could be as I pulled on my leathers and tied my empty sheath to my thigh. The woman had dominion over Attalos, was cultivating an army and her breeding program was well under way infiltrating the Nine Houses of the Nobles. One last glance at Coal sleeping and I retrieved my knife from under my pillow.

So, what did she want?

Boots in hand, I backed out of the room, eased the door closed and held the latch so it made only the softest *tink* as it fell into place. As I stepped back, my foot caught.

"What the—Terran?" I stumbled backward, crashing into the opposite wall. My Jimmy Choo's flew, my skull rattled, and I ended up sprawled on my ass on the plush hall runner.

"Oh! Princess," Terran tried to catch me but managed only to rescue an airborne boot. "Are you all right?"

I looked up at the horror on his face and burst out laughing.

"Turnabout is fair play. I guess you owed me that." Gods had that been just two days ago? Or was it three now? "Thanks for not punching me in the face."

I rubbed the back of my head where I'd connected with the wall and he offered a hand to pull me to my feet. In the aftermath of our collision it dawned on me. "Why are you camped out in the hall? I sent you to bed last night."

Terran shrugged. "I heard you cry out a few hours ago and raced into the hall. When I was about to burst in, you assured Coal it was just a bad dream."

"So, you decided to camp out?"

He picked up my boots and handed them back, his sage green gaze despondent. "But I fell asleep in the doorway. I apologize. I am not the best private guard."

"Ah, no biggie. Besides, you're better than you think. It's not too often I end up ass-planted because someone caught me by surprise. You get props for that."

CHAPTER SEVENTEEN

In the light of day, Rowan's backyard was a pocket of natural seclusion like nothing I'd seen or smelled in the city of Attalos. The security walls, obscured behind ivy, tropical plants, and the soft drooping branches of fig trees, cast the illusion of there being no walls at all. Birds sang an endless melody, hidden amongst fragrant blooms of flowers and fruit, and perched on the edges of the fountain which was now full and trickling the same champagne colored water as the atrium. But the most important feature to me was the lawn. Manicured and even, it stretched on for the length of the practice field back home. Perfect.

The workout was brutal. After wind sprints, weight training and showing Ydorus, Eury, and Terran a few key gymnastic techniques, they took turns sparring with me. It didn't take long before they realized one-on-one wasn't going to get them anywhere so they ganged up, which was exactly when things got entertaining.

"Hits are fast, grabs are slow, boys." I shoveled a forkful of breakfast casserole into my mouth and chased it down with a tumbler of juice. "You can wrist grab or arm bar any time in your counter – before, during, or after your hits. It's a basic fact. Keep your opponent on his toes, make him anticipate, and then take him off guard."

Ydorus sat at the kitchen table icing his shoulder while Leda—Rowan's middle-aged, rosy cheeked housekeeper—piled a mountain of carbs on his plate. He nodded his thanks. "There is no pattern to the way you fight, Princess. No one could anticipate what you're going to do. You're mad."

I laughed and pointed to the basket of biscuits. "Sometimes preserving your life comes down to one insane move. When the enemy can predict your intentions, you're in deep shit."

Terran snorted and, after piling three biscuits on his plate, passed it across to me. "So, predict what our opponent is going to do, but remain unpredictable ourselves?"

"Exactly. *Annnnd* if you can look good doing it, all the better." I snagged a couple of biscuits for myself and passed the basket on. "Terran, we need to get you some better gear. This chamber guard uniform bites in battle."

"Probably because duty guards patrol halls and check window locks at night. Aside from the frequent moments of sibling rivalry, there aren't too many skirmishes in the Eligibles' wing. More often, just romantic rendezvous."

I snorted, remembering the hot-n-heavy we'd almost stumbled into on the grounds the other morning. Something about overhearing those two niggled at me, but I couldn't figure out why. "You fight well, though."

"Not to the level of the Strati," Terran said.

"You're still decent."

He stuffed half a biscuit into his mouth. "Initial training is the same for all soldiers. Proficiency during that time dictates where we go after that."

Eury swiped a pat of butter with his knife. "The Strati are drilled to be a different breed, Princess. Many let the position of power go to their heads and becoming honorless bastards. Not all, of course," he said, flashing me a charming smile.

Ydorus pushed back from his empty plate. "Some of us are stubborn enough to believe we can recapture the united Attalos we grew up in. In years past, Attalos was an incredible place where everyone was safe to live life."

I thought about Elani and wondered for the millionth time if she and Rowan were all right. "How many men does my mother have in her personal horde?"

The three men regarded each other as Leda brought a fresh jug of juice over and a pot of coffee. She sat them down and met my gaze. She was pretty, in an older woman kind of way. Her skin had that hint of green that marked an Earth Faery with soft mocha hair and eyes to match. "Can I get you anything else, Princess?"

I pushed my chair back and undid my top button. "Lexi, please, and no thanks. I'm stuffed. But I could use a change of clothes. Is there something I could throw on so I can rinse my shirt?" I gave a cautious sniff and wrinkled my nose. "Yeah, that would be great."

"I'll find her something." The rough timbre of Rowan's voice had me whirling in my chair. There, leaning on the frame of the archway into the kitchen was the master of the house. He looked freshly washed and well-pressed in grey slacks and a crisp white shirt. He strode across the kitchen and bent to kiss Leda on the cheek. "How have you been?"

"Well, thank you, sir." She brushed a light hand down his muscled arm and smiled. "And incredibly thankful Jonash called me back to service. I've missed this."

Once again I thought of Elora and the way she ran our household back at Haven. The more mouths to feed the better, nothing was ever an imposition and everyone was always welcome. Leda and Elora were cut from the same cloth.

She swept a hand and gestured to the room. "These halls have been silent too long."

Rowan's smile faltered. He turned his back and reached into a cabinet for a mug. He shifted a few around and when he faced us again he wore a mask of perfect contentment. "I left money on your desk for the market. Take care not to draw attention to the fact that we have mouths to feed. The last thing we need is for the Queen's Guard to end up here again."

Leda paled and then gathered our empty plates. "I shall be discreet."

Rowan abandoned the idea of coffee and headed toward the hall. As he passed by, he threw me a gut-wrenching stare.

Was I meant to follow him?

I thanked Leda and hurried behind. His long, smooth stride ate the distance of the massive halls like nothing. He didn't even seem aware that I was with him. Or he didn't care.

After a maze of halls and two flights of stairs my cheeks were starting to burn. "Hey, Doc. What did I do now? Obviously, you're pissed and my keen intuition says it's directed at me."

Rowan turned on me and I fought not to recoil. The eyes that locked on mine were blazing and cold.

"Okay, definitely pissed and definitely at me."

He turned again and the walk of the tempest continued. I followed at a safe distance, watching the tension in his broad shoulders as he stomped through his house. I'd been struck dumb by the strength in his arms and back the other night at the forge, but his butt was rather spectacular too. And his gait, *uh-huh*, he strode like a predator stalking a kill.

I swallowed hard, knowing exactly who the kill was this morning.

What did I do? That question seemed to be at the root of all my troubles through the years—with Bruin, with Jade, with the multitude of people who I had inadvertently offended—but this time, I honestly didn't know.

Around another corner and up to the third floor. When we came to a set of ornately carved orichalcum doors, Rowan jolted to a stop, his palms resting on both handles.

Standing behind him I could see the violent flex and hollow of his stubbled jaw as the rest of him remained utterly still. Without warning he rammed his forehead against the door panels. Once. Twice. I leapt forward as he cranked on the handles and sent them sailing.

Shit. The master suite.

The room was stunning. The far wall backed onto the tiered glass atrium. From this side, I couldn't hear the trickle of water, but the scampering shadows of a never-ending waterfall plummet flickered against the lit glass. A huge canopy bed nudged against it, the lush, heavy draperies hanging in a silver and violet brocade. As Rowan's fingers trailed down the fringed edge of the drapery, the fury in his frame seemed to drain.

"I never came back." His voice was dead as he sank onto the violet duvet. "I didn't want to see this house without them in it. I swore I'd only come back once I reclaimed our family honor and found a way to free Elani from her sentence."

"But here you are."

"Yup, here I am." He fingered the stitching of the bedspread, his head bowed so his hair covered his face. "The Queen's whore, the embarrassment of the Fifth sector, an utter failure as a Noble, son, and brother."

"The game's not over yet. From where I stand, I'd say you're doing okay. You've kept Elani alive this long. Tell me what happened at the palace?"

He winced. "What?"

"Ew, gods, I wasn't asking about *that*, I just meant . . . did the Queen seem angry? Did she know you helped me?"

He shook his head.

"Then we still have time to figure out a plan. We'll get Elani out of the palace and we'll figure out a way to keep the Strati from ever coming for either of you again."

As I fell into the green-gold depths of his gaze his expression hardened. "You're a dangerous woman, Alexannia Grace." He launched off the bed and opened a drawer of the bureau. "I can't afford to believe in your promises. Elani is all I have left."

"I would never do anything to endanger—"

"Intentionally, maybe," he spat, "but you put people in danger. You stir up trouble. You wreak havoc and innocent people pay your dues. I don't think you realize how reckless you are, even after your friend's death."

The fissure left in my heart from Tham's death cracked wider. "I'm sorry you're raw about coming here, Rowan, but you re-opened that wound, not me. I would have found somewhere to stay, if not at Balor's—"

"Please," he snorted, venom thick in his voice. "The Queen's spies would have notified her the moment you set foot near the town-houses. But you knew that, didn't you?"

I gripped the bedding, trying not to lunge. "What the hell does that mean?"

"It means I see through your poor, displaced-orphan routine. There's nothing weak about you, *Princess*." He swept his arm across his front and gave an exaggerated bow. "You're just getting the lay of the land. Hell, you've been orchestrating things since you got here."

"If you believe that bullshit, you don't know me at all."

"I know Terran, Coal, and I have had our lives upended. We used to know how to manage the status quo, now we're skirting death just by being part of your life. Shit, I walked into my own kitchen just now and you had three soldiers sitting up and panting on your every word like puppets." His eyes narrowed. "Your mother has that same gift."

I was off the edge of the bed before his words had even sunk in. "I'm the one caught in the perfect storm here, Doc. I'm riding this wave and trying not to choke on the surf or get crushed on the rocks. In four days, I've lost my home, watched my father's head roll, found out my mother is a demon-bitch from the depths of hell and held my best friend as he died—"

"Poor Tham." He scrubbed his palm across his unshaven jaw and laughed. He actually fucking laughed. "My point exactly. Even with you in another realm your undercurrent was strong enough to tow him in and drag him under."

My fist connected with his face hard and fast. Rowan's head flipped back like a snapped rubber band. I grabbed his crisp, white shirt and swung him to the ground. When he back-flatted on the floor I landed my knee in his chest and pinned him.

"You *bastard*." Choking on fury and anguish my hands wrapped around his throat. "Don't you ever . . . laugh about Tham's murder."

He glared at me, his Adam's apple pressing hard on the flesh of my palm, his left eye doing a serious water and blink from where I'd nailed him.

My temper exploded through every cell in my body and I thought I might kill him. But before I gave in to slamming his skull against the floor I remembered the last time I'd lost my cool. The aftermath of that little tantrum with Mika was something I truly didn't want to repeat.

"Again I thought we were almost friends. My mistake." I released my grip and strode for the open double doors. "Forget it. Forget everything."

I raced past the naked marble statue. Through the room I shared with Coal. The bathroom door slammed behind me and I twisted the lock. I slid down the wall and let my ass bottom out on the cool, marble tile. My trembling arms hung off my knees and my head dropped back.

What the hell was I doing here? Closing my eyes, I fought the tide of emotions threatening to detonate and take out a city block. If one more thing happened, I was going to lose it and it would be a scene or horror like you read about.

Knock. Knock.

I was on my feet. I flung the door open, screeching a particularly colorful string of curses—except it wasn't Rowan. "*Coal,*" I choked, my eyes glassing up. He stood wide-eyed, ginger hair poking away from his head in tufts. I'd forgotten he was sleeping in the bed. I probably scared the crap out of him when I slammed the door. "Oh, gods, buddy. I'm sorry. I didn't know it was you."

The frozen uncertainty blanketing the kids face was more than I could take. Now I was scaring a little boy? My hands were trembling, my back aching, my pulse thundering in my ears. My chest was so tight that I'd swear no air would ever pass through my lungs again.

I sunk to my knees and opened my arms and he didn't hesitate. "I'm sorry," I breathed against his soft neck. The wall of moisture brimming my eyes began to fall. I hugged him tighter. "I'm angry, but not at you. We're good."

I pulled back and cupped his lean face in my hands. He looked so lost it broke my heart. "You and I will always be good. You don't know me well yet, but you're mine now. I'll die before I let anything happen to you, okay."

He leaned back and read my expression.

I lifted my wrist up and let the golden hawk of my Talon brand appear on the surface of my skin. "I swear, on my honor as a warrior and your guardian, that you and I are a team. You aren't alone in this world anymore."

His hug clutched even tighter the second time around.

Rowan appeared in the doorway. "Could I, uh . . . talk to you a minute?"

I let Coal go and brushed my tears away. "I've heard enough from you for a lifetime."

He stared at the marble floor of the bathroom. "I'd like to apologize to you properly. In private."

I stepped behind Coal, pulled him against me and crossed my hands over his chest. He was the tiniest shield imaginable, but I felt better having him there. "The only thing I'm interested in is how to start the shower. Once I get cleaned up, Coal and I will be making tracks."

"You don't need to. I don't want you to go."

"Yeah, well, I don't care what you want. I won't stay here. You've made it clear what you think of me. I won't hear any more from you—"

"Marry me."

My jaw fell slack. "*What?*"

"You heard me." He rammed his fisted hands deep into the pockets of his slacks. "You have to marry a Noble within the next three days anyway and Zale's a womanizing prick—"

"And you're a prick of a different breed," I snapped. "And as proposals go, that sucked by the way."

His jaw clenched and hollowed. "I believe we want the same things for Attalos. You care about justice and people . . . and you can't deny we've got incendiary chemistry."

"So, does a Molotov cocktail, but I won't be hitting the horizontal

with one of those either. Burn me once shame on you, burn me twice .
. ." I shook my head. "Not interested."

He exhaled and ran a rough hand through his bronze waves. "I was
an asshole. No argument. But you can't begin to understand how out
of my mind I am after a night of . . ." He looked at Coal and stepped
inside the bathroom. "Are you really going to make me do this in front
of him? Because I'm not leaving until you hear me out."

I thought about twisting the knife. Laughing at Tham's death was
unforgiveable, but Coal was an innocent bystander in this mess. After
a deep inhale, I bent down and kissed the top of his head. "Hey, buddy.
You slept through breakfast. Why don't you go to the kitchen? Ms.
Leda saved you some of the casserole she made for me and Terran this
morning."

I could read in his eyes that he was torn—hunger versus concern. I
nudged him toward the door and flashed him a genuine smile.

O.K., he signed. It was awkward but understandable.

"I'm good. I promise," I said, beaming that we'd had our first official conversation.

When Rowan and I were alone amongst the elegant porcelain
fixtures and gleaming stone, I crossed my arms and waited.

"I screwed up. I'm sorry." He groaned and propped himself up
against the vanity looking ill. "It was a humiliating night. And then I
back came to this house . . . and you were laughing with soldiers, two
of them Strati . . . and I was thinking about my parents and how Strati
slaughtered them . . . and what they did to Elani . . . and you looked so
good, your cheeks all flushed from your workout."

He turned his back to me and gripped the counter his head
hanging down. "I'm so fucking tainted," he whispered. "I'll never stand
up to your perfect image of Tham. I hate myself for being jealous of a
dead man and I hate him for having the love and respect of—"

"Whoa."

His head came up and he looked at me through the mirror.

The self-loathing in his eyes killed me, it did, but the ache in my
chest didn't thaw. "I'll forgive that you were out of your mind and you
fucked up. I am the last person to judge someone for popping shit, but

you crossed the line when you brought Tham into your little rant of self-destruction. You laughed. He's dead and you laughed."

"I didn't mean it like that. I swear. It won't happen again."

"No. It won't." I turned and opened the door to the shower. "Could you show me how this works? I'd like to get cleaned up before I go."

"Go where?"

I glared over my shoulder. Did he really think he was getting in on my plans to avenge Tham? He must have caught my none-of-your-damn-business vibe because sadness suddenly clouded his eyes.

"Sure," he muttered. "Here, it's easy." He reached for my hand and I pulled it back. He frowned and cleared his throat, but didn't try to touch me again. "These are designed for Water Fae. You place your hand on the control pad and summon the water. Concentrate on the temperature and the force and it will come as you will it."

I looked at the small screen he was indicating. "Good, thanks."

He nodded and backed out of the room. As he pulled the door closed behind him, I could feel how badly he needed me to let him off the hook. Sorry. Nope. Incendiary chemistry or not, it wasn't happening. I already had a date with four very deserving men.

Alone, I stripped off my clothes and left the pile in the middle of the bathroom floor. There was a mountain of thick, puffy towels in the stand-up cabinet and I pulled out a couple. One I tossed on the floor and the other I straddled over the heated rail outside the shower.

With my hand flat on the screen, the skin of my palm tingled and I was in business. All I could think of was getting out on that street come sundown and teaching a few of the Queen's soldiers how it felt to be ambushed.

CHAPTER EIGHTEEN

Standing in the recessed doorway of a fancy-schmansy scarf and accessories shop, I spun my knife in one hand and my newly acquired Attalosean pain-stick in the other. No eyes could spot me even if the streets weren't abandoned for the night. I was hidden, deep in the shadows and well away from the iridescent glow of the city's luminescent field.

The first of Tham's attackers had been child's play—a disappointment actually. A quick this-is-for-Tham-you-fucker and a long smooth stroke to give him a Columbian necktie and I was off to a good start. The bastard hadn't even had the balls to take it like a man, whimpering and snotting as he asphyxiated in a back alley. Pathetic. Apparently, he only had stones when jumping an innocent man surrounded by three other thugs.

The door opened at the bath house across the alley and a male stumbled out in the swath of light. The place was a seedy slap-and-tickle joint and a favorite amongst the Strati soldiers during off duty hours. Ydorus had tracked the other two soldiers to this brothel just after dusk and they had yet to depart. *Smart boys.*

The guy in the doorway stepped out of the harsh backlight and into the full glow of the moon. He was not my target.

I let the minutes tick by, snacking my way through the stash of candy Terran had nabbed me this afternoon, one lollipop at a time. *Mmm cherry.* Spinning the orb of saccharine bliss, I watched that door, waiting for the burst of adrenaline to kick in when my targets decided to put away their cocks and show their ugly faces.

More time passed and the warm wind turned chilly. I tucked the baton into the back of my leathers and patted my too-light vest. Gods, I missed my weapons. Savage had made me those blades and I missed each of them like lost children. I pictured the dozens and dozens of weapons hanging on the wall of my battle class back at the castle: daggers, flails, morning stars, rapiers, shurikens, axes, picks, and sickles. My heart gave a quick pit-a-pat at the thought.

Three more lives to claim and I'd be free to focus on how to get Coal and me home. Surely Zo or Castian could help my family find me. *If they want to find me.*

I shook my head. They might think I'm being selfish and went AWOL to blow off steam, but when I don't show for my own party and they learn what happened to Tham . . .

My heart ached. Surely Zophia had told them by now. I rubbed my fingers across the soft, embroidered choker. Apt name—choker—because it choked the breath out of me to wear it. Gods, I miss you, hotness.

I knew exactly what Tham would say if he was standing beside me. His sultry, suede voice came into my mind and I bathed in its familiar warmth. *You have one minute to wallow in the delicious misery of what you cannot change,* sweeting. *Embrace it annnnd proceed.*

Well, I'd been leaning here listening to the slap of eager flesh for the better part of two hours, so I was pretty much done wallowing. I was ready to get to work. The door opened again, and as if called by my thoughts my two soldiers stepped out of their playhouse and started down the alleyway.

Perfect. A threesome they'll never forget.

The grey sky of morning was lightening, the red line of dawn edging the horizon like a freshly slit throat. The Right of Vengeance dictated that the three lives I'd expired tonight were mine to take and aside from having the kills sanctioned by the Seelie Court, everything was solid. I doubted very much that the courts would come into play, but even if they did, I didn't care. Justice had been served and I'd take the lumps rather than giving up Zophia's assistance.

After blowing a kiss to the heavens, I slipped in the back gate of Rowan's mansion and headed for the ornate double doors. It felt good to right the world a bit and nothing got the blood pumping like skulking around in the dark killing bad guys. I'd saved the best 'till last, though. Tasso would learn about the demise of his three accomplices and understand it for the message it was.

You're next, asshole.

As long as Terran, Coal, and I stayed out of sight today, I'd be in business for another round of fuck-you-and-the-Queen-too come nightfall. It was fast becoming my favorite pastime. I looked to the sky again.

Red sky in morning, Tasso take warning.

"You're in a good mood."

I whirled toward the barrier wall, my blade aimed at the shadows. My eyes had penetrated the darkness all night and were tired but focused. I blinked against the burn and traced the silhouette sitting under the canopy of the outdoor lounge.

Rowan.

I sheathed my blade and turned back toward the door. It was best not to meet his gaze head on. My body hummed with adrenaline and the way that man pegged me with those seductive hazels, I might just pin him down and ride him rough, right here—right on his back patio. Yup, there was something about fighting that triggered my sex drive.

"I'm a big girl, Doc," I said, pleased that my voice was tight. "No need to wait up."

Releasing the handle on the door I strode through the back vestibule and into the living room beyond. The room was even more impressive tonight. With the familiar urge to live large after a battle zinging in my veins, everything came into focus—each smell, sound and sight more delicious, exciting and vibrant than the night before.

A soft snore rose from the oversized sofa facing the fireplace. Terran had obviously been waiting up for me too. Sound asleep, he sprawled on the couch, a bottle of what looked like Scotch and a long/tall sitting on the teak coffee table in front of him.

"Guard 11, turn in for the night. All is well." I squeezed his arm and smiled when his unfocused gaze met mine.

"What timess-it?" he asked, palm-scrubbing his face.

"Almost five-thirty."

I helped sit and spotted a small sewing box at the bottom of the bookshelf. After a quick look inside, I hooked my arm through the handle and got Terran to his feet. As an afterthought, I leaned back and grabbed the neck of the liquor bottle and we headed upstairs.

"You crash in my room with Coal, okay? I'm messy and I don't want him seeing me like this and freaking out."

We climbed the stairs, slow and steady, headed past the naked statue and continued to my room. When I cracked the door open, the light revealed Coal on the bed. Curled up in a little ball like a puppy in a basket, he was out cold. I rubbed my chest as my heart fluttered. Could you fall hopelessly in love in just a few days? Yes. Yes, you could.

"Terran, I'm probably going to sleep late but, with what went down tonight, I don't want either one of you to step out of this house tomorrow, got it?" I watched him shuffling toward the bed, stomping his downed pants with his boots, trying to pull them off.

Terran mumbled some garbled gibberish and I laughed. Setting my contraband in the hall, I steered him to the bed and sat him back. After undoing his boots and setting them on the floor I pulled his legs free from his pants and settled him under the duvet.

"Terran tell me what I said."

"You're sleeping in."

"And?"

He yawned wide as he whispered. "Coal and I are inside until you say otherwise."

"Sweet dreams, boys." I eased out the door and stepped across the hall.

Terran's room was smaller than mine, but it had an ensuite bathroom and that was all that mattered. I lifted the bottle of amber liquid I'd commandeered from downstairs and brought it to my lips. I coughed after the first swig but didn't let that slow me down. Not Scotch, but it would do the trick.

The slow burn that worked its way down to my belly was hollow and unsatisfying. Gods, what a night. Tracking those men down for Tham went a long way in restoring my sense of self, but it hadn't changed anything.

Tham was still dead.

I sucked back another long swallow and cleared my throat. Tomorrow would be better. I had big plans for Constable Tasso. Big. Big plans.

When I'd banked a large deposit in my alcohol-buzz account, I decided that looking in the mirror could no longer be avoided. With my free hand, I snagged the sewing box on the way to the loo and sucked back some more liquid relief. I'd seen Cowboy and my other Talon brothers Martha Stewart themselves, but this was a first for me. No Jade to patch me up tonight.

I washed my hands and arms and reached for one of the two hand towels sitting on the counter. Jonash had taken the time to fold and sculpt the towels into little terry dolphins and for some reason, I hated to kill the poor buggers.

Ironic after all the slaughter I'd just finished.

After drying my hands on my shirt, I peeled my bloody leathers down my thighs and tossed them and my shirt into a heap in the corner. Then I set up shop on the wide marble counter. Flipping open the padded lid of the box, I poked around: needles of various sizes, thread of various colors and tiny scissors.

Cooleroo.

Another hit of anesthetic and a few sloshes over my pointy little tools and I started the grueling process of trying to thread the eye of the needle. I bit my lip and snorted. I should have taken care of this before I numbed up. I made another pass at the cock-sucking little hole and laughed out loud. Who the hell thought this was a good idea?

"Having problems?"

Oh shit. I swallowed hard and took a breath, whipping my inner vixen back into her cage. I was nearly naked, rather drunk and completely jazzed . . . a trifecta of bad decision-making, waiting to happen. I cast the most casual glance I could manage into the mirror and snorted when I met his penetrating gaze. "Nice shiner."

He raised his fingers and probed his eye where I clocked him earlier.

I sighed as the hot pink thread avoided that stupid little hole for the eleventeenth time. "Shit, this looks so easy when Iadon does it."

Rowan set his medical bag down. "Let me help."

I pulled my hands back. "Are you going to be a dick?"

He raised a beautiful brow. "I'm not planning on it, but I make no promises."

After considering my options, I offered him my needle and thread. He waved them away, grabbing a dolphin hand towel sculpture and shaking the life outta the poor thing.

Murderer.

When Flipper had been thoroughly doused and squeezed out, Rowan took a knee beside me and twisted my hips so he was getting an up-close-and-personal with my ass cheeks.

"I, uh . . . bastard number three got a lucky stick when I was dancing with his friend."

"I see that." He stroked the warm cloth down the indent of my hip and butt. "Got you pretty good. Were you really going to sew this up with pink quilting thread?"

"Seemed like a good idea at the time. Besides, Gutterman's good shit, right?"

Avoiding his stupid smile, I distracted myself by fishing around in the little box. "Was your mom handy with all this happy homemaker stuff?"

Rowan focused on the wide gash running about five inches down the outside of my hip and curving across my backside. "She was.

Quilting and needlepoint were her favorite, but she could sew just about anything." He pulled the handle of his doctor bag and set the thing on the floor by my feet.

"So, you get it from her?"

"What's that?" He tapped a small syringe and clear fluid squirted into the air.

"The flare for stitching things. I'd like to keep the scar as small as possible."

Rowan met my gaze in the mirror, his smirk far too sexy. "I'll do my best. Little stick now while I freeze this."

"You've been a pain in my ass since I met you. Why stop now?"

Rowan poked me a couple times, probing and prodding my flesh. As he waited for the freezing to take hold, his eyes took a slow and steady inventory of the rest of me. He traced the outline of the giant red-tailed hawk tattooed on my opposite hip. "This is nice."

"Jade, and I got them when we were accepted into the Talon." His gaze continued a slow, heated sex-ploration of my valleys and curves. "It's not polite to stare, Doc."

He smiled, his eyes lit with a flirtatious light. "You got your fill when I was at the forge the other night. Only seems fair I get the same opportunity."

I thought about that. Man, the way the glow of the fire glistened off the sweat on his skin, his thick muscular arms and shoulders tapering down to those slender hips. I bit back a moan as my nipples hardened against the silky leopard print of my bra and warmth started to spread from my core.

He was focusing on me, gauging his effect on me. This was *soooo* not good. If he didn't start sewing me up soon I was liable to turn just a little and—

"Did you feel that?"

I swallowed and opened my eyes. "Sorry, what?"

Rowan chuckled and cupped the globe of my ass in the palm of his hand. "I asked if you could feel this. I'm guessing the freezing is working."

"Seems so."

"Bend over the counter a bit so I . . . uh, yeah. Yeah that's good. Just. Like. That."

I bit back a growl and focused on not thinking about my derriere being propped in front of him in my next-to-nothing panties, not thinking about his calloused fingers caressing my body just inches from where I wanted him to be. The urge to drink hit me hard. I tipped the bottle back and let it burn a happy trail down my throat.

"Did you get your revenge?" Rowan's voice was husky and rough. "On the ones who killed your . . . Tham?"

"Three of the four." I hissed as he dug into a particularly tender spot. "And he wasn't *my* Tham any more than he was Galan's or Jade's or Aust's. We were friends, not dating."

"Uh-huh?" The surprise in his voice was only surpassed by the disbelief.

"Okay, friends with benefits might be more accurate. He was family though. I loved him like that."

"Seemed like more."

I arched a brow. "Well, it wasn't."

He worked along in a mind-numbing silence while my head whirled and swirled in an uncoordinated dance. "Not that it's any of your business, but Highbornes are an affectionate race. Tham was on his *Ambar Lenn*, his coming-of-age journey to find his place and prove himself a male of worth. He was enjoying himself, tasting the flavors of realm life." I smiled, thinking about his survey of what kind of woman he liked best. "All the flavors."

He hooked the curved needle through my skin and pulled again. The dull ache of my flesh tugging together seemed negligible compared to the pain I'd been living with lately.

"What about Rowan?" I asked. "When you first left home to study medicine in the outer rings, you must have been tempted by all the different kinds of women?"

He frowned and pulled the stitch tight. "I wasn't looking to get laid."

"It was just a terrible by-product of being a rich, sexy, med-student Noble, I'm sure."

He turned away, taking an unusually long time to pull the scissors from his bag.

I'd struck a chord and not in a good way. "Sorry. I was teasing."

He shrugged but didn't look at me. "It galls me that I squandered that time when I could have been here with my family. It's pretty hollow to remember, when I know what it cost me."

"You couldn't know. And I bet your parents were crazy proud of you the whole time."

After he cut the end of the thread, he peeled open a package and pulled out a wide gauze pad with sticky edges. With exacting attention to detail, he smoothed it over the wound. His palm lingered as it cupped my ass, setting the protective layer.

I met his stare in the reflection of the mirror, his faint blush bringing on a hot, hard lust from somewhere deep inside me. He cleared his throat. His hand slid to the outside of my hip as he straightened behind me. He had that look again—that panty-combusting, wantonness that I'd seen and had a taste of at Terran's family home.

"Uh . . . I'm finished here. Let's get you cleaned up so I can check you over properly."

"Cleaned up?" I pivoted, but he didn't step back. As a result, I was pinned between the vanity and a very large, very aroused man. He really was in sublime physical condition. My hands came up and traced where his heavy shoulders sloped down to rock hard pecs. I swallowed. "What are you suggesting, Doc, a sponge bath?"

A devilishly wicked grin spread across his jaw. It caught my breath. His eyes searched mine, his tongue wetting his full bottom lip. He wanted to kiss me. For a moment, his eyes sparkled with it. His hand lifted, a finger traced down my jaw.

When it touched the edge of my velvet choker, the sparkle dimmed. He stepped back as if a few feet would cancel out the sexual tension filling the room. "Do you remember how to start the shower?"

"Why'd you shut down?"

He lifted his fingers and counted off his reasons. "The Queen's claim on me, Elani's safety, your impending marriage, my state of dishonor, your grief for Tham, your being drunk . . ." He reached to touch me, then crossed his arms tight against his chest. "There's more to consider here than how badly I want to seduce you."

There was a vulnerable wonder in his voice that made me ache. No seduction necessary.

"It's a bad idea. All around."

Coward. Even though I knew something of penis-related rejection, and couldn't argue with what he was saying. I also couldn't help the sexual frustration. "I'm half-drunk, actually, but I'm also covered in blood and sweat. Frankly, I don't sleep well when I'm sticky."

I undid the clasp of my bra and tossed it, then down went the slip of leopard print silk from my hips. "You go make your list of excuses, Doc. And while you're lying in your big ole bed tonight, rock-hard and you give in and take things into your own hands—and we both know you will—remember that *you* walked away. And when you've got your rhythm and your chest is pumping and heat is radiating like your internal furnace is about to ignite, think about me standing here naked. Remember you didn't have the stones to take what you want."

He sucked in a breath and scowled. "Keep the water from wetting your dressing. Focus your ability. I'll check on you in the morning when you're sober."

"Oh, bite me," I shouted over my shoulder and slammed the shower door.

CHAPTER NINETEEN

*L*onely, horny and just this side of being a quivering, moist mess, I summoned the water on as hot as I could stand and let the spray sting my skin from four separate shower heads. For Goddess sake, who needed four shower heads?

I wanted to cry. All this pent-up energy ebbing and throbbing through me and Rowan had found his reasonable streak. Sex wouldn't have to mean anything. I just wanted to climb him like a jungle gym and release some of this energy. I tipped my head back and washed my hair, concentrating on keeping the water flow from my bandages.

A rush of cool air made my nipples tighten and my eyes jerk open.

The shower door was open and Rowan was stepping into the spray. "Damn, woman, mind if I turn this down?" Rowan passed his hand over the screen and the temperature adjusted, then he closed us in together.

The powerful muscles of his upper body shifted and flexed as he moved, but that wasn't what had my lips parting. His erection was massively thick and by the way it stood, from his groin to his navel, proud to be in the game. Spectacular.

I tore my gaze from his sex and something in me melted. The fear and hopelessness in his eyes ripped at my heart. "I didn't walk away because of the reasons I told you . . . though all of them are still true."

"I'm a big girl, Doc. This doesn't have to be anything more than it is. What's—"

"What if I can't?" He swallowed, his tawny complexion gone pale. "What if I can't get the feel of her off me? I don't want to bring her into this." He bit his lip and dropped his head back. "I swear to the gods I've scrubbed my skin 'till I've bled and yet I always feel her touching me. What if I'm with you and ruin things because of her? I'll lose my mind."

"Has it happened before?" I read the answer in his silence. "You haven't been with anyone else the past four years?"

He shook his head. "How could I? I'm polluted."

"It's not your fault. Any of it. You know that, don't you?"

He let the water darken and soak his chestnut hair but never took his eyes off me. "What if I can't get the feel of her off me?"

We moved in slow, sensuous tandem, shifting our feet, our bodies edging ever closer. "If you need more, take it. If you need rougher, do it. If you need me to twist you inside out, tell me." I laid my hands on the wide flat planes of his chest and he shuddered. "That woman has no place here. I'm willing to bet that once the two of us get started, we'll sandblast her from your body and your mind."

The ridge of tension in Rowan's brow eased a little. He reached past me to retrieve a cloth and a bar of sweet-smelling soap from an inset shelf. After wetting the cloth under the stream of water, he turned the soap in his palms and created a frothy lather.

"Raise your arms for me and hold on," he said, eyeing two of the shower heads above me.

I did what I was told and forced myself to remain still as he washed away the blood and sweat of my evening. With slow sensual strokes, he started at my neck, down my shoulder blades, and spent considerable time sliding those silky bubbles across my chest and circling both my breasts.

Lower. Please gods, lower.

He continued down my navel, the heat of his need filling the steamy chamber surrounding us. His attention slid to the outside of my hips, followed the controlled stream of water avoiding my bandaged injury, and spent extra time on the other side, visiting my tattoo. "You have the sexiest ass I've ever seen."

I reached to the back of his neck, my fingers tangling in wet curls. "Then you've never seen your own."

He shook his head and pointed to the nozzle of the shower head. "Arms up. Doctor's orders."

Water trickled along his sharp cheekbones, outlining the curve of his jaw. He chuckled when I released my hold on him and pushed out my lip. He reworked the creamy bar into the cloth for a fresh round of sweet-smelling suds. "I told you I would get you cleaned up for a closer examination."

A moan tore from my chest and a rush of heat flooded what I prayed would be the next stop on his home-care house call. "You *did* say that," I whispered, my heart racing.

He knelt in front of me, his touch slow and languorous, his lips caressing my skin, light and maddening. I shifted my footing, practically panting for him to take me, to kiss me, somewhere, anywhere —*everywhere.*

Right when I thought he'd lean in and go for gold, he dropped his washcloth to my ankles and started working his way up. "Tease."

"Almost there, Trouble. Be patient."

"Not my best event." I growled and shifted my feet to give him access. "I'm more of an instant gratification kinda girl."

Warm, strong hands caressed my calves and massaged my flesh as he made his way upward. I bit my lip, my breath coming fast and shallow. Magic and heat, pure blue flames and electricity—that was what was licking its way through my body and building in my core.

He pressed my thighs apart and his cloth slipped between my legs. I cried out as his touch skimmed and washed me right where my need raged.

"I've wanted you since the first moment I saw you," he drawled.

I groaned and tilted my hips into his hand. "Nothing like a girl puking on your shoes to kindle the flames of passion."

He nipped the flesh of my good hip. "My cock's been as hard as my anvil since you showed up and eyed me the other night. I almost came in my jeans right there at the forge."

The cloth dropped to the tile floor with a wet *plop*.

My flesh prickled with the most amazing pleasure as the water rinsed and swirled over my skin. I sucked in a gasp. The flow of the shower had a life of its own, stroking me, twisting around my nipples, tingling over my every pore. It flickered over the tight bud of nerves at my core and warmed until I cried out. "What are you—Oh, gods, Rowan are you—"

He chuckled appreciatively as his tongue dipped in and out of my navel.

"You're doing that?" I dropped my head back as he kissed his way up my ribcage and suckled my nipple into the heated depths of his mouth.

"Mhmm," he hummed against my breast. He finished with that side and shifted to the other, taking care to divide his attention equally between the two.

"Rowan." Desperate to feel him writhing inside me, I was willing to beg. "Please, it's so good. *Too* good."

He straightened and stood, his broad shoulders looming above me. The swollen crest of his erection pressed against my stomach. "Too good?" Wrapping his muscular arms around my waist, he lifted me off my feet. In two quick steps my back was pressed against the smooth, slick wall of the shower and his hands cupped the rounds of my ass.

"I don't want your stitches to—"

"I'm good," I breathed, as the first wave of release started to grip me. "Fine. Go. More. Now."

His lips swallowed my cry as he pinned me against the tile and slid smooth and deep inside me. Inch by rapturous inch he impaled me and groaned into my mouth. My muscles gripped and pulsed, tightened and rose. The pleasure was incredible. It lashed at my senses and burned through my system.

Another strong thrust and I hit my breaking point.

He moved his kiss to my collarbone and rode out my release. I pulled in deep, humid breaths, my head spinning, either from the orgasm or the steaming air, I didn't know.

I didn't care. As my heart fought to free itself from my chest, his pumping gained momentum and my hunger raged on, desperate for—

"More."

Clutching his hair, I wrapped my feet around his hips. I dug into his quads, pulling him closer as he pounded into me. "Give me more. Give me all of it."

His tongue thrust into my mouth matched the desperate thrusts between my thighs. I met him stroke for stroke, that incendiary chemistry igniting and bursting until we were both aflame. He was exquisite, temple-pounding gorgeous, and rough. Gods, how I loved rough.

"Come for me again," he rasped, fighting for breath. "Doctor's orders."

As he pitched his shoulders forward and found his own release, my body obeyed. The pleasure unraveled my soul. It spanned the jagged fissure in my heart and stopped the desperate ache. As the full weight of his frame crushed me against the shower wall, I realized Rowan had gotten under my skin.

Momentary panic overwhelmed. How had that happened?

Rowan held me, easing back to let the water wash between us. I winced as I lowered my legs and tested my injured hip.

Not bad.

"Dammit Lexi, I used you too hard. I'm so—"

"Amazing," I said. Staring at him from beneath lowered lids, I stroked my mouth over his. His lips parted for me, his tongue meeting mine in a playful sweep. The contact sent another shock of pleasure through my and I moaned. "You were amazing. My stitches are fine."

The sharp edges of his worry drained away and he pulled me tighter against him. His hips ground against me in a sultry sway, his interest on the rise again.

I bit his bottom lip and drew back. "A mattress at my back would be nice for round two."

Rowan's eyes lit and his smile was brilliant white. He stopped the water, grabbed a wide, fluffy towel off the heated rack and wrapped it around his hips. With the second towel, he dried me before scooping me against his chest and whisking me into the bedroom.

Damp brown hair curled against Rowan's neck as he laid me down and gave me a sexy half-smile. "Better?"

I reached between us and untucked his towel, tossing to the floor. His ass was a work of art. It was a shame not to take time to appreciate it. I slid my palms down the smooth skin at the base of his spine and over the contours of his body. "Better."

Heat ignited between the two of us and we were lost again . . . and again.

Sex with Rowan smoothed a balm over every ragged wound I'd been hemorrhaging from. It allowed me to forget—if only for a time.

The deep-seated disappointment of my Haven family was gone. The ache for a father I would never know forgotten. The weight of soul-shattering guilt over Tham's slaughter lifted.

By the time my stitches throbbed and the sun had risen, I collapsed and sank into the delicious golden glow of satiation. I slept. Slept harder and deeper than I had in weeks. Months. Tucked tight against Rowan's wide chest, with his forge-sculpted arms encircling me, and the scent of sweat and sex in my head, I felt safe. Truly safe—if only for the moment.

Tham came to me in my dream and we walked along the Haven stream with the wolves. Nightrunner, the pack alpha, and Faolan walked with us. Faolan's belly was heavy with a litter of unborn pups. I told Tham about Rowan and Terran and most of all Coal.

"With your capacity for love, *neelan*, you shall make a fine *naneth* for the boy."

I snorted and bumped him with my shoulder. "I don't know how to be a mother. I grew up without one and now that I've met her, turns out she's an evil bitch."

Tham skipped a flint rock across the still surface of my pond hidden in the forest below the Dens. "In that case, you know precisely what not to do, so you are halfway there."

We talked about people we both missed and things he wished he'd had the chance to do before he was killed. It was wonderful to spend time with him but, when the chill came into the wind and the sky darkened, Tham sent me back.

I woke, still wrapped in Rowan's embrace, his morning erection prodding the small of my back. By the weight of the arm draped over my side and the long, deep breathing warming the back of my neck, I knew he was still out.

I thought about the days that led the two of us here. We'd both been so angry at each other, the people around us, and our lives. And last night . . . I'd been drunk and riding an adrenaline high from stalking Tham's killers. Maybe things would look different to him this morning.

Maybe I was stupid to think it was more than a night of sex. Great sex . . . but sex all the same.

"What's on your mind, Trouble?" Rowan nipped the back of my neck, the pinch of flesh tingling up my nape as his breath warmed my skin.

While I struggled to put my anxiety into words he propped himself up on his elbow and studied my face. Since when was I shy on saying what's on my mind? I shrugged. "Just morning-after-the-night-before stuff. Absorbing everything before the world crashes in."

His gaze narrowed. "Morning after the night before? So, what's the verdict, good or bad?"

I reached up and gave him a soft kiss. "All good on my side. I can't speak for you—"

A set of knuckles rapped on the door and Terran popped his head in.

"You awake Lexi, Coal wanted to bring you—" Terran's eyes popped wide as he glanced to the bed and made a quick shift to block the door. "Sorry."

Is Coal out there? I mouthed, pulling the sheets tight to my chest.

He nodded. Rowan launched off the bed in a glorious streak of tawny skin, scooped his dress shirt off the floor and tossed it to me before heading to the bathroom with his pants in hand. Terran played the part of the privacy screen while I buttoned up and adjusted the covers so all my parts were covered. I laughed as Terran tried to hold his position, his hips and body jerking as he was obviously shoved from behind.

I gave Terran the nod and he stepped out of the way.

Coal threw him a dirty look and grunted at him. His pajama bottoms dragged over the ends of his feet as he shuffled over to the bed. The tray of breakfast he carried was almost as big as him.

"What this, buddy?" I asked, signing the words as well.

He handed the tray up to me then scrambled to climb onto the edge of the bed. The mattress barely registered his weight. He looked at the tray and then at me, a hint of frustration darkening his previous smile.

I pointed to the items on the tray and showed him the signs as we went. "Juice, potatoes, waffles, fruit and coffee."

He watched my hands and mimicked my movements the best he could. He was so incredibly smart. Did all mothers think that of their kids?

"That's right." I nodded, as we repeated them a few more times, his smile returned. "Thank you." I picked up the little pitcher of syrup and poured it over the whole thing.

Rowan came out of the bathroom bare-footed and bare-chested, wearing only his grey slacks. His hazel eyes were lit with green, his loose brown waves thoroughly rumpled.

Rounding the foot of the bed, he examined my haul. There was plenty for both of us, even considering my usual appetite. Coal looked at Rowan and then at me and I could see him piecing something together. Did he know about sex? Would he feel threatened by me spending private time with Rowan?

When his hands came up, I braced myself.

He raised his eyebrows and tilted his head. After pointing to me and then to Rowan, he made the sign for 'happy'.

I set my fork down and signed as I answered. "Yes. Are you happy?"

He thought about that for a moment, pointed at Rowan, then to me and then hit his fist into the palm of his other hand.

My heart broke. I swallowed past a lump in my throat before I could answer him. "No, sweetie, I'm sure he doesn't hit . . . and I would never let him."

After a moment, he nodded and hopped off the bed. Jogging to the window he pointed at himself and then outside.

Right. I'd restricted them both to the house until I learned about the fallout to my little outing last night. "Sorry, today is an indoor day, maybe tomorrow. Is Ydorus or Eury here?" Coal shrugged, looking sad. Man, this kid was going to wrap me around his little finger. "Give me a few minutes to eat and take a shower, then I'll head downstairs and see what's doing. Are you getting dressed today?"

He shrugged again and I couldn't stand it.

"Well, it doesn't matter to me, but you'll do better at hide and seek if you're not tripping on your pant legs. And we can work on your signing some more too if you want."

Coal brightened and scampered off across the hall.

Rowan kissed my forehead and the two of us descended on the food like vultures on a fresh kill. We'd burned a hell of a lot of calories this morning.

Terran stood at the doorway staring and shaking his head.

"What?" I said, stuffing a forkful of seasoned potatoes into my mouth.

"I thought you were a lesbian."

Rowan choked, juice spraying into the air as he bent over, sputtering.

I pounded his back. "*What? Why?*"

Terran handed Rowan a napkin. "The leather pants, the short hair, the fighting, the language . . . and the boots."

"What's wrong with my boots?"

Terran shrugged again. "I've studied the Modern Realm. Tough women who wear boots and cut their hair short are often—"

I snorted and rolled my eyes. "Well, that's a widely sweeping stereotype but I'm not. Not that there is anything wrong with that . . . but I am definitely one-hundred percent hot-blooded hetero."

Rowan seemed to find the whole topic incredibly funny. I scowled and he raised his hands. "Hey, I like your boot. You being a lesbian never even crossed my mind."

I shoveled another forkful of fruit-covered waffle into his mouth. "Cinderella is living proof that footwear can change your life. Can you imagine me stalking around last night wearing sling-backs and a skirt? Gimme a break."

Terran trotted to the hall and grabbed a bag off the floor. "That reminds me, Leda asked me to bring this up."

"What is it?" I reached up and accepted the large bag.

"A gift," Rowan said. "I had her visit the third ring to pick up some things from one of the other realms black market boutiques." Rowan shifted the tray off the bed so I could have a look. "Terran said you offered him your left nut for proper ladies' workout wear."

The two of them chuckled as I reached in and pulled out a pair of yoga pants and dug further. "Thank you, baby Jesus, *underwear*." I looked down at the thoroughly feminine wisps of silk and satin. "You made Leda pick out underwear like *this* for me? Gods, what will she think?"

Rowan peered into the bag and bit his bottom lip. "I don't care what she thinks and no, I called that order in myself, Leda just picked it up."

"You did this yesterday? Awfully cock-sure, aren't you?"

He bit his bottom lip, his hazel eyes glowing with a look my body recognized in an instant.

I swallowed.

"Well look at that, Terran," Rowan said. "I do believe our Princess is blushing."

I snatched a pair of panties and stretch pants and carefully slid out of bed. Tugging Rowan's shirt down my thighs, I preceded to the bathroom.

"Not so fast, Trouble," he said as I turned to shut the door. "I want to check your stitches before you go conquer the world. Hop in the shower, but leave those pants off until I have a look."

"Stitches," Terran repeated, his face going rigid. "Are you all right, Lexi? You said you were fine last night. I remember that much—"

"I *am* fine," I assured him, my focus trained on Rowan stalking toward me. "He just gets off playing doctor."

"Goodbye, Terran," Rowan called over his shoulder. "Lock the door behind you."

Terran cleared his throat. "Ah . . . okay, so, I'll be down with Coal when the two of you finish up here."

I swallowed at the wicked grin Rowan flashed me. "Yep. See you in a bit."

When the latch clicked shut, Rowan had me up in his arms and then sitting on the cold, smooth vanity. When he spread my knees and stepped closer, I bit his chin. "How are you feeling this morning, Doc?"

He freed the top button on my shirt from its mooring and moved down to the next. "Thoroughly sandblasted . . . and ready for another house call."

CHAPTER TWENTY

$\mathcal{Y}$dorus and Eury arrived just before noon, but they hadn't come alone. Four other Strati had joined them, and by the time Rowan and I descended the main stairway, the new guys had each been thoroughly fed by Leda and sent out to the back-yard to wait.

"What's with the reinforcements?" I asked as we entered the kitchen.

Ydorus rose from his seat at the table and glanced to where Coal was handing his lunch dishes to Leda.

"Coal, buddy," I said, ruffling up his ginger hair, "why don't you grab those hoops and ball we saw in the cubby in the backyard? Maybe you and Eury can figure out a game to play for a bit." Eury bowed his head and I held my knuckles out. After a quick bump from Coal, the two of them slid out the back door. "Right where I can see you though, 'kay?"

I took a look at the wooden chair tucked under the kitchen table and winced. My sextacular morning hadn't done my gashed ass a bit of good—not that I'd tell Rowan—and now, the stitches stung from the ointment he'd slathered. The idea of sitting on a slab of teak didn't give me a warm and fuzzy.

"Let's take this conversation to the living room," I said. Accepting a coffee from Leda, I gestured to the overstuffed furniture set against the back of the house. Rowan smirked and opened his mouth to comment. "Careful, Doc, you've already got one black eye from me."

Terran snorted and Rowan tested the shiner I'd given him for him laughing about Tham. It was an ugly shade of puce this morning, rimmed with purple.

Without comment, Ydorus sat in the far chair and crossed his arms over his leather soldier's vest. "There was quite a bit of commotion in the streets this morning," he said.

I eased into the sofa opposite the back windows and I let out a breath. Much better.

Ydorus waited for me to get comfortable and then continued. "Three of the Queen's Strati were found dead, killed by some skilled assassin in the night."

"Were they really?" I said. "And?"

Ydorus gestured to the back patio. "Those are good men, Princess. The two on the left are my Uncle Nicoli's boys and the other two Eury has known his entire life. We went through training together. You can trust them."

"Trust them with what?"

He leaned over his knees and frowned. "With whatever plan is underway to overthrow the Queen. You can't expect to do it alone."

What? "I think you've got the wrong idea. There's no mutinous scheme underway. I'm just exacting justice for Tham, and keeping Coal away from Lir-dickhead."

Ydorus ran a finger down the stitching line of his uniform pants. After picking of a couple invisible pieces of lint he looked up. "Permission to speak candidly, Princess?"

"Always . . . and it's *Lexi.*"

"With the tripling of military guard storming the streets and the implication that you are behind it, you would be wise to come up with a plan. And quickly. The Queen will not—*cannot*—allow this uprising to go unchallenged."

"And why would suspicion fall on me? It could have been anyone who killed them. The people of Attalos certainly have just cause to want the Strati dead."

Both Rowan and Ydorus gave me a *well-duh* stare, but it was Ydorus who continued to speak. "The three men killed were seen in the city streets with your Elf friend in tow. It's no secret that he was killed, or that you took it badly. The Queen is accustomed to her tactics drawing people under her control, not fighting back."

"Yeah, well, the Queen is bat-shit crazy and should never have been allowed to rule."

"Not always," Rowan said. "There was a time your mother was a great and compassionate ruler."

I snorted, took a sip of my coffee and burnt my tongue. "In what lifetime?"

Rowan rested his arm across the back of the sofa and crossed his feet on the coffee table. "What was it . . . about eight cycles past?"

"About that," Terran said, "Pater worked in the palace orchard back then. He told me the Queen fell gravely ill and was never the same. She didn't go totally off the bars, just slowly became the woman she is today."

"Off the *rails*," I said, blowing across the surface of my mug. "And what kind of illness?"

Terran shrugged. "No one ever really knew. She was unconscious a week or more, and the healers thought she was beyond aid. The entire city held a vigil and prayed for her."

I found it hard to imagine the citizens of Attalos flocking to offer their well-wishes. How the mighty had fallen. "Would there be records of the time she was ill, Doc? Eight cycles would be more than thirty years ago."

"I should think so," Rowan said, accepting two sandwich plates from Leda and passing me one. "They'd be in the archives of the Palace temple if there were. The City's clergy are the guardians of documents like that. Why? What do you think her illness will tell you?"

I mulled that one over. Could a mysterious ailment from three decades ago have any relevance to her decline into maniacal insanity?

"Can the Queen be found incompetent? If something from that illness compromised her mind, could she be removed from the throne?"

Rowan wiped his mouth and shrugged. "I'm not sure. That would fall under the jurisdiction of the Noble Council. My father's volumes of the laws are up in his study. You're welcome to go through them, but it will take all night. And then, even if she could be removed, how would someone enforce it? The Noble Council and the Strati follow her without question."

I shrugged. "Attalosean laws are absolute, right? If we found something, maybe we could use it to our advantage. It's a starting point, anyway. You and Terran wade through the books and see if you can find something we can use."

Rowan scowled. "And where will you be?"

"I have plans tonight."

Rowan set his plate on the side table, the oh-no-you-don't written all over his sexy puss. "Weren't you listening? Ydorus said the guards have tripled in the streets. If they've connected those three men to Tham's abduction, they're going to know you'll come after the fourth. Tasso will be bait for the largest ambush this city has ever seen."

"He's right," Terran said. "There will be eyes on Tasso from now until you're brought into the palace. It's too dangerous."

I was on a low boil as I stood. No fucking way was I not taking out Tasso for what he did. That asshole's life was stamped paid and was mine for the taking. I drew a deep breath and reminded myself that these two weren't trying to control me, really, they weren't . . . really. "I appreciate what you're saying—"

"I won't let you." Terran rose from his chair and almost looking confident as he squared off against me. "As your personal guard, my duty is to ensure your safety. You will not go hunting tonight."

I pulled back and raised a finger. "Watch it Terran. Talk to me like I'm some female who needs protecting and I see a black eye in your future too."

He met my glare and pushed forward until we were nearly nose to nose. "I know how to duck."

Okay that was funny. I tried to hold onto my anger, but it was no use. The tension dissolved. "Look, I'm going, but if it stills the waters, we'll come up with a solid plan. Ydorus, Eury and their boys can help and then we'll take it from there. You two need to stay here to go through those law books and keep my little man safe though. I'm counting on you."

Terran didn't seem to like it, but nodded. Rowan, however, just glared.

"Good," I said, "now everyone get their thinking caps on and we'll finalize our plan before dinner." I walked to the large picture window facing the backyard and knocked on the sea-green glass. Coal's smile broke wide. "But for the next half hour we're all taking a moment to live a normal life and play hide-and-seek with Coal. *Not it.*"

CHAPTER TWENTY-ONE

"If it be a sin to covet honor, I am the most offending soul." With Shakespeare's words warm on my lips, I thought how impressed Reign—and our Centaur tutor, Chiron of Delaran—would be that I actually remembered something from all the hours of tutoring they'd invested in.

Rowan kissed my forehead, his lips soft on my skin, his anxiety choking the air between us.

Avenging Tham by eliminating Tasso had to be done and it had to be now. Coal was in bed. The sun had set, the full moon had risen, and the iridescence of the field over Attalos was lighting my way to where I needed to be. But for the first time in my life, I was torn about leaving to fight. "Ydorus and the others are waiting for me."

"Let them wait," he whispered, studying my face. Gentle fingers traced the line of my jaw, and caressed my neck. Freshly showered, he smelled delicious, his loose brown curls damp against his neck. His hands moved lower, his touch pausing on the pockets of my battle vest.

My heart beat faster. "Thanks again for the weapons. I love them."

He shrugged, his smile not touching his eyes. "You're not really the kind of girl I'd buy flowers for."

I chuckled.

He didn't.

"Hey, don't." Stretching up on my tiptoes, I claimed his lips. His kiss was stiff, but I persisted, nipping and kissing until he loosened up a little. I pulled my lips from his. "I'll be fine. Promise. You'll be so busy with those law books, you won't even miss me. I'll be back before you know it and you can sew up any damage. We can have a repeat of last night."

His glare was an ocular version of a fully extended middle finger. "Swear you'll be careful."

I held up my arm and let my Talon brand appear. "On my honor, I do so swear."

He dropped his lips to the top of my head and pulled me tight. "You're not nearly as invincible as you think you are, Princess." To prove his point, he spanked the gash that wrapped from my hip to the cheek of my butt. Hard.

"Hey." I hissed. "Be nice or I'll reconsider my after-party plans and cuddle in with Coal."

He almost smiled. "I don't think so. *If* you get back here alive there will be a thorough exam of all your parts and pieces. Doctor's orders."

I wrapped my arms around his neck and kissed him until we were both breathless. "It's a date."

Iridescence shimmered along the inner surface of the dome. It danced in greens, blues and pinks, illuminating the black night sky like the Aurora Borealis. Moving amongst the long shadows of sleepy homes, I ghosted through the abandoned streets. The city was quiet, the citizens all tucked safely in their beds. I doubted they were sleeping. The air was charged with violent intention. Mine. The Queen's. The citizens' themselves.

My skin rose in goosebumps as I neared the rendezvous point. The evening breeze crept over my skin, leaving the faintest sticky feeling of salt and sweat on my flesh.

"Princess," Ydorus whispered.

I shifted my gaze to the dark void between two buildings and found him.

"Everything all right, Princess?"

I nodded and joined him. Drawing a deep breath, I fought the ache that had been growing in my chest for days. It felt wrong not having Bruin and Jade watching my back and Julian orchestrating the attack over comms. But they weren't there and I was. I bit back the pain that I was now on my own.

"Everything is perfect. Let's do this."

As Ydorus led me the rest of the way, I tried to shake the feeling that I'd missed something, something just beyond my mind's eye. I scanned the streets again as he tucked us into a nook at the edge of the courtyard. Tasso, the pompous bastard, stood opposite us, standing against the guardhouse chatting with two men.

Ydorus leaned close. "Besides Tasso and his friends, there are two guards inside the guardhouse, four watching from buildings surrounding the courtyard, two dressed as citizens in the gated patio of the restaurant across the way and there might be one hiding behind the bronze sculpture at the center of the fountain."

Did they really think I would tromp right into an ambush? *Yes. Obviously, they did.* They'd probably even laughed about it, me being an emotional female and all. Well, their underestimation of me was to my advantage. Thankful once again for Reign raising me, I drew on my years as a Talon warrior and as a teacher of battle strategy.

Shifting my feet, I stretched my neck from side to side. The moon was almost directly over the main square and when it was, these men would see just what kind of strategist I was. I ran a hand down my newly mended leathers and smiled. Rowan was a handy little sewer. He had many talents, actually. I patted down the front of my vest, glad for the weight of weapons.

I loved all my new knives, but the best for this battle was the hand-held compound bow with orichalcum bolts. I slid my fingers over the butt of the weapon and stroked the polished wood. Now all I needed was to get close enough to shoot one of these nasty little fuckers right through Tasso's eye socket.

That was going to be damn satisfying. *Truth.*

Ydorus and I sat tight, waiting for the working parts of our plan to sync up. It was Tasso and his men who began the shift and fidget. Maybe they figured I'd get sick of waiting and just go for it. Yeah, think again.

One of Ydorus's cousins from this morning, dressed as a male server, came out from under the awning of the restaurant with a dessert tray. As planned, he set the tray on the table between the two soldiers trying to blend in and the courtyard beyond. I rolled on the balls of my feet, watching as he busied himself, screening those two sipping at their doped drinks.

"They're starting to waver," Ydorus whispered, drawing his pain-stick baton. "Won't be long."

We watched as first one, and then the other, slumped in his chair. Two down.

Taking out a lighter, Ydorus's cousin pointed it toward the tray and I drew my dagger. The whoosh of blue flame was massive, the patio bursting alight. He must have used a stein of booze to ignite the thing because the awning caught fire and in seconds, flames leapt in every direction.

Chaos ensued: the scrape of chairs, the scream of patrons and the rush of two more hidden soldiers to investigate.

The whistle that rent the air was Eury's signal that he was on the move to secure the guardhouse. That was my cue.

As the waiter and his brother faced off with two very surprised fellow soldiers, I darted from shadow to shadow, edging closer. Despite being close enough to see the feral grin on Tasso's face, I couldn't get a clean shot. I ducked low and rolled to the side, coming up against the trunk of one of the metal sculptured trees. Holding up the bow up, I sighted Tasso. Shit, almost there.

I needed him to step out from behind the streetlamp.

The restaurant commotion was still in full riot when a merchant woman burst from her shop and started screeching at the two Strati hiding on her balcony. Waving a broom and a flashlight, she screamed about privacy and the perversion of men watching from the shadows.

Eury rammed a metal bar through the door latch of the gatehouse and blocked the exit for the Strati inside. Whether it was a flash of movement or the Fates deciding to screw me, Tasso turned exactly the wrong way, at exactly the wrong moment and chased after him.

Shit. Tasso was headed out of the courtyard.

Abandoning plan A, I launched into the alley nearest me and gunned it in the same direction. My thighs ate the distance as my heart raced inside my chest. Tasso was mine and no way was he taking Eury down for helping me.

As the commotion of the courtyard grew faint behind me, I cut through a side street. The rhythmic sound of heavy footsteps connecting with stone echoed hollow somewhere on my right. Male voices grumbled and shouted. Something clattered loud behind the candle shop. I raced on.

The moon slid behind the clouds and the luminescence of the field was gone. The sudden loss of light had me blinking to adjust my vision. Footsteps resumed to my right and I pushed into the darkness by sound alone. Eury and Tasso were coming down the next street, had to be.

Adrenaline pumped the thunder of my pulse into my ears. They would be intersecting just about—

The rollercoaster drop had me flailing mid-air.

Water scrambled my mind as I splashed and sank. My muscles tightened as icy darkness enveloped my body.

The canal.

I must have run off the edge of the walkway and landed in a canal. Struggling to find which way was up, I broke the surface and choked my lungs clear. The clouds were passing, the glimmer of moonlight casting a path back to the edge. I was a strong swimmer, but the lip of the alleyway was at least five feet above my head. No ladders. No edges to grab.

The scuffle of a vicious fight, echoed above. Cursing. The dull thud of bodies connecting. The grunt and crash of hand-to-hand. *Shit*, Eury.

I needed out of this canal. I needed to be up there. A surge of water pushed at me from below. Did I do that? But I could barely work the shower.

The sounds of the battle above tightened in my gut. I couldn't tread water here all night while people were getting hurt. With all my might, I focused on the water raising me to the edge. I needed a lift. I needed out. I needed—

The catapulting effect was immediate and far more powerful than I expected.

The stone of the walkway came hard and fast. My tuck and roll barely saved my head from cracking. My shoulder hit and bent behind me. White-hot pain shot through my hip. I blinked, my vision spotty.

Tasso was there, not twenty feet away, beating on Eury like a dog in the street.

I scrambled to my feet, ignoring the lethargic response of my left leg or the road rash on my palms. Fuck, where was the crossbow? Canal, likely.

Hand-to-hand it is. Crossing my arms over my waist I grabbed the two hilts protruding from my battle vest and drew steel. Tasso and Eury were still hard at it. Didn't even hear me slip in behind them when—

I froze. Shaking my head, I breathed deep again to make sure. *Scourge.* The rotting stench of the undead clung to Tasso's uniform . . . how?

My hesitation wasn't long, but it cost me. Tasso spun and back-fisted me to the face. Staggering to the side, I breathed through the hit. He whirled me around. The instant I spun to face him, I rammed my knee between his legs and locked my hands on the fucker's throat.

An earthquake of emotion ripped through me.

Gone was the strategic, Battle Master of The Academy of Affinities, gone was the Talon Enforcer for the Realm of the Fair, gone was any thought or emotion beyond the violent menace erupting from my core. My skin ignited with a burning heat.

A hard punch to the gut and my breath left me in a rush. Struggling in an all-out brawl, my body moved on autopilot, slashing and hacking at the bastard who had taken pleasure in killing Tham—the sweetest male ever known.

With my vision still on the blink, the images Zophia had shared with me flashed like a never-ending lightning storm behind my eyes. My muscles and bones ignored the damage, ignored the teeth-rattling strikes Tasso landed.

I was action. No thought. No feeling. For the first time in my life, my temper exploded and I didn't reel it in.

Struggling in a close melee, I unsheathed my Guardian from my thigh and brought it up in a hard arc. The blade fought through his ribcage, positioned to pierce his heart.

"That is for Tham." I jammed it in, hard. "And for me, you fucking piece of shit."

Tasso's eyes widened and then we both sank to the cobbled ground.

Sometime later—a long time later judging by the ache in my muscles—I became aware of Eury's low moan. I yanked my knife from Tasso's body and crawled over. The buckles of his chest plate were slick with blood and tough for my cramped fingers to manipulate free. Shit. He was drenched and in bad shape.

"Princess?" I gripped my blade and whirled, blade poised. No need. It was the merchant woman with the blue wings from the other day. She approached slowly, her hands up between us. "Princess, you're hurt. Let us get you in off the street before more soldiers come. It's not safe here."

"Him first." I wiped my blade on Tasso's cape and sheathed my knife. "Eury's worse off than me. He needs Rowan." When she just stared at me, I snapped. "Lir-Rowan, Noble of the Fifth House, get him for me."

She recoiled. "This man is a Strati soldier. Leave him to the night. You need to—"

"He's with me," I said, resting a protective hand over Eury's chest.

"Not all soldiers are the Queen's men. If you care anything for what remains of Attalos' honor, I demand he receive shelter and care."

She pursed her lips but didn't hesitate long. Whistles sounded a few streets over. Men shouted. Nodding, she waved to the three young men. They scurried out from the shadows.

With booted feet, two of them rolled Tasso like a rotten log and kicked him into the canal. The third grabbed a large sheet of wood from the alley and dropped it onto the bloody stone walk beside Eury. He and the woman shifted Eury onto the board and dragged him down the alley to a door.

The voices grew closer.

When I made to follow, my foot skidded. Pain ripped through my knee as it hit blood-slick stone. I tried to catch myself, but my body didn't obey. My vision fritzed again.

The thundering of soldier bootsteps were almost on top of us. The last thing I remember . . . strong hands scooped me up and pulled me in tight.

"We've got you, Princess," a voice whispered. "We've got you."

CHAPTER TWENTY-TWO

"*E*asy Trouble. Don't try to get up. You're safe." Familiar hands stroked my bare arm, the gentle scratch of callused palms calming me like a balm on a wound.

My eyes were not so much closed as on lockdown. The world was spun, my head throbbed, and my stomach felt as if it were filled with writhing eels once again.

I laid statue-still and pictured my surroundings. A fire hissed and crackled nearby. The dim glow of lantern light danced on the outside of my lids. I inhaled deep. Earthy. It smelled the same as Balor's hidden underground home.

I shifted my leg. My clothes were off. Rough blanket fibers rubbed against my belly and thighs, but not where my underwear and bra covered me.

My stomach sloshed. *Oh, gods.* My lips pursed.

"Oh, I know that look." A quick shuffle beside my head and Rowan was rolling me to my side. "You've got to stop—"

My ears cut off all sounds as I gripped the basin. My throat burned, my sides ached and my head was about to spew grey matter in every direction. When the retching stopped, Rowan laid me back and wiped my face with a damp cloth.

"You have a concussion," he said, wiping my bangs back from my face. "Would you have anything for her to drink?"

"Of course. Tea? Water? Ade?"

"Whiskey," I croaked.

"No. Not with a concussion," Rowan said, a smile in his voice. "Water is best."

Soft footsteps shuffled away and returned within moments.

"Here, Trouble. Drink this."

I cracked my eyes open and played good-patient while focused on the masculine beauty in front of me. He'd been to the smith's shop. I could smell forge smoke on him. He looked tired, but relieved. "So, by the smirk I take it I'm not going to die?"

"Not tonight. No."

"And Eury?"

Rowan pointed to the pallet on the floor by the fire. Eury lay still, a threadbare blanket draped over his hips. His clothes had been removed and most of the blood had been cleaned up. He was bound in gauze and bandages and looked like a black and blue piñata that had had his insides beaten out of him. "He'll survive too."

I leaned back and closed my eyes. Bad idea. Open was better. Definitely better. "We need to get out of here. The Strati will be all over those people if we—"

"Don't you worry about that, Princess," the woman with the blue wings stepped closer. "You're safe enough down here and the boys cleaned up the walk outside."

"Tasso's body—"

"It's taken care of, Princess," she said. "Please, lay back and rest."

I guess I did, because the next time my eyes opened, daylight streamed in through wide solar tubes fixed into the soil ceiling above. By the quality of the light, I'd guess it was approaching midday. A muffled moan had me rolling over to check on Eury. His swollen face stole my breath, his brow drawn so tightly he looked like he was reliving the whole nasty ordeal in his sleep.

I swung my legs off the little bed and let them sit flat on the woven mat. So far, so good. After tightening the blanket under my sore shoulder, I tested my balance and shuffled across the floor. "Hey, my man. Ease up."

I slid down beside him and traced the crease of his brow. As my thumb pressed over his forehead, the scowl began to lessen. I continued to smooth out Eury's stresses, avoiding the cuts and bruises the best I could. After a time, I felt the weight of someone watching from the door and cast a glance over my shoulder.

"My brother Bruin," I said to my hostess, "used to have terrible nightmares when he first came to live with us. His family and entire community were killed and he had a hard time during sleep. My sister and I would take turns trying to soothe him."

"Did it work?" she asked, setting a small tray on the chest by the bed.

"Usually. Once he stopped fighting, he'd sink into a deep sleep and we'd take turns watching over him." As if he were listening to my voice, Eury eased and settled. "Eury just relaxes, Bruin would change form. That's how we knew he was really out cold."

"Change form?"

"Mhmm, my brother is the Alpha Were. He's the Bear King of the Realm of the Fair."

"So you *did* grow up as royalty," she said, surprised. "The company you keep has everyone wondering."

I didn't miss the judgment in her voice and took an extra few minutes straightening Eury's blanket to simmer down. Tugging the thing up over the shallow rise and fall of his gauze-bound chest, I folded it back a bit and struggled to my feet. "Where I'm from, it doesn't matter if you're an orphan, a warrior or a barmaid, my father makes sure everyone knows their value."

She raised a brow and rose from the cot to give me back my bed.

It felt good to sit, my little tour of the room had drained most of my energy. "Attalos could learn something about looking beyond appearances."

"No offense, Princess, but idealism gets people killed."

"Oh, it's not idealism. We've got bad guys too. Scourge, that's what our enemy is called." The memory of Tasso's stench hit me again.

"Are these Scourge like our Strati? Like our Queen?"

I considered that. "Evil is as evil does, I suppose. The Scourge are nasty bastards who allow a sorcerer to suck their souls in exchange for power and what they think is going to be immortality. Really, they just become rotting undead, and raid and kill indiscriminately."

"What does the sorcerer do with their souls?"

I shrugged. "We haven't figured that out. He's obviously siphoning off power from them somehow—he's very powerful—but my other brother, Julian, figures with the number of Scourge that have been inducted, there must be something much bigger happening. Something we're not seeing."

I thought about that for a bit, my mind still occupied by Tasso and his funky stench last night. I needed to talk to Terran and Rowan. "Has Rowan been by this morning?"

"Yes, but we assured him we could take care of you ourselves and sent him on his way. I doubt he'll be back."

"What? What did you say to him?"

Her eyes widened as if my reaction surprised her. "We were protecting you, Princess. Your doctor friend is in league with the Queen." She bit her lip and brushed her forehead with the tip of one of her wings. "It won't do to have people thinking the two of you are—"

"Are *what?*" I drew a deep breath and tried to hold back the anger burning in my gut. "Rowan's a good man and, as a Noble, he should be respected by his people. Where do you get off judging what he's had to endure?"

"Endure?" She arched a brow. "He's the Queen's whore, Princess, a Noble no longer. He turned his back on our people and chose a coward's path to survive. He's done nothing but shame himself and the members of the fifth district for years."

I jolted up, the sheet pooling to the floor. Clamping my hands, I took a measured step away from the woman. Like last night, I experienced true ferocity. I reached for my shirt and awkwardly pulled it over my head. "Rowan's sacrifices safeguard his sister's life. She's the only family he has left—"

"Despite whatever lies he has spoken, Princess, his sister is dead. Killed a full cycle past with his parents."

I shook my head. "Elani is a prisoner at the Palace, a pawn in the Queen's game. When Rowan steps out of line, the Queen hurts her." I pulled my pants up my thighs and steadied myself against the wall. I needed air. Sliding my vest over my shoulders, I tightened the lacing and met her eyeball to eyeball. "What would you do to save your children from the Queen's evil? What wouldn't you do?"

"There is nothing."

I nodded. "If that's true . . . and if there really are no secrets in Attalos, I want everyone to know Lir-Rowan, Noble of the Fifth House, has done nothing but protect his sister. It's his district and the citizens of Attalos who turned their backs on him, not the other way around."

Before I said too much I turned to the stairs. As I lifted my foot to the first step, I looked over my shoulder. "If it's safe, I'll send for Eury at nightfall. I expect he'll be well cared for until then."

She met my gaze straight on and bowed. "Of course, Princess."

CHAPTER TWENTY-THREE

uty soldiers and Strati swarmed the city streets like angry wasps. They stood at every intersection, patrolled the alleyways and perched on rooftops, watching from above. Obviously, it would be smarter to stay hidden. Safer to go back into that cellar and wait till nightfall. I wasn't in the mindset to play it smart or safe.

I needed to find Rowan. Needed to find my boys. But first, I needed to find Sera and learn more about what she and Balor had done to me. What was I capable of? How did my connection to the elements work?

Stealth was a polished skill of mine. It was the work of twenty minutes and I was down the hidden stairs in the back of Balor's townhouse and searching the underground apartment.

I knew before I finished looking around that Sera had cleared out. Balor's things remained in place but the apothecary room was cleaned out. The only thing left was a piece of paper sitting on the mixing table with a single sentence written on it. *From the one with forethought and prudence, a leader shall rise.*

Allrighty then. So, Sera would be no help.

I made my way back to the street and considered my next move. Beeline it to Rowan's mansion, check on Coal, and see what the legal ledgers of the Nobles said about ousting the Queen. Rowan still owed me and my injuries a private once over. My current need to get naked with Rowan was more than a biological urge to satisfy and more than easing the hurt and anger of the way his own people judged him.

A brush with death had a way of bringing the world around you into hi-def, surround-sound focus. It made you want to live out loud and crank up the volume. And time spent skin-to-skin with Rowan was exactly the kind of sensory explosion I was amped for.

Ousting the Queen could wait. Our troubles could wait.

I skirted down a side street and jogged along the backside of a low retaining wall. My leg was still kicking up a stink and my shoulder felt as if it had been ripped from its socket and knocked back in place with a sledgehammer. Boo-fricking-hoo. In the long list of 'things that have gone to shit' that was the least of my problems.

I tucked behind a stone monument as the rhythmic footsteps of a military run of soldiers approached. A faint, metallic *k'tang . . . k'tang* rang in the distance. Lifting my head, I caught my bearings and wondered if I could find his blacksmith shop without Terran or Coal to guide me.

The formation of Strati soldiers passed without incident and I ducked through a merchant's yard and then down a side street. After slipping behind a dozen bronze architectural buildings and down another alley, I peered around the corner and saw the modest one-story building with huge paneled walls and smoke rising up through the chimney.

My heart beat as if I'd run a marathon, but it had nothing to do with my outing and everything to do with the man bent over his forge, glistening in the sun like an ancient Greek god.

After double checking the way was clear, I slipped inside and hid in the shadows by the back wall. "Hey, Doc, mind closing up shop for a bit?"

Rowan dropped his hammer, his hazel's filled with an emotion I didn't understand. He cursed under his breath. "You shouldn't have come here. You just don't think, Princess."

Princess? "I was careful," I said, jutting my chin forward. "Gods, it's stifling in here. Why are you working in the middle of the day?" It dawned on me that he'd told me he only smithed at night for just that reason.

I gauged his posture. His shoulders were stiff, his jaw clenched so tight I could see the hollow of his cheeks twitching. The hair on my arms rose just as the door to his back room opened and Strati flooded inside the open walls.

I drew steel, but before I could engage, one of the soldiers poised a blade at Rowan's ribs.

"Think well, darling," Zale said, strolling out from the back room looking like a well-dressed peacock in full preen. "You don't want more blood on your hands than you have already, do you?"

My gaze snapped back to Rowan and the Strati standing at the forge. The odds were bad, but I'd fought worse. Rowan had a sword billet right beside him. If he made any move for it, if he did anything to defend himself . . . anything other than let them take him hostage I could—

Zale's stupid face broke out in a gloating grin." You should know, Princess, we have your little scorch. If you want your pet unharmed. . ."

Coal? They have Coal. What about Terran?

My breath left my lungs in a rush. As quickly as my mind and muscles could react, I broke my stance, laid my blades onto the back bench and raised my empty hands.

"All of them," he demanded.

My hands shook terribly, whether from fear or fury I didn't know. It took great effort to empty my pockets. In the end, every gift Rowan had given me was left abandoned.

"That's my girl," Zale said, his smirk lifting with malicious intent. "I told your mother you could be trained—given proper motivation. We just need to get you in the mood for our wedding and then I'll have you all to myself."

I stared over at Rowan and swallowed the bile burning up the back of my throat. How could things have gone so wrong, so fast?

Rowan met my gaze. Disgust and anger burned in his eyes and

struck me like a physical blow. Rowan and Elani would suffer for this. They would both pay for him getting involved and helping me in my fight. In just a few short days, I had ruined everything he'd endured to protect his sister.

Bruin's deep timbre growled in my mind. *"It was an accident you've said. You didn't mean it, you've said. Fuck, Lexi, your actions have consequences. You hurt the people around you and don't even see it until they're lying there bleeding."*

My reflection stared at me from the polished surface of the metal wall. I clutched my chest, sure my heart had shattered. Mika, Tham, Eury, Coal, Rowan, Elani. All of them either had suffered or soon would because of me. Bruin was right. I hurt people. I did this.

Darkness hit fast as my mind shut down. I let the blackout take me. I deserved nothing less.

"You have to go back, Lexi," Tham said, swinging the hammock with one leg draped down and his toe against the forest floor. With the gentle sway of our bodies, we watched the dappled afternoon light dance between the lacework of leaves above us. "As much as I love our time together, you can't stay here with me indefinitely."

I snuggled tighter to his chest and breathed in the suede and outdoor scent that was Tham. "Stop being logical. A few more minutes, 'kay?"

Tham squeezed my shoulder and kissed the side of my head. "It is your dream, *neelan*. You hold all the power."

I sighed. Dream, vision, or visitation from beyond the Fade, I didn't care. Tham came to me when I needed him and that was enough for me. "If only that transferred into real life, maybe I'd know how to get everyone out of this mess."

"You will, *sweeting*. I have faith in you."

"Well, that makes one of us." I closed my eyes and soaked in Tham's warmth. It was unnerving to not hear his heart beat beneath his open vest. Dead or not, he possessed the biggest heart of anyone

I'd ever known. "Will you stay with me? It's silly, but I feel stronger knowing you're watching over me."

"I swear it."

The moment the sky clouded over and Tham sat up, I knew the evil was back. Cold tendrils crept over my body, seeking, probing. The icy slither snaked its way into my mind and into my chest. The evil lured and coerced, grew to be more and more seductive each time it entered my dreams.

Whatever it was . . . whoever was inching inside me wanted to possess me—take me over and consume me. I felt it to the depths of my soul.

"Lexi," Tham said, shaking my shoulders. "Go now. Fight for the others as you fought for me. Go. Find your boy and get him away from that female."

"But, I . . ."

"Go," he shouted. "By the love of all things holy, listen to me now and go, *neelan.*"

I sprang bolt upright and kipped to a ready stance. My legs trembled as my fingers grasped at my chest. The darkness of evil dissolved into a phantom chill. Honestly, if it wasn't for Tham shaking me from the illusion each time, I would never have the strength to fight off the abyss that threatened to consume me.

"Princess? Are you well?"

My neural pathways were tangled like boxed strands of Christmas lights. Bits of reality flashed in strobes inside my head. My palms tingled, itching for the weight and feel of steel and hilt. I scanned the room and tried to clear the fog from my mind. Where was I?

Silk draped walls, ancient frieze, Greco-Roman carvings, gaudy, oversized desk . . . *fuck.* I was in the Queen's private study. Sitting tall and regal upon her throne, she watched me, her long black hair framing her elegant features.

It was something in her emerald stare that set off the alarm bells in my scattered mind. Disappointment? No. Frustration. She looked at me as if I had once again thwarted some cold, evil plan . . . and I had, hadn't I?

A chill ran down my spine. I don't know how I was sure, but I was. She was the entity trying to get a foothold in my head while I slept. My bat-shit mother. She might be jaw-drop gorgeous squeezed into haute couture, but she was as lethal as a viper.

"I asked you a question," she said. "Are you well?"

"Peachy." Always, wildly feminine the woman possessed a seductive power that I didn't want anywhere near me or my boys. I swallowed the bile at the back of my throat and hit head-on. "What have you done to my friends?"

She arched a brow, picking up the slim-line dagger from the leather blotter on her desk. Turning it over in her hand, she sliced a flower off its stem from the vase between us. The corners of her mouth twitching in a twisted smile. "Your little urchin and your chamber guard are safely tucked away for the time being. Do as you're told and they will remain that way."

"And Rowan? What have you done with him?"

"Mmm, a great many things. He is a gifted male."

While she twirled the tip of the letter opener against the pad of her finger, I gauged my chances of launching myself at her and slitting her throat with it. I calculated the distance then eyed the two Strati soldiers standing guard in opposite corners of the room behind her. Damn.

"Pity he aligned himself with you and forfeited our arrangement. Especially considering that was the one thing protecting both him and his sister."

My heart stilled. "Why are you doing this? Don't your people mean anything to you? Don't *I*? I'm your *daughter*. You're supposed to be my *mother!*"

For the briefest moment, her eyes softened to a pale moss green. Gone was the hard edge. Gone was the hateful bitch. Instead, a sad expression of loss and confusion clouded her eyes. My mouth dropped open but, before I could think of what to say, the illusion shattered.

Gathering myself, I limped to the curio cabinet. I poured a glass of amber liquid and one-timed it. I downed another while I tightened up. When I had control of my voice again, I closed the glass-fronted door. "What is it you want?"

"A great many things," she said, amusement in her melodic voice. "I want puppets to remember their places. I want the hopes of some grand rebellion to die. And I want you to join your sister Eligibles at the leap year celebration and accept Zale as your husband."

"Why? What could me marrying that asshole possibly do for you?" But I knew. She wanted control of the Nobles Council and was infiltrating it every way she could. To break my will and force me to be one of her pawns would send a very clear message to others.

If I could believe her, Coal, Rowan and Terran were alive—that was the important part. As much as I wanted to run the silver point of that dagger through the top of her glamorous skull, I couldn't jeopardize their lives.

I needed to curb my natural impulse to strike and step back before I did something really stupid. I set my tumbler on the desk with a subtle thump. Maybe it was the booze interfering, but I couldn't see any plausible way to get around her and ensure that everyone remained safe.

"Fine. Tell me about the fucking wedding."

The Queen's lips narrowed into a fine ruby-red line. "Correct answer, but I don't appreciate your tone."

"Sorry. I have several others. Contemptuous. Angry. Snide. Aggravated. How about we settle on extreme sarcasm and get this conversation over with?"

My egg-donor cast a gaze to the desktop in front of her and with a careful hand took a moment to ensure everything was straight and in its place. "Leave us."

Her words were barely more than a whisper, but the two Strati statues came to life behind her and scurried away like mindless mice. "I should put you to death for speaking to me in such a way. Have you no sense of self-preservation?"

I shrugged. "I know exactly what you're capable of."

A thin smile tugged at the corners of her mouth. "No, Princess, you still have no idea."

I rubbed my damp palms down the thighs of my leather pants and tightened my hold on my temper. "If you're referring to your little sleep invasion, I already figured that out. You can stop trying to get control of me with tricks."

She barked out a menacing laugh. "Tricks? Oh, I have much more than tricks, Princess. I am the tingle at the back of your neck when you walk in the dark. I am the sound in the shadows when your heart races and you fight the urge to run. I am every terrifying, throat-clenching horror you dream of when you wake damp with sweat and chilled to the bone."

The boogieman rant was more than creepy, but I'd be damned if I'd let her know that. She smiled, pointing the tip of the dagger at me. As she turned it over and over, the light caught the metal, flashing along the beveled edge of the blade.

"But, it doesn't have to be that way. You have true character, Alexannia. Potential beyond your own imaginings. Despite Balor's betrayal —or perhaps because of it—you are the only progeny of mine to possess the strength and conviction to lead my army beyond the walls of the city. You are the only one of my offspring to ever be truly *Eligible*."

Ahhh, so there really was more to the title than farming us out to the Nobles.

"If you wish to gain your freedom in Attalos," she continued, "to turn down your marriage, to keep your pets safe, to have my ear and my approval—instead of standing in my way you will stand at my side."

Long, graceful fingers reached toward me and beckoned me closer. My mind made the connection between the words and the shock of hearing them with the speed of a lightning bolt. She wanted me to join her, to rule her evil army against who? Members of the other realms?

Drawing a deep breath, I looked at her outstretched hand and fought the little girl in me who'd always dreamed of having a mother. Maybe, if I joined her, I could pull her away from the ledge of maniacal insanity. My legs trembled, ached to go to her. The gods and I both knew I would do almost anything to have the love and approval of my mother . . .

But stand at her side?

I stepped back. "I see the dictatorial terrorizing you inflict on the people of Attalos and I can't be part of it."

"Even if denying me puts the people you care about in more danger?"

"I'll have to help them another way. There must be something else you want from me."

She tilted her head as if thinking that one through. "You marrying Zale tomorrow and smiling for our guests would be a good start."

"You realize he's a self-serving, egomaniacal dick, right?"

The Queen laughed. "He, like everyone, serves a purpose in the grander scheme of things. The only question is will you play your part so that your friends may live?"

Try as I might, I could think of no other option. "All right. For now, I'll play submit to your game of quid pro ho."

Her melodical laugh rang like church bells in a graveyard. She turned the dagger again and pressed the flesh of her finger into the point. Intentionally, she drew the blade across the flesh of her finger. "Wonderful. Compliance is at least a step forward. Tomorrow is a big day. Perhaps things will look different after a time and you'll see how things are meant to be between us."

Pat. Pat. Pat. I watched the violet drops fall from her finger and splat on the leather blotter. As the blood converged into one larger drop, my resolve solidified. I would never be absorbed into her rule. Dead or alive, I would fight her control and search for a way to help free Coal and the others.

Turning on my heel I headed for the door. What had I agreed to? Gods, if this was the work of the Fates fucking with me, I was going to skin the three of them.

With my hand on the grip of the door, I paused and stared at the ornately carved panel. "You may have forced me to accept Zale and the farce of this marriage, but don't take my compliance as submission. You can kill me, you can kill people I love, but I'll never be who you want me to be. I'll never stand beside you."

The rustle of fabric alerted me and I dodged to the side as the dagger sunk into the door. My heart *thumped* once as I ripped the weapon free and spun. With a flick of her finger, the dagger had changed course and bulls-eyed the pool of purple blood on the blotter. *Thump.*

Staring at the dagger's hilt twanging right in front of her, she clapped. "Alexannia, you are such a breath of fresh air."

CHAPTER TWENTY-FOUR

In the days I'd been AWOL, my suite at the palace had changed. Somewhere in the back of my mind, I expected to find my belongings still rummaged through and a sickening blood stain in the foyer. Instead, the rooms shined as gold and opulent as they had on that first morning almost a week—or more like a year—ago.

Everything picture perfect. Like nothing ever happened.

Movement in the bathroom had me stalking further into the room, searching for . . . right, no weapons. But as a frail young girl with auburn hair walked through the vanity area and into the bedchamber I bolted to her side.

"Elani." I flung my arms around her tiny frame and felt her stiffen. Right. Through Rowan, I felt as if I knew the girl, but she didn't know me. Likely didn't even know I was close with her brother. I took a step back. "Shit, sorry. I didn't mean to freak you out."

Her dainty fingers clasped together as she drew a deep breath. "No, Princess, of course not. Are you all right? No one has . . . hurt you, have they?"

I knew by the tightening in her voice what she worried about on my behalf. And though my mother had chosen physical brutality to keep her and her brother in line, she must have known that tack would never work with me. "I'm fine. Are *you* all right? Rowan was so afraid that the dirt I stirred up would settle on you. Have the Strati come after you? If they came after you because of me, I'm so sor—"

"He *told* you?" She whirled away, her arms wrapped tight around herself. "He swore no one would ever know. I can't believe he broke his word. What you must think . . ."

Stepping behind her, I squeezed her shoulder. "It's not what I think, but what I know. What happened isn't your fault, Elani. None of it. I've dealt with this kind of evil before and it's sick and twisted and—"

She shook her head and turned to me, her eyes glassy. "What the Queen has done cannot be undone . . . but to know my brother speaks of it . . ."

"Oh, gods, Elani, I'm sorry. Don't be angry with Rowan. I swear, he only told me so that I can help end this nightmare." I remembered the pained expression on Rowan's face as he'd warned me what they did to his little sister if I didn't stop. Now, I couldn't stop and he would never forgive me if Elani paid the price. "And Rowan? Have you seen him?"

She shook her head. "One of the Queen's Strati will come and take me to the consort quarters after. It is the only time he's allowed to see me . . . and only if he pleases her."

I pressed my fist against the sharp stab in my gut. My stomach being empty was the only thing that kept me from throwing up. *After.* That one word stole my breath.

A bright-eyed girl burst through the door and scurried into the foyer. "Everyone, she's here. She's back."

Everyone? Yep. Half a dozen people popped into my personal space, all of them eyeing me like a prize sow at market. I was *sooo* not in the mood. "What is this?"

Elani transformed from the weepy young girl I'd been speaking with into her servant-girl persona. Emerging from my walk-in closet, she offered me a sad smile. "Your marriage to Lir-Zale is the final event of the Leap Year Celebration. There will be five Eligible's marrying. Your sisters arranged the ceremony months ago, but there are dozens of last minute preparations to be made. You will begin with beauty treatments, gown, hairstyle, paint colors, what gems you want in what pattern—"

Oh gods. Only by sheer force of will, I struggled against my instinct to kill someone. The dye was cast. Denying Zale would only put everyone in more danger. Gesturing to the little army of carts now lining both sides of the outer bathroom I sighed. "Okay, so what's all that?"

"Your illusionist's tools for your beautification."

"My who . . . for my what?" I followed Elani's pinched gaze to a skinny, green-skinned male wearing a glittery silver vest. "The Nobles and royal guests are here, gathered for the formal reception tonight. The festivities go well into the morning ending in the outdoor theatre. As the sun rises for the dawning of the new day, you and your sister Eligibles will be presented on stage and wed."

"Gods, this is all such a nightmare."

The expression on Elani's face was far too old for a girl so young. I had seen the same look in too many faces since I came to Attalos.

I looked at the spot where I'd found Tham's body and closed my eyes. I could still see every stab wound, every score of his ivory flesh, every bruise. What if that was done to Coal, Terran, and Rowan. This was so much bigger than me.

So many others had it much worse than I. If the only way to evoke change in Attalos was through the Noble Council then I needed to get access to the people on that council. With a sickening dread, I solidified my resolve.

Marrying Zale had become the option of necessity.

Mrs. Lir-Dickhead.

"Princess Grace." A voice from the doorway had me turning. It was Stitch. Pale green hands fidgeted with the tie of his cloak and freed the knot. When he tossed it over the back of the sofa, his hair swayed like a baby duck's down in a strong breeze. The sight of his mourning band sucked the air from my lungs.

He rushed across the floor. "Thank the Fates you are well. When you failed to return to my shop and I heard about the killings . . ." He pulled a kerchief from his pants pocket and rubbed his face.

"I'm fine." With an arm across his back I helped him to the sofa and away from prying ears. "I'm sorry you worried. Things happened and I—"

He touched the soft black choker on his throat. "I know what happened."

Thankfully, before he made reference to Tham, the wedding makeover team kicked into high gear. It seemed, my mother wasn't convinced a couple of illusionists could whip me into any shape worth presenting to her royal ass-kissers. I ranked having the entire flock swoop in, squawking and flapping like geese. Ordinarily I would have ejected the whole gaggle but as long as no one was safe, I couldn't make waves.

First came the acid peels, foot scrubs and all manner of spit and polish, thankfully minus any actual spit. Next came the pluck and primp. My put-yer-eye-out hair-spikes were replaced by downy soft curls while my skin was conditioned and my follicles scraped, shaved, moisturized and then massaged. The man was gifted. After stalking the streets on my assassin spree the past two nights, I could have suffered through that kind of torture all afternoon. I even managed an hour of sleep while he worked on my back.

The final makeover brought on the artistry. My nails and face were painted and then two supercilious teenage girls with iridescent wings went to crazy-town gluing tiny purple gems in intricate patterns of filigree down my right side. Their little Bedazzling trek moved across my forehead, down my neck and then headed south, decorating the modest curves of my breast, ribs, hip and thigh.

"I don't recognize myself," I said once they finished.

"Success," the giggle twins chimed in perfect unison, "that's what we were going for."

Allrighty then.

In the end, every pore was breathing, every bruise was concealed and with all the customizing of my girl parts I was starting to panic.

"Attaloseans don't get married nude or anything kinky, do they? I will be wearing *something* at this reception, right?"

My entourage exploded into another fit of giggles as they headed for the door. Even Elani and Stitch chuckled.

"The jewelling is for the pleasure of your Noble," Elani said, closing the door behind the troop. "It's tradition."

That gave me an idea. Shuffling to where I'd dropped my clothes, I retrieved my vest and removed the small spy camera disguised as a rhinestone from the front snap. A little dab of the giggle twins' gluey-goo and it blended in with my decorated forehead and became my third eye.

The size of a postage stamp and almost as thin, I removed the control pad from where it remained hidden in the lining of my vest pocket. I turned it on and tucked it in my bra. "If anything happens to me, make sure this gets to my family in the other realm. They'll finish what I started and make things right here, I swear."

Elani retrieved a fabric garment bag from the back of my closet door. "Come. Let us dress you."

Happy to be offered something to wear, I tested the stick of the gems as Stitch and Elani helped me into my outfit for the evening. No need to worry. Those sparkling little stones weren't going anywhere.

Awed, I straightened in front of the mirror wearing Stitch's masterpiece.

"It's wonderful," I breathed. Regardless of the growing dread that the Queen would hurt Coal if I didn't marry Lir-douche-bag, and crazy about what she might be doing with Rowan in her consort quarters, the outfit was perfect.

Sleek gold slacks with Stiletto boots might seem understated for a wedding, but with the violet, backless top that dropped into a full-length train it was more than elegant. I ran my fingers up the crushed velvet halter to where the delicate ivory and gold lacework bib clasped around my neck, just below my mourning band.

Elani slid the dangling, gold leaf earrings in place and all I could do was stare.

"Your sisters chose traditional gowns," Stitch said, "but I thought you'd appreciate something more functional. I gave you as much mobility as I could and incorporated hidden pockets in the underside of your skirt to hold your weapons. I would have put some in place, but the Strati are screening everyone entering the Palace. I'm sorry."

My ache from having no knives swelled. And the fact that Stitch had recognized that had tears rising in my eyes. "It's perfect. Thank you. I appreciate the thought."

He bowed. "From the one with forethought and prudence, a leader shall rise."

That must be an Attalosean proverb or something. I stepped back to the full-length mirror and it dawned on me. "What's your true name? It's not really Stitch, is it?"

He shook his head. "My given name is Bay. My matris is of water and my patris is of earth. Bay, fits both."

Something occurred to me. "Elani, why is your brother named Rowan if your parents were both of water and your grandmother was of fire? Rowan is a tree."

"Patris had a childhood friend who was like a blooded brother. When Rowan was born his friend became an Abbatis priest at the Fae Trinity Temple and forfeited his given identity. Patris said that since his friend no longer needed the name, it would put it to good use."

"Rowan is a good name," Stitch . . . no, Bay said. "It is strong and vital and a man's name must reflect his identity in the community."

I felt the presence of someone entering the room and turned. "In that case," Zale said, "he should have been named Pornos, because that's all he is and will ever be."

I squeezed Elani's wrist and considered the benefits of strangling Zale. He strutted into my suite as if he owned the place, primped, polished and preened to near perfection. He really was an Adonis until he opened his pie-hole and the spell was broken.

"Would the two of you excuse us?" I asked. "My fiancé and I need a moment."

Elani glanced to the mantle clock and back to me. Time marched on.

"I'm sure Zale can escort me to the reception," I said, gesturing to the door. "Go back to your suite in case anyone is looking for you. Bay, thank you. This outfit is spectacular. No one could have gotten me and my tastes better."

Bay dropped his gaze and bowed. "You honor me, Princess."

When Zale and I were alone, his smile spread until it lit a malicious gleam in his eyes. "Well, well. Don't you look the part of the blushing bride. New clothes, new hair and thanks to your mother's forethought in giving you my little slave boy, a new attitude."

He pressed a finger over his lips and looked me up and down. "Submissive is far more becoming than the slumsnipe bitch you've been thus far."

"Oh, I assure you, it's just the hair and makeup."

"Well, with you on your best behavior, and me—well, simply being me—all eyes will fall to the two of us."

"I'm sure we'll be the talk of the ball." I snorted. It was taking all my strength of will to play coy with this asshole, but for my boys, I needed to be in control. "What about Freya Love? You mean the three of us, don't you?"

Zale rubbed his fingers over his mouth, covering a smirk. "This will be interesting. And since, the consummation of Noble marriages must be witnessed, the council is already abuzz. They pretend to be enlightened, but down deep they're just as perverse as the common."

"*Witnessed?*" Oh, this was getting better and better. "As in . . . a threesome peepshow?" When his smirk widened, my stomach flipped. I needed to find Coal and get my boy somewhere safe. "Voyeurism isn't my thing."

"That's a shame. I've already arranged a surprise for you." Zale strode to the bar console and slid the marble countertop backward until some hidden mechanism clicked. A moment later, a viewing-screen rose from inside the cabinet. He swiveled it toward me.

I was just about to tell him where he could shove his surprise when the screen flashed to life. *No. Oh, hells no.*

CHAPTER TWENTY-FIVE

*R*owan naked was a beautiful sight, but not like this. I closed my eyes but the image of his hands running down the silk sheets, contouring my mother's curves, had seared in my mind. Wearing nothing but a gold slave band around his neck he kissed her arm, her shoulder, her collarbone.

Rowan—No, don't!

I swallowed but my mouth remained dry. My fingers clamped against my thigh, searching for a hilt to grab hold of. My first impulse was to find a knife and the consort chamber and peg her through her shriveled black heart. My second was to turn the blade on Zale. Or maybe on Rowan.

In any case it would involve pain, a lot of pain.

"Truth is tough to stomach, isn't it?" Zale said, smug amusement thick in his voice. "While you're here worrying about your little urchin, how to escape, and what tomorrow will bring, your whore boyfriend is sheathing his sword inside another woman and telling her every little secret you ever whispered in his ear."

Anxious, hurt, and generally mind-fucked, I stared at the screen. *Rowan would not betray me.*

"He was only too happy to let us ambush you, Gracie. He invited us in, even hid me in the back room."

I wanted to smack the confidence from his perfect pretty-boy face. Rowan couldn't do that—he wouldn't—unless Elani was threatened. Then, maybe.

"See what he does when he's not with you."

My eyes widened as Rowan pulled back the sheet. My mother wore a midnight black baby doll, so sheer that I could see his hand as it slid beneath the fabric and cupped her breast. In the back of my mind I wished that she had declined more, sagged more, aged more. But no, she was a sleek cougar on the prowl and Rowan was caught in her clutches.

Her head fell back, mouth open, no doubt to let out a moan. Gods, I could feel it.

My skin tightened as a phantom memory caressed my skin, gentle in touch, but the slightest bit rough in texture. My eyes stung. I blinked quick, and then not at all. Gods, what a picture she made lying next to him, her long black hair strewn over the pillows, tangled around Rowan's thick biceps, her eyes as emerald green as Jade's.

Zale prattled off beside me, a steady stream of verbal diarrhea bouncing around in my ear. I was pretty sure that's where the buzzing in my head was coming from. Either that or my cranium was about to explode.

Shut the hell up. "So what, Zale? The Queen and Rowan have sex tapes. That's old news where I come from." My chest cavity hadn't been this cold since my meltdown at the pond, but I kept my tears at bay. "Does my mother know you're circulating her porn?"

Zale scowled. "Just watch, this is where it gets good."

Rowan lay perfectly still as she slid her hands up his chest and behind his neck. She fisted his hair and yanked his head back. I stiffened.

Zale's smile broke wide.

As Rowan got pushed onto his back, the Queen mounted him. I drew a labored breath searching Rowan's lifeless gaze as he stared straight up at the ceiling. Misery shone in his eyes—utter desolation—

as the Queen leaned forward and moved her mouth slow and demanding over his. Broad mechanical arms wound around her, stroking up her back as it flexed and relaxed.

"Seen enough?" Zale asked. "Your white knight is quite literally a mother-fucking whore. You'll do well to realize that, and stay in line for the next twenty-four hours. I'm respected in this city. I won't have you embarrassing me." All his posturing made me want to knee him in the crotch. "Ready to go to our reception and play your part?"

"Oh, I'm ready all right." I met his smile with a genuine one of my own. He'd made one mistake in his screening. The Rowan in his little film noir didn't have a shiner. His skin was beautifully unmarred. No sign of where my fist had connected with his face and no scratches on the back of his shoulders where I'd marked him during our own sextathalon.

This tape was old news. The knowing didn't erase the ache in my chest completely, but I could breathe again . . . and worry. If they had to use an old tape in their ploy to break me, what was happening to Rowan right now?

Lifting my chin I sucked in a breath and cleared my throat. "Let's get this party started."

Following the crescendo of lutes and harp, the chamber orchestra slid into a light and lovely couples' dance. The glittering crowd spun and twirled, hands and bodies linked, gowns trailing in graceful arcs. It was an Attalosean who's who. All the Eligibles, past and present, wore all the right gowns and drank all the right multi-hued drinks. We sat on display on the raised dias, lined up for inspection while the aristocrats of the Noble houses, the Strati commanders, the upper echelon of the city and the respected clergy twirled around on the ballroom floor below.

The Princess to my right—Hope, I thought, but could have been Faith or Charity, they were all the same to me—was a bubbling fountain of intel for the evening's festivities. She knew nothing of any use, clueless about where prisoners were held, or in which part of the palace I'd find the Queen's personal consort chamber rooms.

". . . after the introductory dancing, there will be a feast and then the actors will come and the finest dramas of the past cycle will be acted out. I attended one last year that. . ."

Blah. Blah. I gritted my teeth and scanned from right to left. Seventeen sisters sat erect in their cushy, junior thrones with intricate updos and golden armbands roping up delicate arms. Their ample chests were corseted and plumped up for view and their gowns were a veritable rainbow, reflecting the visual interpretation of their given names.

I scowled at my flat bodice. Thanks, Balor. When he'd done his magic enhancements, couldn't he have given me more in the T-and-A category? I had the strength of earth, the passion of fire, but I got totally robbed in the boob gene pool.

As a tray-wielding waiter passed by, I swigged down the remnants of my flute and swapped it for a freshie.

Freya Love, sitting prim and proper to my left, scowled. "Could you at least pretend you have manners? You reflect upon the Ninth House now. Who raised you?" She gave a polite wave to a couple swooping by on the dance floor.

"Maximus Reign," I said, pasting on a smile. "The most feared warrior and slayer of the Realm of the Fair." I batted my eyes at the men standing with our douchebag fiancé at the side of the room. "Reign was more concerned with his kids coming out on top of a fight than which fork to use. You know, he never even mentioned holding up our pinkies as we stabbed through the chest of our enemy."

Freya rolled her eyes. "You don't scare me."

"I guess I'm the twin who got the lion's share of the brains."

"Gods, don't say that aloud. It's bad enough you're a sister Eligible, but to be my biological double—it's horrifying." She smiled for the crowd, keeping her gaze straight ahead. "Why don't you go get yourself killed? Then, Zale and I won't have you thrust upon us like someone's unclaimed laundry."

I snorted. "Trust me, I have no interest in playing house with you, Zale, and the sister wives of the Ninth House."

"So, go." She sipped on her glass flute. "Slip away after the feast and be gone. No one will even know you're missing until the dramas conclude and that won't be until after dawn."

"That's a great plan, in theory, but I've got unfinished business here in the palace. I can't just take off. Besides, where would I go?"

"Back to your pathetic little mountain, of course." She paused as the song ended. Some of the dancers milled around before us, waiting for the next song to start while others escorted their partners back to find someone new.

I busied myself with my champagne glass until the music picked up again. "I can't access the portal pond. Believe me, I've looked into it."

Freya slid her gloved hand into the silk clutch looped around her wrist and pulled out a sapphire brooch. As she delivered a Cheshire grin to the masses, she slid the jewelry into my palm. "Give this to the night watchman at the portal. His wife loves trinkets and he's willing to bend the rules to keep her happy."

My skin got hot as the hair on my nape stood straight up. "Why would you do this for me?" She looked over at Zale and I had to laugh. "You know Zale's got a thing for me and you want me out of the way."

"Please," she scoffed. "He's not interested in you any more than a man watching a dog fight. You're a novelty he doesn't understand."

"And can't possess," I said. "He's not used to being slighted by Eligibles. I'm not part of the collection he's built for himself."

"Two is hardly a collection." She swept a wayward curl and tucked it back in place.

"Two?" I snorted again. "No, he's up in the double digits. According to the guards, he sneaks them out behind the bronze wall and gets his grind on quite regularly. I actually stumbled upon him myself the first morning I was here."

"You're lying," she snapped. An unattractive vein pulsed beside her eye. "You would say anything to cause trouble."

"I guess that wasn't you then, moaning and panting as the sun came up."

She turned on me, her pale purple gaze hardening with fury. "Zale loves me. He told me I would be head-wife—"

"You too? He told me the same thing. Said I intrigue him beyond the others." I laughed as she raised her hand to cover her mouth. "Oh, please. Is that the line he used on you? Come on, you've got to see that he's a player, right?"

"Get away from me, you . . . you freak." Freya Love's veneer of perfection cracked like a fault line. She squeezed her eyes tight and when she opened them, her mask was back in place. "If you think I'll let you ruin what Zale and I have, I promise you . . . you'll find yourself on the unpleasant end of a tragic but fatal accident."

I had to laugh out loud. "Let me get this straight. You've heard the allegations that I'm the person who stalked a senior Strati in the dead of night, evaded an army of soldiers and left four men with their throats hanging open and your first thought is to blackmail me with the threat of violence? Really? You're going with that?"

While I was still chuckling over that one, a middle-aged man in a scarlet chiton stopped directly in front of us. "Princess Grace," he said. "Would you care to dance?"

"No. I'm fine, thank you."

"Please, it would be my honor," he said, raising his hand.

I was about to decline a second time when the curled fingers of the hand being offered caught my attention. Upon closer inspection, I saw the crooked bridge of the man's nose. It was the priest who sat beside me at the luncheon on my first day here. Zale scowled at me and suddenly, there was nothing I wanted more than a tour around the ballroom dance floor. "On second thought, I'd be delighted."

With our raised hands linked and his crippled hand at my back, we merged with the flow of the crowd. After the initial adaptations to move as one with a stranger, we relaxed into a rhythm. The rise and fall of the music pulled us along like a gentle wave. For just a moment I let my fear for my boys slip away and took a moment to really breathe.

Reign had insisted on formal dance lessons for Bruin, Julian, Jade and me from the time we hit puberty. *'You'll thank me one day,'* he'd said. *'Treaties and negotiations get hammered out as often on the dance floor as they do in a war room. Politics is nothing but a fucking dance . . . and a headache.'*

When the song ended and the clergyman retained possession of my hand, I assumed we were going again. His eyes were whiskey brown and kind. Maybe I could trust him with my questions. "Uh . . . would you happen to know of a priest of the Fae Trinity Temple formerly known as Rowan?"

We began to move for the second time, his brow creased but his smile remained in place. "Perhaps," he said. His voice was even but his body tensed noticeably beneath my hands. "What would you want of him?"

"Nothing serious, I . . . uh, was just hoping to ask him a few questions."

We stopped. As the other dancers whirled past us, he squeezed my hand tighter and dropped the hold on my back. I met his gaze and after more than a decade of living with warriors, I read the minute he decided to reach into the fold of his tunic for a weapon.

I clasped my hand around his wrists and twisted. A knife. Nice. "That's a lot of steel for a priest, don't you think?"

He struggled against my hold, eyes wide. "You're stronger than you look, Princess."

"I've heard that. Now, how 'bout you drop the weapon."

"Or you could let go of my arm before you snap my wrist, and I'll slip the knife into your skirt as planned."

"Planned? What plan? Who—"

"Your followers." He leaned closer and I caught a good look at his priest's collar. It was actually a mourning band, the same as the one Bay made for me. "Those of us who think you're the one. The one who will bring change."

I searched his gaze and didn't catch any deception. "Nice words, Padre, but flattery won't get you under my skirt. I'm not that kind of girl."

A wry smile crept across his face. "Reaching under a lady's skirt isn't an everyday occurrence for me either, but I smuggled this knife in for you—regardless of the danger—and we are beginning to draw attention." Zale was making his way toward us from one direction, while two senior Strati eyeballed me from another. "Please, Lexi, trust me to do this."

His familiarity took me aback. "I don't know you."

"True," he said, stepping against me, our hands concealed between our bodies. "But you know my namesake, biblically by what I gather. Help him, Lexi. Help both of them. Bring my godchildren home where they belong."

CHAPTER TWENTY-SIX

*I*f Bacchus had been in the building, he would have found the progression of the evening a true and accurate tribute to drunken revelry. After the dancing began the feast. A heavy aroma of spices and grilled meat rose up in thick swirls from the six, long tables running the length of the dining hall. Golden rainbows arced from teardrop crystals in the chandeliers as glasses were filled and refilled with rich amber, burgundy and russet brown liquors. The roar of slurred voices and laughter blended and rose to a cacophony of merriment.

Zale sat to my left, soaking in the warmth of the pre-wedding spotlight. Social charmer or manipulative attention-whore? Whatevs. I had his number.

As mesmerizing as it was, I studied the Nobles as the flowing spirits worked their intoxicating magic and loosened lips. The women drank with slightly more reserve, tittering and gossiping, and then running to the loo in packs of swirling gowns.

I sat quietly, drinking what was poured for me, gathering intel, listening for any hint of where prisoners might be taken or held. Apparently, though, the crowd I was seated with was more interested in the restoration of the main square's bell tower and the ongoing debate of whether the new steps being laid at the Temple should be marble or orichalcum.

I tipped back my glass and the moment it was empty, someone swooped in and refilled it.

I stilled my jumping leg under the table. The presentation of the couples was next and then, once the dancing resumed, I would be free to slip away unnoticed.

"—I know, such a shame for the people of the Fifth sector. I heard. . ."

My focus shifted to the nearest six-pack of ladies floating toward the hallway. I lifted my napkin and set it on the table. Zale's fingers tightened around my wrist as I stood. To the other guests at the table, it might've looked attentive as he twisted my hand to his lips and kissed my knuckles.

Picturing Coal scared and alone, I unclenched my fist and relaxed. I did, however, shoot him what I hoped was a clear and immediate warning disguised in refinement.

His gaze grew hard, but he eased off his grip. "Where are you off to, Princess?"

"Just freshening up before the big presentations." He released my hand, the smug look of triumph irking me more than I could take. With a charmer of a smile I met the gaze of the table. " And I need to stretch my legs. My ass is fucking numb. You'd think the Queen could spring for chairs with a bit more cush, wouldn't you?"

I smiled politely as the ladies gasped and the Noble males looked to Zale with sympathy. His Lir-ness excused himself and grabbed my elbow as we made our way to the hall.

"Really?" I said, with a laugh. "What trouble am I going to cause between the dining hall and the ladies' room?"

He scowled. "I'm just keeping an eye on my investment. You've fast become the talk of Attalos and I aim to make sure that works *for* me, not *against*."

There was no sign of the feminine six-pack in the hall and I prayed they were in the washroom. I reached for the handle of the door but he still had a hold on me. "Will I be permitted to piss on my own, or will you be escorting me into my stall?"

He released my elbow and scrubbed at the back of his neck. "You have three minutes before I come in after you."

The outer powder room was buzzing with primping ladies, but this wasn't the cluster of bodies I was looking for. As they recognized me, the room silenced to a dead hush. Nice. I pushed into the washroom and cursed. Nothing. There was no one here. Deciding to take advantage of the momentary solitude I used the bathroom and washed up.

The next half-hour was going to be the worst part, standing up in front of a ballroom full of people while they formally announce both Freya and I accept Lord Dirtbag of Knobsbury as our husband. *Gods. Save me.*

My head began to swim as my skin flushed hot. I bent over the sink and splashed water on my face.

Dining with the Nobles had taught me one thing. When I was married to Zale I'd be in a much better position to change things. The door opened as I patted my face dry and I rolled my eyes.

"The presentations are beginning," he said. "Time for the performance of your life."

I swallowed the bit of barf that rose into my mouth and forced a smile. "All right. Let's get this over with."

Zale held the door open and waited for me to exit. The host's voice carried from the ballroom into the hall. He was announcing the Eligible allocations. I froze. Could I do this? There had to be another way. I couldn't stomach the idea of spending one moment alone with this prick.

"Pull yourself together Gracie," Zale hissed, gesturing to the open door of the ballroom. "Unless you want another piece of your scorch removed. The boy still functions with his tongue cut out, but you never know what I might remove next.

"What? You—"

Zale smiled and waggled his perfectly arched brow. "He'll never interrupt me again."

My hands were around his throat before the thought even registered. I swept his feet and held his body pinned beneath mine on the hallway marble. I watched from some detached distance. His olive complexion deepened to red.

"You cut out his tongue?"

How could anyone do such a thing to a little boy? Zale's eyes widened. His fingers scrabbled at my wrists. As the gods stood witness, I would squeeze the bastard's last breath out between my palms. "You are *so* fucking dead. When I get finished with you—"

Strong hands yanked me by the waist and lifted me off Zale's body. I struggled against the Strati's hold, massive arms restraining me from behind. The soldier crushed my arms against my chest and pinned them. I tried to head butt him, but he anticipated it. I kicked at his kneecaps, but he shifted and evaded. "Calm yourself, Lexi," the soldier hissed in my ear. "Be calm."

Ydorus. I stopped struggling and he loosened his hold. Zale braced his hands on the floor and gasped for air. He looked near death. *Shit.* What had I done?

The blood pumping hard through my body rushed from my head. Ydorus pulled me tight against his massive chest and kept me from keeling over. *Shit.* People heard the commotion and were rubbernecking it from the doorway. They'd seen me try to kill Zale. He would go crazy over this.

My soon-to-be husband staggered to his feet, hands curled in fists, thighs engaged as if he were about to spring forward. When he caught sight of our audience he straightened and moved closer. "You're lucky we're expected inside," he whispered, his voice a hoarse croak. "Make no mistake, once you're mine, you will suffer." He wrenched my elbow and yanked me toward the door. "Now, paint on a smile or your little bastard can kiss his arms goodbye."

The next hour passed in a blur of nausea. Images in my head flashed in a never-ending loop of nightmare: Coal being dismembered,

Terran missing and bleeding somewhere, me trapped under Zale's weight and powerless to fight back, Rowan being used as his soul died a little more, Elani being stripped and raped while my mother laughed—

"Stop growling," Freya said, smiling like a cover model at the dancers on the floor before us. "You are such a freak."

I grasped the arms of my chair. Was I growling? "Look, I need to get out of here."

"Good. Go."

"Yeah, like Zale's going to let me leave."

"Honestly, if it gets rid of you, I'll take care of Zale." Freya rose from the line of Eligibles and floated down the four steps. With her hand extended toward Zale, he broke from his conversation and met. He leaned forward to allow Freya to speak into his ear and after a moment he straightened and signaled to a couple Strati to follow.

Freya gathered her skirt and climbed back up to our perch looking pleased. "Fine. Zale asked those soldiers to escort you back to your suite and stand guard for the night. He said he'll check on you in a few hours when it's time for the ceremony."

I hid my smile as I recognized one of the two Strati standing at attention waiting to escort me out. "Well, then I guess I'll see you at the altar."

Freya rolled her eyes and I practically launched myself down the stairs. My Stiletto boot caught in the train of my skirt and I tripped forward into the arms of my guard. Ydorus caught me and set my back on my feet. "Easy, Princess," he whispered. "I got you."

Zale saw my stumble and headed over, probably to keep me from embarrassing him. I waved him off, discreetly flipping him the finger and after straightening the hem of my bodice, made for the door. Ydorus and the other soldier walked just behind me as I strode down the hall, past the washrooms, around the corner and toward the pocket of privacy alcoves hidden behind grand tapestries of the south hall. The click of my boots drowned out the soft, heavy thud of theirs as we got some distance from the noise of the ballroom.

As we cleared another corner I spun and Ydorus responded exactly as I'd hoped. He wrapped his arms around the other Strati while I clocked him a solid right hook to the head. Within seconds we'd dragged him into an alcove, bound him with a drapery tie, and left him to sleep it off. Back in the corridor, I ensured that my styled hair hadn't moved so much as an inch and lunged toward my friend.

Muscular arms picked me off the floor. "Oh Lexi, we were so frightened for you."

Just as my boots once again met the floor, a handsome, dark haired Noble exited the draped alcove right beside us. I recognized him. He and his spindly little wife had been seated just down and across the table from me. I straightened myself and Ydorus cursed. Cue wide eyes and raised brows all around. *Oh, shit, if he tells Zale—*

His tryst partner stepped out from behind the curtain and it was definitely not the Noble's wife. In fact, this man had also been sitting at our table. Seeing us, the two gentlemen righted themselves and flushed fifty shades of scarlet.

"Princess . . . I, uh—"

I held up my hand. "Enjoy your evening, gentlemen."

"Uh, thank you, Princess. And you as well." The aristocrat smiled in a way that didn't reach his eyes, but recognizing their dismissal the two made tracks. Ydorus stood beside me, eyes front, hand on the grip of his pain stick. When the two were gone, I tugged on his chest plate, stepped into the alcove and drew the drape.

"What if they say something?" Ydorus whispered.

I shook my head. "Don't worry about them, they won't risk a scandal. Okay. First tell me. Do you know where they're keeping Coal?" His face screwed up and my heart stopped. "Have they hurt him? I'll fucking kill them—"

"They don't have Coal," he whispered. "We do."

"But Zale said—" I closed my eyes and fought the scream trying to peel from my throat. I had bought their lies because it was too dangerous not too. "You're sure Coal's safe?"

Ydorus nodded. "Estes and I secured them ourselves."

"Them? Terran's with him?"

"Yes. He was torn between staying with Coal and coming for you. We all agreed you would want him watching Coal."

Tears welled and spilled as I drew my first deep breath since the Strati took me from Rowan's swordsmith's shop. "How," I choked. "How did you avoid the Strati?"

"Before they took you, Rowan called Terran to give an update on you and Eury. When the Strati burst in on him we overheard everything and Estes moved them out to the Earth ring. Trust me, Coal will be protected. He's with Terran, among his own people, and they know he belongs to you."

Knowing that Coal and Terran were safely tucked away changed everything. It had been paralyzing to worry what was being done to them and how my words or actions would affect them. Gods, it was exhausting trying to keep from making mistakes. My heart ached for Rowan. He'd been doing the same thing for four years. It had to stop.

After making sure the coast was clear, I headed straight for the servants' quarters. "You and I are going to find Elani and get her and Rowan out of here."

"And then what?"

There was no holding back the smile on that one. "Then we're going to kick some major Strati ass."

CHAPTER TWENTY-SEVEN

*Y*dorus and I Nancy-Drewed our way through the stark servant areas on the other side of the palace. As we strode along, I recognized the main corridor as the one Terran had brought me down on that first morning, a week ago.

Tonight, the halls had been abandoned. Made sense. With the Eligible ball in full swing we hadn't seen anyone milling around in the entire servant wing.

Ydorus's heavy hand fell on my shoulder and pulled me into a doorway. He pointed down the hall. "There."

Yep. Elani was being escorted by a Strati soldier down the far corridor. So, it was done. Rowan had pleased the Queen, and now Elani could spend the rest of the night with him.

I gestured to follow and we ghosted along behind them. As I thought about Rowan at the mercy of the Queen, the tightening in my lungs heightened to an unbearable level.

Rather than detonate and stab someone, I dropped my gaze to the floor, studiously tracing the intricate veining in the marble tile. Shiny. Clean. *Better.*

After a while the monochrome creaminess of the servant areas transformed to a full spectral wonder in the royal areas. Gone were the bare walls, replaced by murals and bronzes and antiquities. Gone were plain mirrors secured directly on ivory walls, instead I watched the reflection of a loyal Strati soldier and a Princess stride past a gold, gilded work of art. Those two people didn't even look like us and it hit me with gut-wrenching clarity how much I looked like Freya all dolled up.

Scary thing this Eligibles business, little Princess clones infiltrating the voting ranks of the Nobles. Gods, the whole thing gave me the heebs. By inserting placeholders into the Noble Council and building an army of vile soldiers, how far could my mother get if she unleashed them on the Realm of the Fair?

The remembered scent of death-rot clinging to Vasso's body struck me dumb. Had she joined forces with the Scourge? Would she condemn her men to be inducted into Abaddon's soulless forces or just fight alongside the scum of the realms?

Gods, I needed to talk this out with Reign and my family. There was something about this that I was still missing.

Ydorus held up his hand and the two of us paused, peering around one final corner. The Strati soldier guided Elani down the corridor and stopped before an ornately carved orichalcum door. With rough hands, he pulled her before him, slid some kind of collar around her neck and then shoved her inside.

When the tail of his cape disappeared around the corner we held our position. Why wasn't anyone guarding the door? It didn't sit right, but what choice did we have.

Right. Okay, here goes everything.

After moving closer, my hand closed around the handle and froze. Just stalled out. No twisting action. Nothing. What if I looked at Rowan and freaked? What if he was sitting on the bed doing nothing and all I saw was him fondling my mother or getting ridden like a prize pony?

"Princess?" Ydorus whispered. "We have no cover here. We must move."

I nodded and brushed my fingers over my coiffed hair and touched the gemmed design running down the side of my face. A quick straightening of my crushed-velvet bodice and I told myself to suck it up and get through that door.

Damn, my hands were shaking. I pushed my shoulders back. Dried my palms against my thighs. Stomped my boot on the marble tile. Okay, what the hell.

"Princess."

I could do this. It wasn't Rowan's fault. Whatever happened here tonight wasn't anything Rowan wanted. I swallowed hard.

Ydorus' anxiety snapped in the air around us. With a growl, his powerful hand fell on mine and forced the issue. The door gave way and we stumbled, as one, into the suite.

"Princess," Elani gasped. She sat cross-legged on a plush area rug in front of the fire. Lounging amongst a mountain of pillows her brother laid beside her. I kept my sights on Elani as Ydorus secured the door.

"Why are you here and not at the celebration?" she asked, launching to her feet. "Has something happened?"

"We're getting you two out of here while everyone's drunk and distracted." I grabbed Rowan's black bag from the table by the door and waved for them to get a move on. "Let's go."

"We cannot leave." Elani turned to Rowan and waited. When he said nothing, she turned back to me. "The alarms on our collars are set for this room. The guards will know the moment we cross the threshold and track the collars."

Annnd that's why no one was watching the door.

"Then we'll get them off you and leave them here. Now, let's hurry."

Elani's copper curls danced as she shook her head. "The collars are heat sensitive. Without our body, the alarm will sound as well."

That complicated things, but I was still determined to remove the two of them from the line of fire. If I could go into tomorrow without worrying about anyone getting hurt, I might actually be able to work a little magic.

"Okay, so does anyone check on you?"

Elani shook her head and out of the corner of my eye I saw Rowan striding toward me. I couldn't look at him yet. He knew me well enough to read my face and if he knew I'd seen that sex tape he'd be mortified.

"Whatever you're thinking. Stop," he said, easing closer. When I expected him to hug me, he paused. "What's up, Trouble?"

"Nothing." I stared straight at the line of buttons plummeting down the center of his broad chest. Thank the gods he had clothes on. Bare skin would have been too much. Too close to the images flashing behind my eyes. "I, uh . . . need to have a look at those collars."

Ignoring the twenty-questions routine that followed from both of them, I examined Elani's slave collar. Between what had been said and my experience with devices like this, I knew the security protocol was arranged in stages. First was the metal lock which we had no key for, then the body heat sensor, then the proximity alarm set to keep them in this room, then the tracking system if they were stupid enough to run and likely a pain inducer to drop them if they did.

I admired the forethought, but *fuck*.

"Okay, here's what we're going to do. I'm confident I can get the locks open. Orichalcum and I seem to have a unique understanding." I could feel its energy, almost as if it was speaking to me. "So, let's assume I get them unlocked, Ydorus and I will put on the collars and wait till morning. Meanwhile you two will meet Estes at the launch and—"

"Like hell," Rowan growled. "I'm not leaving you here for the guards to find in the morning. They'll kill you for setting us loose."

"They can't kill me. There's a palace full of Nobles and guests waiting to watch the twins marry Lir-Douche of the Ninth House."

"You think that matters? The Queen can kill you without ever laying a hand on you. She'll reach into your head as you're standing at the altar. You'll have an aneurism and no one will know it was her. But you'll still be dead."

I stepped around him to gain some distance. I didn't think the Queen would kill me. She still had hopes I would join her in her war plans. "I'll figure it out, but I need you two safe."

"Elani yes." He grabbed my wrist and pulled me around so I had no choice but to look at him. "But I'm staying. You'll need my help."

"What help?" I snapped, staring at the painting just over his shoulder. "I'm a warrior, you're a civilian. You need to get her out—"

He moved his face into my line of vision and scowled. "I may be only a lowly civilian, but I' am a man. I'm not leaving you to fight my battle."

"Yes. You. Are." I closed my eyes and scrubbed my face. With what was going on in my skull I wondered if anyone's head had ever actually exploded. If so, I couldn't be far off from a total detonation.

"Lexi, look at me. What's wrong?"

I kicked up my chin, but couldn't bring myself to follow the order. "Nothing."

"Bullshit. You haven't looked at me once since you stumbled through the door. What is going on with you?"

"Nothing, I . . . uh." The room swept by in a blur as I was flung over Rowan's shoulder like a sack of potatoes. "What the—"

He stomped the two of us into the bathroom and ass-planted me on the counter. After ensuring I was steady he retreated to the door and locked it. "If you need to make me suffer, fine, but don't do it by ordering me away, because I won't go. I'm sorry, okay. I'm so fucking sorry."

The shame in his voice that had me meeting his gaze. The agony of it bit me in the chest and stole my breath. "Why would I want you to suffer?"

"For allowing them to use me to bait the trap for you. For letting them round you up and not lifting a finger to protect you. I was a coward. Nothing like your warrior family. And I'm sure . . . nothing like Tham."

Nothing like Tham? "Don't be stupid. I told you to watch out for Elani first. I can take care of myself."

Rowan rubbed his chest. "The Queen told me they had Coal and Terran too. I don't even want to imagine how much you hate me right now—"

"Yeah, well, the Queen's a liar. And I don't hate you." Staring up at him, I felt a warm rush tingle under my skin. It spread from my chest, skittered down my arms and legs, heated my bare shoulders and back. How could I have feared looking at his ruggedly handsome face? Rowan wasn't to blame here. I was the one acting bat-shit.

Realization hit me in the head like a flail to the temple. It spun my world off its axis and then righted itself again. Gods help us both, I was in love with him.

"Lexi?"

How had that happened? I was a champion at keeping my emotions out of my affairs. Men were satisfaction, comfort, strength, but I was self-sufficient. I didn't need the love of a man. I was a freakin island. Damn him. Rowan had inched his way into my life and into my heart when I was alone and I had fallen for it. Gods, now I was a goner.

"Trouble? You okay?" His voice grew more forceful and I saw when he flipped into doctor mode and began examining me from across the bathroom.

"Marry me," I choked. "Tonight. Before anyone can stop us. I'll take Elani's collar and stay with you. Ydorus and Estes can get her out of the palace and deep into the Earth ring where Terran has Coal hidden. You and I will stand together against my mother, Zale and her army. Let the chips fall as they may."

As Rowan strode toward me that heat beneath my skin ignited in my veins. His massive upper body shifted, his muscles flexing side to side as he stalked ever closer. He didn't blink. His gaze burned, fixed on me like the fire in him was about to consume us both. "I'd prefer if we weren't the chips, if we can help it, but it's not a bad plan."

It was the way he said "plan" that seared through my heart.

"No," I said, my voice breaking as I caught my breath. "I'm not suggesting you marry me to save my skin or to screw my mother. Rowan, I'm in love with you. We don't have to act on it and I don't know if you feel the same way, but, if we're heading into this together that's what I want. So . . . yeah . . . that's all I got."

Rowan opened his mouth to speak. Nothing came out. Pressing my thighs open he stepped against the counter. He was not gentle as he scooped my ass cheeks and pulled me against his straining fly. I moaned as his head dropped and he scorched a kiss down my neck.

"So, is that a yes?"

"Hell yes. Fuck yes. A million times yes." He brushed his lips along my jaw and ran his fingers across my bare back. "If Elani's safe, I'm yours 'til death do us part."

Annnd that would likely be in ten hours when the guards returned. Right. What did we have to lose?

With his jaw cupped in my palms I focused on his face. "Are you sure? You have to be positive this is what you want. If not, I'll find another way—"

A completely lucid, almost spiritual resolve cut across his chiseled features. "I'm sure. I want you as my own. Whether we die tonight, tomorrow or grow old and grey, I'm sure."

The kiss that followed was better than any handshake to seal a deal. With his arms tight around my back he pulled me to the edge of the countertop. My ankles linked behind his thighs as his erection pressed against my belly. I swallowed hard as a wild rush of damp lust hit me.

I gasped. "Let's get Elani to safety and get this honeymoon started."

His smile grew dark and erotic. "Great idea."

CHAPTER TWENTY-EIGHT

Removing Elani's collar was easier than I expected. The orichalcum vibrated to life under my touch and obeyed my will, much as the water had in the shower and again in the canal. Linking the mechanism closed around my neck, I marveled at the warmth of the metal against my skin. Rowan looked like he might faint. I was jazzed.

Maybe Balor knew what he was doing with Sera. Casting aside the fact that I felt like a Franken-Faery, the combined strength of the four elements was a boon. The passion and fight of Fire made me strong and with the added command of Water and now Earth, who knew what I could do? Nothing had shown up from Air yet, but I had no doubt it would. The question was—how would it help me in the future?

After Ydorus called Estes and arranged to meet him at one of the remote launch sites off the staff wing, Rowan and Elani said their goodbyes. He didn't want her to know about us planning our impromptu 'I do's', because she would panic about the obvious conse-quences and he'd never convince her to get onto the launch. So, we said nothing.

While the two of them said their goodbyes, I scanned the room for the peepshow camera. From the angle of the video Zale had shown me and the fact that it caught the whole room—aha, not even a challenge.

The finial of the curtain rod on the far wall was exactly where Julian would put it too. I adjusted the curtain to cover the lens and continued to search for cameras and bugs.

If I were the Queen I wouldn't want my personal business hard-wired to some security room somewhere with guys drooling over my sex tapes. That seemed a little much. Still, I had to be sure no one had eyes on us or this plan was busted.

Moving to the bar by the window I opened the cabinet doors. *Bingo*. Nothing seemed to be active so I was fairly sure nobody was monitoring the room.

At the click of the lock, I turned. Rowan stood staring at the back of that closed door.

"Here, Doc, drink this." I handed him a snifter of an expensive-smelling liquor and he sucked it back like it was water. It must have been the booze burning its way down into his gut that brought him back into focus because he choked and pounded on his chest, sputtering rosy cheeked for a while.

"Again?"

When he nodded, I tipped the decanter and handed him round two. This time, he swirled the contents against his palm and moved to the fire. Leaning one hand on the mantle he sipped at his glass, watching the orange-gold of the flames flicker and snap. His worry for Elani made my chest ache—family—there was no bond like it.

It gave you the greatest strength and comfort when all was well, but hollowed your guts and left you raw when it wasn't.

I downed my drink and blinked fast. My siblings and I might be struggling, but Reign had raised us. He worked every day for the past two decades to build our family's unshakeable foundation, one shit-storm at a time. Our family was stronger than mistakes made and words spoken in anger. It was stronger than new loves taking hold and stepping on toes. It was stronger than . . . everything.

How had I forgotten that?

My mind filled with the images of the fight at the Gatehouse. They were trying to make me see that they were worried. I didn't listen. They had come at me hard, but that was our way. I knew that, still I ran and hid. Like a Princess.

"Do you think she'll be all right?"

I blinked and met Rowan's worried gaze. "Yes. I do. Ydorus will get her safely to Estes, find your godfather at the dramas and be back here before we know it." I laid my face against the broad span of his shoulders and wrapped my arms around his waist. His front was sizzling hot from the heat cast from the hearth. "Don't worry. S'all good."

Rowan snorted, his body bouncing with amusement. "Yeah, it's a Faery tale come true."

I'd give him that one. The weight of what we were facing washed over me. One minute I was fine and the next, it felt like I might be crushed. "I wish my dad was here. Reign would cut through all this dictator bullshit before the Queen and the Strati even had time to crap their pants."

"That's quite an image. Tough man, is he?"

"You could say that."

Rowan set his glass on the mantle and turned in my arms. "And what will this tough man have to say about me marrying his daughter without his permission?"

I tried to smile, but fell short. When Rowan's face began wavering behind a wall of tears, I knew I was in trouble. "This wasn't supposed to happen." I swiped fast at my cheeks. "Reign was supposed to be there . . . give me away."

Crying in earnest, Rowan laid me on the mound of pillows on the floor. He smelled like home and while the fire warmed my butt, his strong hand rubbed circles on my back.

None of this was happening like it was supposed to. I'd dreamed of finding my birth parents since I was eight. I'd planned how it would go, what they'd be like, but never, in all the variations of that daydream did my father get beheaded by my bitch Queen of a mother.

"I'm not usually such a . . . girl."

"Don't apologize. Members of the Noble houses rarely get to prove their substance. You're doing me a favor by letting me comfort you." Rowan offered me a handkerchief. "Why the tears?"

"I wanted a mother," I sobbed, wiping my face. "Jade and Bruin used to tell Julian and me stories about their mothers and I wanted one."

Rowan kissed the gems by my temple and whispered close to my ear. "And no matter how old you are, there's a part of you that will always need your parents."

I snuggled closer and laid my head on his arm for a pillow. "Rowan? If we survive . . . can we have a real wedding with our family?"

He laced his fingers with mine and pressed our joined hands against his chest. "I swear to you, if we survive this, I'll marry you here, and in your realm, and in the Modern Realm, and with as many guests and flowers and bottles of champagne you can organize. Your father can give you away or your brothers or your friends. Whatever you want. Anything you want."

I wiped the last of my tears away. "You might live to regret that. You've never seen me in party planner mode. I want the whole show. Cake, dancing, tossing the bouquet . . . I'm going to take that flower grenade and toss it yelling *crawl for it bitches* . . . cause that's what girls do."

Rowan barked out a laugh. "Done. Besides, you're going to be a Noble of the Fifth House. The bigger you go, the better you'll fit in."

I nipped the edge of his jaw and giggled. "I'll never fit in with what the Noble Council considers appropriate."

He shrugged. "The Noble Council can stick it, it's the citizens of the Fifth sector we need to worry about and they already love you."

"They do?"

"Mhmm." His kisses followed the trail of gems down my neck, along my collarbone, and down further. "Everyone is wearing chokers, like yours."

"I figured they'd lost people and appreciated the sentiment of the mourning bands."

"I'm sure that's part of it," he whispered against my bodice, "but they wear them for you. It's a show of support. Those are your people."

"My people?" I giggled as he nuzzled under the fabric and edged toward my breast. "Who in their right mind would follow me anywhere?"

Rowan lifted his head, his eyes glowing serious. "How can you not know what an incredible woman you are? You're strong and smart and kind and—"

"And my brother Bruin is stronger, my brother Julian is smarter and my sister Jade is . . . well Jade tops the charts on pretty much every other scale. I'm just Lexi, the spoiled, hot-headed Princess."

Yeah, that was about it. I was never as much of anything as my siblings.

Rowan scowled. "I find that hard to believe. From where I sit, you're amazing on every scale. In fact, if we weren't bound to this room until morning I'd take you out and let the citizens show you how much you mean to them."

I rolled my eyes and was about to argue when a rap on the door had us jumping to our feet. After drawing the knife from beneath my skirt, I stepped behind the door and gave Rowan the nod. He turned the lock and opened the door a crack, then threw it open wider and ushered Ydorus and Father Rowan into the suite.

"Elani?" Rowan said before the latch had even closed behind them. "Is she safe?"

Ydorus nodded. "I put her on the launch myself and watched until Estes steered it out to the main canal. He won't have any problem from there."

Rowan exhaled, his wide shoulders easing. "Thank you."

Ydorus patted him on the back and gestured to the Abbatis priest standing next to them. "Is this the man you were looking for? Lexi said the priest she danced with and since he is the only person she danced with. . . ." He held up his hands.

The priest met Rowan chest-to-chest and they clapped each other on the back. "How are you, my boy?"

Rowan stepped back and pulled me to his side. "I'll be better once we're married."

Father Rowan looked from his godson to me to Ydorus, who wore the same stunned expression. "But aren't you getting married to—"

"Lir-dickwad?" I said. "No. that's not happening. If I have to be married to a Noble on my fifth birthday, we'll alter the plans a little. Nothing they can do about it, right? I've been told a million times—the Laws are Absolute."

Rowan snickered at my attempt to capture the pious tone that everyone used when using that statement. "Who wants to be Lady-dickwad anyway?"

"Exactly. And since it's after midnight, it is my birthday. This Eligible is ready to get hitched."

The fire let off a *crack* as if in agreement and once the pillows were cleared from the floor, the priest positioned us in the center of the open space in front of the hearth.

From his satchel, he retrieved a feathered fan and a smudge wand. He held the tip of the bundled wand against the embers of the fire until it started to smoke and the scent of white sage drifted in the air. Walking a counter-clockwise circle around us, he swept the feathers through the air as if metaphysically cleansing the space.

"Face each other and join hands. Clear your minds of conflict. Troubles of the day have no place here. For two souls to stand the trials of time as one, you must unite as one in a place that is not a place, in a time that has no time."

I exhaled and shook out my hands before accepting Rowan's. A million thoughts fired in my head, made me second guess, but when I looked up and met Rowan's gaze, the chaos stopped. His grip was ready and steady. Solid. The room around us faded away as our connection took hold.

Priest Rowan completed the first circuit and continued. "Tap into the Sacred around you. Feel the Divinity of the space. The power of the Veil, the god and the goddess. Focus on the energy arcing between you, within you."

The third time around, he set the feathers on the carpet to my left, the smoldering wand on the hearth, and took a vase of flowers from the mantle. He set the bouquet on the ground to my right and the water-filled vase behind me.

When he rounded back to the fire he faced the flames. "Castian, god of gods, join us. We ask you guard and protect the joining of these two souls. Fire is passion, heat, anger and transformation. It consumes the old, making room for new growth in a relationship. Let it be so."

He moved a quarter of the circle and stood before the vase. "Water is the mother of us all. It nurtures us and cleanses our souls of inevitable slights and misunderstanding through meditation, introspection and dreams. Let it be so."

He continued, standing before the flowers. "Shalana, goddess of earth and woodlands, bless this union of your creatures. Earth is the foundation of life. It gives love built together grounding, wisdom, and prosperity. Let it be so."

At his forth stop, he gestured to the feathers. "Air fills our lungs when we live life and tightens our chest in warning. It is the element of thought and intelligence. In a marriage, it brings creativity, invention, and inspiration. Let it be so."

Stepping to our side, he smiled at his godson. "Rowan, Noble of the Fifth House, before the god and the goddess, speak only truth. Is this union a true and earnest desire?"

"It is," he said, his smile radiant.

"Then swear to the powers of the Veil that you will honor Alexannia Grace, Princess of Attalos until your dying breath."

"I do so swear."

Priest Rowan nodded and turned to me. "Alexannia Grace, Princess of Attalos—"

"Hells yes. I do so swear." I glanced up at the heavens. "You hear that, Castian? And if your meddling nieces get any ideas about screwing this up for me, I'll be pay each of them a visit. I do so swear that too."

Rowan chuckled and patted the priest's shoulder, who was looking a little lost. He recovered and brought three candles out of his bag.

"The traditional binding was done by blood but that ceremony transformed into the joining of light—"

"I vote for blood," I said, drawing the blade hidden in the train of my skirt. My cheeks warmed as the men blinked at me. "What? I'm a traditional girl. No pain, no gain, right?"

Rowan snorted holding out his palm. "Right. Why light a wussy candle? We'll do things the warrior way."

The priest accepted the weapon from my hand and scored each of our palms. When the line of blood rose from the wound, we clamped our hands together.

"This joining represents the union of two. From this point on, your lives, passions, and futures are one."

The fire whooshed in a sudden flare and it was done.

Married . . . 'till death do us part.

CHAPTER TWENTY-NINE

We fell asleep entwined together. After a few, sensual hours of consummating, we sank into the comfort of a perfect moment. No nightmares beckoned. No nocturnal visits from Tham. No invasion of the bitch Queen.

The night remained ours and ours alone.

In the dim light of pre-dawn, I rolled over and found Rowan's body in the sheets. He was warm and willing, hardening almost instantly to my touch. A deep inhale raised his broad, landscaped chest as I crawled across him and tugged the sheet lower.

"What are you up to, Trouble?" Rowan asked, his voice graveled and tired.

"Mischief," I said, biting my bottom lip and eyeing the beautiful plains and ridges of his naked body. "You just lie back and relax. I'll take care of everything."

A throaty chuckle escaped his chest as I continued my descent. While my fingers explored, I circled his nipple with my tongue, then nipped my way down his pec and over his tight abs. He groaned when I got to his navel, his hips undulating toward me, his erection pulsing for attention. A crystal tear appeared at the tip. Gods, I could taste him already. With a slow, firm hand I stroked him once from crest to base and took him into my mouth.

He gasped, his body tensing like he'd been electrocuted. He was hot. He was huge. And he was *mine*.

While he settled, I started with a slow up and down. He shifted his hips and widened his knees. I took advantage of the space, cradling his weighted sac in my palm. He was flawless. Perfection, from his wide shoulders, to the sexy indents of his hips, to his long-muscled legs dappled with silky brown hair.

"You have the sweetest tongue," he growled. I closed my eyes, absorbing every twinge and tightening of his muscles, every quake of pleasure, and every breath that tore from his lips. "You should have warned me, that being with you would steal my very sanity."

I laughed and his hips jolted again. He had treated me with such exquisite care over the past hours, passionate but gentle, every moment about me, about my pleasure, about letting me take what I wanted. This morning, I wanted the same for him.

Strong hands squeezed my shoulders and tugged me upward. "Give me your mouth, wife," he whispered pulling me up to his lips.

It took all my willpower to give up my hold on him, but this was his moment after all. Heat pounded through my veins as I ran my hands up his ribs. In one smooth motion, I straddled his hips and took him inside me. Both of us groaned as I sat back and he sank deep into my core.

"Kiss me, Lexi, before I lose my mind."

Leaning forward, yielded to his request. With a thrust of his hips, he pushed in further and I caught myself with my palms on the mattress. A stinging pleasure lit off inside me and almost distracted me from my goal. "Oh, no, Doc. This one's about you. Now behave."

Our gaze locked just inches apart and he stared back at me. Rowan was power and tenderness, strength and reserve. He'd seen my best and my worst, and loved me anyway—maybe even loved me because of it.

His lips met mine with possession, his hands tightening in my hair.

With every push and pull, I grew hotter. And so did he. Within moments, lightning was gathering in my core and I pulled back to focus.

His hips undulated in a slow rise and fall beneath me. Using the spasms of his muscles beneath my fingers as my guide, I rode him out, tormenting him when he came close, suspending his release. "The longer you burn, the more you'll combust when the time comes."

He chuckled and his erection surged inside of me. The sensation was wickedly peculiar. "You're a cruel, cruel woman, you know that. But I love you."

"I love you too." Reality hit me then. What if this was our last time together? What if the guards came and killed us both . . . or worse, just him. Tears pooled.

"Don't think about it, baby," he whispered against my mouth. "Stay with me. Right here. Stay with me." With a soft curse, he pulled me against his chest and rolled us over. Face-to-face, with his weight between my legs, he took control. As he stared down at me, his expression held an intense mixture of love, fear, strength, sadness. . . .

His eyes rolled closed and his pace picked up. The rhythmic shift of the bed grew louder. The friction of skin-on-skin grew hotter. His breath came in short, tight bursts and then as he pounded harder, faster, he stopped breathing altogether.

I moaned as the veins popped at the sides of his neck and he threw his head back. The cry of pleasure was like nothing I'd heard before and it filled me with such a sense of satisfaction that I was lost.

Release washed over the both of us. Not the earthquakes of the past hours. Not the sex with a purpose, desperate to hang on to each other when the time was fast approaching to tear us apart. No. This was languid, hot and luscious.

This was making love.

When it was over, I laid on my side looking at our candle and Rowan curled his massive body around me. After the blood bonding, we'd opted to do the candle tradition too. The two of us lit individual candles and used the flames to light a bigger, sturdier candle together.

Neither one of us had wanted to blow the thing out last night, so it burned on. His arm draped heavy over my side and his palm stroked my chest and settled against the mattress, cupping my breast. "What are you thinking, Trouble?"

I kissed the mound of his bicep where it rested under my cheek. "That you're the first man to ever make love to me."

"I am, am I?" His voice was breathless, but that didn't hide his skepticism.

I frowned, wishing I could read his face. Without turning, I sensed him wanting to say something more, but hesitating. It was the same awkward tension that had come between us so many times before and it made me twitchy.

"I didn't say you were my first in bed, just that you are the first to truly make love to me."

He gave me a squeeze. "Sorry, I didn't mean to upset you. I'm . . . honored."

The apology was worse than the doubt. "Forget I said anything."

We laid there and suddenly, I was thankful to be facing the candle instead of him. I wanted to get up and head to the bathroom. I wanted to put my clothes back on because I was feeling *waaay* too naked.

He pulled me tighter as if he knew I was about to bolt. "I honestly didn't mean to ruin what you said. I am *honored*. It's just . . . I was in your bathroom when you tended to Tham. I saw the way you bathed him. You were so gentle and so familiar. You said you were just friends, but you loved him, I know you did. And the way he looked at you before he died . . . I just thought he would have been—" He sighed. "Never mind. It's none of my business."

I sat up, not sure if I was angry at Rowan or at the fact that Tham never got to have share himself with someone. "Don't be stupid."

"Stupid? How am I stupid? I was trying to be accepting of your sexual relationship with another man."

"I told you. Highbornes only have intercourse with their mates and then are paired for life. Neither of us wanted long-term. We fooled around, but nothing beyond that."

I resisted the urge to stomp away. Locked in the darkness, skin touching, with only the sound of our breathing breaking the silence, I reined in my I-am-an-island instincts. "You were stupid because you said it's none of your business. I'm your wife. If you have questions, you should ask them. I want you to ask them."

He sighed. "It's not so much questions as me not wanting to compete with a ghost."

I shivered, thinking how close he was to the truth. How many times had I thought about telling him about Tham coming to me in my dreams? Whether it was real or not, Rowan would think I was clinging to a lost love and doubt his place in my heart. He wouldn't understand and I wouldn't risk hurting him like that.

"Tham was a handsome man," he said, his breath brushing my cheek. "He was obviously crazy about you. And the way the two of you connected. . ."

Despite the heat of our combined bodies, my shiver grew into a chill. I grabbed his jaw and leaned close. "You aren't competing with anyone. I'm yours, right? Tham was a huge part of my life the past few months. I'll miss him forever but there was nothing romantic going on, not in the bedroom and not emotionally either."

He threw back the sheets and launched off the bed. "Forget I said anything."

I untangled my foot from the bedding and followed. "No. I want to hear it. This relationship is a first for me. I want to be part of what you're thinking."

He scrubbed the back of his neck, the long elegant lines of his body flexing as he moved. "I'm thinking that with the past four years and what you know about me . . . you'll realize you regret marrying me and move on."

The air froze in my lungs. "I'm not going anywhere." *Hopefully.* My heart sank as I had to amend that. "As long as I have a choice, you're stuck with me . . . but, if *you're* having second thoughts that's a totally different."

His stare pegged me with all kinds of WTF. "No. None."

I nodded, crossing my arms over my bare chest. "Fine then, we're happily married."

"Yeah . . . fine." Turning his back, he strode to the bar and grabbed a glass. Reaching down to the center cabinet he opened the small fridge and grabbed a bottle of juice. When he slammed the thing shut the door next to it swung open.

Shit. Rowan moved to close the door to the camera equipment and froze. His body tensed, the muscles in his shoulders tightening with an unnatural stillness. "Lexi, before you declare your loyalty to this marriage, there's something you should know . . . that your mother might use to hurt us."

"I know about the tapes."

He straightened. "How?"

My mind spun faster than I could think. The truth was ugly. It would make him feel worse about himself. Lying wasn't really the best answer. Distraction wasn't going to—

"Answer me, Lexi," he growled.

My head snapped up at his command and he had the good sense to flush.

"I'm sorry." He blew a long breath out and when he spoke again, his voice was tense but calmer. "What do you know of the tapes the Queen makes?"

I cursed, deciding to go with the truth. "Zale tried to get under my skin by showing me one of the two of you yesterday afternoon."

"Bullshit. The Queen hasn't . . . nothing's happened since the night we got back from laying Tham to rest in the Earth ring. I swear. I haven't been with her since you and I—"

I lifted my finger to my cheek and tapped below my eye. "I knew it was an old recording. You didn't have a shiner. Besides, nothing they do changes how I feel about—"

The beep of a keycard swiping through the hall scanner had Rowan shoving me into the bathroom. "Stay here."

Stay here? Staring at my tousled, bejeweled reflection I realized those might be the last words my husband ever spoke to me. Was that our goodbye? Would our final moments be us fighting about sex recordings and him being the Queen's plaything?

The muffle of male voices in the next room had me gripping the door handle. Morning inspection. There were three, I thought, and someone was coming toward the door. *Shit.* I was naked and supposed to be his sister.

"My sister—"

"Is in the shower. Yeah, I heard you. Nothing I haven't seen before."

I grabbed a towel and bent at the waist, twisting my hair until the black was covered. The tail of the fabric fell over my shoulder as I tucked the second towel around my body. Elani and I were similar in size and sadly, build. Maybe, if the Fates were busy screwing someone else's life I might get away with impersonating—

The door bumped me in the ass as the Strati stepped in. I dropped my gaze and assumed a submissive pose.

"Elani," Rowan choked. "The soldiers are here to reset your collar."

I shifted my rounded shoulders like Elani did and gave the soldier access. While he opened the clasp to the controls of the collar, I adjusted the tail of my terry turban hiding the pattern of jewels smattering down my neck and collarbone. I didn't dare breathe. My eyes were locked on the thighs of the soldier. If he saw my purple pupils he'd know who I was.

At first, he seemed oblivious to me, inserting a miniature USB thing into the neck piece. When that beeped, he closed the clasp and I prayed that would be the end of it. But no. As he moved behind me, he gripped the towel at my hips and pushed me up against the counter. Before I could turn he swung the door shut and closed us in together.

Rowan cursed and by the muffled scuffle and thud going down on the other side of the door, the other Strati was dealing with Rowan's protests. My heart skipped a beat then kicked into high gear. Should I fight back and expose us? Could we still get away with him thinking I was Elani?

A meaty hand grabbed at the tuck of my towel and I raised my hand to stop him. He was ready for me, capturing my wrist and pulling it behind my back. "Feeling feisty today are you, little girl?"

I drew a deep breath through my nose and kept my head down. Raised voices bled through the door. Rowan was about to lose his shit. I had to make a decision here, one way or the other. When fingers slid under the hem of my towel and grabbed my bare crotch I snapped.

Spinning around with my elbow I caught the bastard in the temple. The force of my blow sent him into the wall and I swept his supporting foot. As he ass-planted on the tile floor I plowed him one in the face.

Dazed, he scrambled to block my fists.

"Fuck you," I growled, pulling my fist back for one more strike. "Not used to little girls fighting back are you, big man?" The fire in my gut ignited and it felt so good to let that shit fly. I lost track of the pummeling I gave him, but when I was done, I picked the blood splattered towel off the bathroom floor and tossed it over the piece of shit. That taken care of, I grabbed a fresh towel to wrap around myself and snagged big man's pain stick.

One down, three hundred to go.

It took a bit to cover my hair again and give myself a quick rinse off. I moved as quickly as I could. After the scuffle in the bedroom, it had gotten far too quiet out there. I needed to get to Rowan, but if everything was cool, I didn't want to tip our hand either.

Opening the door only enough to slip through, I closed it behind me.

"Done so soon—" The other soldier was pouring himself a drink at the bar.

I kept my gaze down but found Rowan sitting by the fire in his boxers, looking like he was fighting not to explode. He had a split lip to go with his shiner and didn't that make my blood boil. His gaze locked with mine and I nodded.

S'all good, Doc. Stay cool. I got this.

The soldier realized something was wrong almost instantly. The energy in the air changed and everything slipped into a slow-mo action sequence like in the movies. His glass slid onto the top of the buffet with a dull thud and I curled my fingers tight around the leather grip of the Strati weapon hidden behind my thigh.

His fingers edged toward his hip. "Where's. . . ?"

In one powerful surge, I sprang the distance and engaged. When you're light on steel, there's nothing like the advantage of a surprise attack. I took him to the floor with a flying tackle, catching him around the neck and shoulder and wrenching him around like a pretzel. We landed hard, his considerable weight more than double mine. My hip screamed like a bitch. He managed a solid hit to my gut, but even as the air punched out of my lungs I smiled.

Gods, I love a good fight.

The combination of my strength and him underestimating me from the get-go—probably thinking I was Elani—made it possible to deliver a paralyzing blow before he even clued in he was about to be expired.

Straightening over the body, I felt Rowan's gaze burning into my spine. Damn. He'd never seen me in action before. Would he be horrified that his wife was a killer? As the silence droned on, I took a long inhale and gathered my shit. After I reclaimed my towel I pivoted and met his stare. He was focused, his eyes peeled wide.

"Are you okay?" I asked, raising my palms to him. I stood my ground, giving him a minute to see that I was still me. Lexi. His wife. "I'm sorry. Sometimes when I work, I get—"

"Don't you dare apologize," he said. "You told me you were a warrior. You said you could take care of yourself, but I had no idea. I never imagined."

"Is that good or bad?"

With his gaze locked on me, he rose up and stalked forward. "You amaze me. More every moment."

I exhaled the breath frozen in my chest and stepped into his arms. "How's your lip?" I gave his face a gentle prod and he shook his head.

"Please don't think I'm useless."

I eased back to see him better. "Why would I think that?"

"Both times we've faced trouble, I've done nothing to help you." He stepped back and gripped my shoulders, looking serious. "I swear, I can hold my own. I'm not a coward. I want you to know that. I was just trying to keep you safe."

"Whether you can fight or not, I don't care—"

"I can fight," he said. His grip on my shoulders was getting painful and I understood why. I grew up with warriors. It was the universal law of cock and balls: Men protect their women.

I reached up on my tiptoes and kissed his lips. "Let's get cleaned up. If we're taking down my mother, we need ammunition."

CHAPTER THIRTY

"Why couldn't it be this way?" I gestured down the stark empty hallway that led away from the hustle and hoopla of the palace kitchen and sighed. "But no," I whispered. "Since we need secrecy, the room we want has to be splat in the middle of the fricken circus that is our lives."

I followed Rowan down yet other boring white hallway and prayed for once that the Fates stopped screwing with me.

Rowan chuckled and nodded that the coast was clear. "That which doesn't kill us. . . ."

". . . better run like hell, because it's not getting another shot at us."

Rowan kissed my hand and pulled me along, his shoulders bouncing as he laughed. "And *that's* why I love you, Lady Rowan."

Lady Rowan. Man, I loved the sound of that. With my one dagger sheathed behind my leg, I was hoping not to run into anyone other than staff. From my experience with chance encounters in the staff areas of the palace, they were like timid little mice. A living example of 'they're more afraid of you then you are of them' and that totally worked for me.

"Do you even know where you're going?" I asked.

Rowan's head tilted from side to side as we descended a set of stairs. "Mostly."

"Mostly?"

I was just about to start our first fight as a married couple when we rounded a corner and collided smack into a staff kid rolling a liquor trolley. Bottles clanged and toppled and the three of us scrambled to save as many of the glass soldiers from death-by-marble as we could. The crash-and-smash of three unlucky fellows echoed in the halls like cannon shots.

The poor boy looked horrified, but Rowan was on it. He adjusted the bottles to fill the space and told the boy that if anyone noticed bottles were missing to say that two Strati took them and headed toward the orchard. No one would go looking for them. The boy seemed hesitant at first, but shoved the broken glass to the side with his boot and nodded.

With our trolley friend off on his way, we resumed the search for the Fae Trinity Chapel and hopefully the palace records room.

"Here." Rowan took the key his godfather had given us and opened the door. As we stepped inside, the lanterns flared to life and he locked us in. Four, long chapel pews carved with tomes—scenes from ancient battles, men fighting, women swooning, children clutching to the gowns of their mothers—segmented the rectangular space.

On the wall behind the raised altar was the same depiction of the Fae Royals that we had over the main entrance of the castle back at Haven. Castian, of course, was front and center, his brother Dane to his right, Alyssa, Shalana, Zophia and her three bitch-sisters all looking sultry and resplendent and—oh, they still had Rheagan in this family sculpture.

Rheagan had been removed from all Pantheon depictions of the Royals in the Realm of the Fair right after Castian exiled her. *I guess Attalos didn't get the memo.* I wondered if the fallen Fae goddess knew Abaddon and the Scourge were fighting to set her free. After ten thousand years of being banished as a sea beast, would she even care?

"Lexi? You with me?"

Right. Following the priest's instructions, we made our way to the dais and found the crescent moon brooch on Castian's cape. Rowan grabbed the marble dial and fought to turn it once all the way around. When it settled back into its original position, the wall let out a click and a seam appeared where a moment ago there was none.

Bingo.

"Hurry," I said. "Zale and his band of bastards will know I'm missing by now and be searching. If they think to check the Queen's playroom for you, we're busted."

With both of us pulling at the exposed lip of the door we managed to pull it far enough for me to squeeze through. There was no way my brawny husband was fitting. "You keep watch, I'll check it out."

Rowan frowned. "I don't like the idea of you—"

"What's the worst that can happen, Doc? I get stuffed-up from mildew and dust." I rolled my eyes and grabbed a lantern from the wall. "You know what they say, *Don't sweat the petty things and don't pet the sweaty things.*"

"Who says that?" Rowan snorted.

"They. People. You know. Them."

Rowan shook his head. "No one says that. Now get your perfect little ass in there so we can get done and out of here."

"Roger that." I slid inside and lifted the lantern. My heart sank. Books and parchments and scrolls and tomes in every direction. From what I could see, no alphabetization, no order, in fact, I was pretty sure Mr. Dewey Decimal was rolling over in his grave. "Don't priests take a vow of neatness or something, cause uh . . . *wow.*"

Rowan peered through the crack at the door. "I think they're more concerned with poverty, murder, adultery . . . that sort of thing."

"Well, that's not going to help me in here." Leaning over the one long table in the room, I hooked the lantern on the pendant hanging from the ceiling above and started flipping through some of the piles. It was still amazing to me that I could even read this.

Blah. Blah. Blah. Land registry. *Blah. Blah.* Old marriage records. Some architectural drawings for the addition of the amphitheatre. *Blah. Blah.* Law books. Nothing.

I straightened and caught sight of—"Oh, these look promising."

Skipping past an avalanched pile of leather-bound books, I fingered the spines of a set of journals bearing the royal seal and the same serpent-entwined rod that was embroidered on the side of Rowan's medical bag. Skimming through the pages I read the documentation of an appendectomy preformed two years ago on Princess Forbearance. I snorted. "Maybe Grace isn't so bad as designations go."

I slid that journal back in place and pulled one out further down the line. It was older, but still not far enough back. A few more tries and—

"Someone's coming," Rowan hissed. "Get the light."

I willed the flame to snuff as he slid the door a sliver from being shut tight.

"What are you doing in here?" A voice barked in the chapel.

"Enjoying some privacy," Rowan answered. "Is there a problem?"

I held my breath and stood statue still. The sound of shuffling feet moved closer. My heart thrummed double time. Was the opening of the door noticeable? Could I get out to help Rowan if things went south?

"What's this?" the Strati asked.

I drew my knife from under my skirt and readied to launch. The ping of a phone stick seemed to echo off the chapel walls. "No, not her, but I found the Queen's whore in the chapel . . . yes sir . . . on our way."

I swallowed hard, but the lump in my throat remained. *Don't take Rowan. Don't take Rowan. Please, Fates if you've ever listened to me, don't let him take—*

"Come with me," the Strati commanded. "The last of the dramas has begun. The Nobles are readying to begin the marriage ceremonies."

"I'll be right up," Rowan said. "I just need to—"

"—you're coming now, whore," the soldier boomed. There was a quick shuffle, then a dull thud and Rowan choked for breath. I moved with as much speed and stealth as I could, intending to blast through the door, but stopped just short of the door. The chapel was silent. I leaned close to the crack in the door and searched the chapel beyond.

They were gone.

The thought made my stomach queasy and my palms sweat. Gods, my heart was not so much beating, but flipping out in my chest.

He's fine. We were just going our separate ways for a bit and then I'd find him and everything will be fine. Yeah . . . right. *Damn.* I couldn't even believe my own bullshit.

Turning back to the journals I brought the lantern back to life and continued reading what I'd found. There were dozens of entries during the period the Queen had fallen ill. Speculations and panic from healers, the doctor at the time, clergy, and any number of others they hoped could shed light on what was happening.

What caught my attention were the references to her eye color. In the beginning examinations, her eyes were listed as moss green and clear. Later, during intermittent exams, while she'd lain unconscious for weeks, her eyes were listed as being a deep emerald.

There were also mentions of fitful dreams and her healers complaining of an evil entity trying to possess her. They dismissed it as hoohaw. I shivered as the memory of the icy chill entered my chest. *Hoohaw my ass.* The notes from the final examination on her blood work that gave me the quakes.

No. Fucking. Way.

Reduced to mono-syllabic thoughts I fought to think of another answer. It couldn't be. But what else could it be? Nothing. Apparently, after weeks of her lying in a fitful coma she'd just woken up. Her eyes had popped open and she sat up, right as rain. Under protest she'd agreed to a final exam which was when they'd discovered that her blood had changed from the normal scarlet to a rich, royal violet.

Royal . . . violet.

I dropped the book and bolted for the crack in the door. As I tugged at the stone edge I let my mind fly through the impossibility of what I was thinking.

The only people I knew that had purple blood were the Originals. The royal family of the Fae Pantheon. Castian had it. I'd seen the depiction of his seven drops of purple blood creating the Elven race a zillion times on the walls of the castle stairway. Zophia had it.

The door gave way enough for me to barely squeeze out. Not all Originals had emerald eyes . . . only Castian, his brother Dane and his half-sister—Rheagan.

The golden train of my outfit caught on the stone of the door and tore as I forced my way into the chapel. The carved frieze on the wall seemed to be mocking me. Why hadn't I figured this out when she pricked her finger in her study . . . the purple blood . . . the emerald eyes . . . my mother was possessed by Rheagan, and the bitch was making a play for a comeback into the Realm of the Fair.

I fell to my knees and for the first time in my life I prayed—prayed as though my life depended on it.

Because it did.

CHAPTER THIRTY-ONE

The pounding of my boot heels into the marble floor vibrated in my head. My thighs burned as my strides cut the distance between me and the amphitheatre. I flew around a corner, the tattered train of my dress billowing behind me as the halls disappeared in a blur of white.

The Queen would be in the amphitheatre, overseeing the dramas, manipulating my mindless sisters into half a dozen arranged marriages. I sort of felt sorry for them. They were sheep. My heart pounded in my chest, the tightness of breath the same now as when the Queen had tried to possess me—

No. *Rheagan* tried to possess me. The same way she possessed my mother. *Gods, was there any chance my mother—the true Queen—was still somewhere inside herself.*

With my insides balled up and writhing in my gut I paused inside the archway to the amphitheatre. The place was packed, the audience seated in ascending stone benches arcing from one side of the stage to the other, rising in rings to a hundred feet near the back. The crowd, absorbed with the drama on stage, was a scene from a Greek tragedy themselves. They were puppets and they either didn't have the distance to see it, the courage to question it, or were too entranced by the illusion Rheagan had cast to realize it.

My gaze was drawn straight to Rowan, sitting in the Nobles box across the open forum. He was alive and unscathed. I breathed deep for the first time in half an hour.

His gaze locked on mine. I nodded and he tilted his head so slightly no one would have noticed. He glanced to my right. Ydorus, dressed in full Strati garb, moved up my flank and slid the hilt of a second dagger into the palm of my hand.

"Princess Grace," one of the attendants said, waving to Zale. *She's here*, he mouthed, pointing and turning with a light of excitement. "Praise the gods, Princess Grace. The nuptials are about to begin." With a firm hand at my back the little man whisked me through the crowd. "We've had people searching for hours. Your intended feared you had met with some ill fortune."

"Yes. I'm sure Zale was beside himself." I climbed the stairs, joining the Eligibles and their mates waiting for their married lives to begin. The murmurs of the crowd rose as the actors fell silent and still. Ahh, I had everyone's undivided attention.

"Sorry to keep you waiting, folks," I said, finding Rheagan perched in her seat of power at the side of the stage. The Queen sat straighter but made no move against me. Her gaze narrowed. Any moment she could flip her wrist and her Strati army would come down on me like hail. Stall. I needed more time. "As you've probably heard, a lot has been going on."

Zale cursed and stormed to my side. He wrenched my wrist and towered over me, his threat as palpable as the smell of fear mixed with his fury. "I don't know what you're up to," he said, "but you're an Eligible and in a few minutes, we'll be married and you *will* do as you're told."

I shook my head. "I can't marry you, Zale."

Zale's cold, dark eyes narrowed. "Now is not the time for grandstanding. This is your celebration day of your sixth cycle. The laws are absolute. Go sit with your sisters—"

I laughed and pulled my wrist free of his grip. Ydorus situated himself to the side, not far from Rheagan's throne.

I gained a bit of distance from my betrothed and raised my voice. "Poor Zale, so worried about me tarnishing his image by coloring outside the lines. Regretting your vow to marry me? Well don't worry about the nuptials. Been there, done that, got the Noble husband to prove it, fuck-you-very-much."

Rowan strode onto the stage and moved close behind me.

"In fact, I'am quite pleased with the upgrade. Oh, and there's nothing you can do about it, because like you say . . . the laws are absolute."

Rowan kissed the top of my head. "Thank you, darling."

Zale's glower moved from me to Rowan and back to me. "You're lying."

I shook my head and tapped the rhinestone camera glued to my forehead. "No, I'm not. Priest. Rings. Blood bond, blessing of the gods, the whole deal. Too bad we don't have time to watch home movies."

I stepped to the center of the theatre and faced the crowd. "Citizens of Attalos, for those of you who don't know me, I'm Alexannia Grace, the long-lost Eligible you've all been whispering about. As of this morning, I am also the wife of Rowan, Noble of the Fifth House."

The audience erupted in a wave of mumbling chaos.

Since I had everyone's attention, I held up my arm and willed the golden brand on my arm to glow. "I am also a Talon Enforcer and newly consummated member of the Noble Council. It is in that capacity that I declare martial law and suspend the Queen's reign."

Voices exploded as Strati soldiers rushed the stage and Rowan, Ydorus and I spread our stances. I glanced over my shoulder to see Rowan windmilling a sword and three Strati moving in. Ydorus was similarly occupied to my left.

And then everything suddenly stopped.

The Strati halted mid-attack and assumed a ready stance. Following their line of sight, I pivoted to the approaching Queen. She practically floated across the stage in her floor-length red gown. It was a grace shared by her brother and niece, though I'd been slow to make the connection.

"Well, well, Alexannia, it seems you have quite a lot on your mind today. I would love to hear it. After all, I believe it is my right to face my accuser, is it not?"

I lowered my blade but remained ready to strike. "I know who you are, Rheagan. It took me a while, but—"

Her head tilted back as melodic peals of laughter echoed in perfect resonance throughout the amphitheatre. She clapped slowly, laughing as if there weren't hundreds of citizens, soldiers, and Eligibles watching.

"A while?" she said. "In a mere week, you discerned what these mice have been scurrying around for almost thirty years. I was right to choose you."

"I told you before I won't—"

She waved her hand at my words. "You did, but you also didn't understand what I was capable of at the time."

Images of Tham bombarded my mind, his attack at Haven, his death in my room, his pyre burning until the silhouette of his body was consumed by the flames. I struggled for breath, the ache in my chest and back debilitating.

Sirens screeched in the distance.

Rheagan spun to speak to one of her soldiers. With her distracted, my mind cleared. I realized then that Rowan had gripped my shoulders and was urging me to fight the mindfuck that bitch was unleashing on me.

I steadied and nodded to him that I was tight. She wouldn't get inside me again, or if she did, I'd at least be prepared.

Pivoting back to me, Rheagan raised a delicate hand. "I tire of this game, Princess. You're much stronger than your mother, but still no match for me. Realize that before more people you love get hurt." Pointing a long, slim finger toward the back wall of the open theatre, she waited.

I glanced up, then back, ready for the distraction to be a trick. It was the tone of Rowan's curse that had me taking another look. No. No. *No!*

A hundred feet above the level of the stage, at the highest part of the amphitheater wall Terran, Coal and Elani were dragged to their feet. They stood bound and helpless against the Strati soldiers guarding them.

The blood pounding through my mind plummeted from my head and I fought not to faint. She had them. How could she—then I saw him. Estes. Estes descended the stairs, a wicked grin on his traitorous face.

"Why?" I cried. "I thought—"

His laughter sent shards of fury through my betrayal. "For a trained soldier, you were too easy to fool. Your need for someone to trust made you gullible."

"But you helped me with Tham and with Tasso."

He hit the bottom tier of steps and joined us on the stage. "I needed to show your mother what you were capable of, Princess. A credit to your father's raising. At first, I thought Bruin was the special one of you four. But that wife of his, more trouble than I anticipated. I learned a lot from them though. Mistakes that won't be repeated."

My muscles tightened. "What the hell are you talking about? Who are you?"

With cruel delight dancing in his dark eyes, Estes swept his hand down the length of his body and the mirage he wore wavered and disappeared. The acrid scent of dark magic singed my nostrils as his visage changed.

"Abaddon."

My mind spun with the reality of what I'd stumbled into. The Scourge's big play. They'd been searching for a way to resurrect Rheagan for millennia and Abaddon had done it. Here, isolated from the Realm of the Fair, taking over the lives of these people. Abaddon had somehow broken the banishment Castian had imposed on his sister and raised her to life again.

I glowered at the woman who should have been my mother. "You won't get away with this. Your attempts to take over the realms didn't work back then and won't work now. Castian will never allow it."

Intense hatred flooded the Queen's beautiful face until she was almost unrecognizable. "You will help me, child, one way or another." An evil chill hit me like a wall and I staggered back into Rowan. You just need to be reminded the price for denying me what I want."

Rheagan raised her hand toward the top of the wall and two Strati nodded. In a frenzy of arms and fists and streaks of red capes Terran was flung up and over the back wall.

I lurched forward but before I could make it more than a few steps Coal and Elani were pulled into position.

Oh gods, no. Not them too.

The chaos in the amphitheatre raged on as the city's sirens wailed. Eligibles, Nobles, and citizens stampeded toward the exits. Dozens of rebel Strati drew weapons as Ydorus barked out commands and a violent rush of palace guards, soldiers and citizens joined our fight.

With nothing in my sights but Coal struggling at the top rail of the theatre I launched for the steps. I pushed hard, dodging the scatter of people and leaping over marble benches when the stairs were blocked.

Heavy footfalls followed my every move. Rowan was right there with me, racing to help his sister, taking my back.

"*Castian!*" I screamed as a steady stream of frantic citizens pushed us back from our goal. "Your fucking Pantheon is influencing the shit out of these people. Get in this game. *Please, Castian.*"

"Is that you asking for help?" Rowan grunted behind me as we were blocked by Strati. He clocked his guy in the face with the hilt of a sword. Blood spattered across the shimmering gowns of the crowd. A lucky elbow to my cheek had me seeing stars. I blocked my foe's follow up and shattered his kneecap with a well-placed boot.

My thighs burned, my face stung and those goddam sirens were ringing in my head. Only three tiers left to climb.

No. Zale had joined the Strati. Together, they lifted the sobbing children. It happened so fast. Before I could get to them, Coal and Elani were flipped over the back rail.

Gone. My boy . . . gone.

Zale turned back from the ledge and flashed me a triumphant smile.

I slammed into him. The hot singe of steel pierced my side, but didn't touch my agony. I clubbed him behind the ear as my knee connected with his quad. The bastard was strong but more wife-beater than fighter. He snagged one wrist but I kept the other free. Palm thrusting his jaw was like slamming my hand into stone.

His knee jabbed my ribs. Over and over. My vision spotted out and a thundering whoosh filled my head.

Do. Not. Pass. Out.

Quick jerk and I flipped around his leg, grabbed his balls and twisted so hard I swear I almost ripped the suckers off. The hiss of his breath was so fricken satisfying. While he wheezed and curled like a shrimp, I locked my hands around his throat.

"Face your reckoning, motherfucker."

His chest heaved and his throat flexed. A hard twist and his neck snapped in my clenched fingers. Cold eyes widened as his lips stretched off his teeth in a sneer that ensured I wouldn't be sleeping for a week.

The crack to the back of my head knocked me stupid. I tried to shake my head clear. Fuck. Rowan was down, his face obscured by a bench.

Scrabbling, I pulled Zale's blade from my side and staggered to my feet. The half of my body that I could feel, screamed in protest. Vertigo sent me listing to the side. "Hang on, Rowan. I'm coming."

Ydorus and his men battled the Queen's Strati in every direction.

My knees cracked against the stone floor. "I'm here, Doc. I've gotcha."

Rowan's bloody face blurred behind a wall of despair and I laid my head on his chest. The rise and fall was slight and then nothing moved at all.

Till death us do part.

My body erupted in blinding agony. Writhing, I screamed as early-morning light pierced the blue sky above the transparent dome. Pain burned though me. It blinded. White spots and tears obscured my vision. Let death come. I was done anyway. I'd failed.

They were dead because of me.

The inconsolable grief of my vision paled to what twisted in my soul. Now, I could make out their faces: Tham, Terran, Coal, Elani and my beloved Rowan.

I would never breathe again.

CHAPTER THIRTY-TWO

"Giving up so soon, child?"

Blinking past the blood in my eyes, I dragged my sights up the scarlet silk gown of my enemy. I bared my teeth. The fire in my spine was debilitating. My entire body trembled beyond my control. "Fuck you, bitch. You want me dead? Have at it."

Rheagan laughed, the chorus of her voice cutting through the waning battle. "Dead? Never have I wanted you dead, my foolish Alexannia. I want you broken."

The gleam in her eyes made my blood burn in my veins. I swiped blood, tears and snot from my face and pushed up to my hands and knees. "You are insane. I claim my Right of Vengeance as wife of Rowan and mother of Cole. I claim your life as mine to take."

"You won't kill me." She cooed, pacing a slow circle around Rowan's fallen body. I shifted, repositioned to place myself between him and her. She smiled. "Kill me and you kill your mother. She's in here you know. Still fighting to regain control. A tenacious thorn in my side. Much like you."

"You're lying." I choked and spat blood.

"Willing to take that chance? You love with a depth and loyalty few comprehend. It's a weakness I enjoy exploiting."

I spat blood and eyed Rowan's dagger lying discarded by his shin. "Love and loyalty are *strength*. Not that a hollow . . . egocentric bitch would understand."

She chuckled, her long hair shining blue-black in the dawning sun. "Then I shall exploit that strength until you take your place with my forces. Bruin, your Were-king brother would be a dangerous target, as would your father, Reign, but Julian, the gentle genius of your family or Jade, pregnant with twins . . . they could easily be the next pawns in our game. And after them, we have Galan, Aust, Lia, Nash—"

I lunged.

Rowan's orichalcum dagger surged in my palm and slid through silk. I followed the thrust, ramming until the tip hit the marble pillar at her back. I twisted. And lifted.

Mustering all my remaining strength, I gutted the woman who should have been my mother. Blood streamed from the wound in my side. I couldn't feel my limbs. On adrenalin alone, I held fast. This woman would die.

As long as air filled my lungs I would bring her down.

I locked my knees and listened to the portal sirens. "The gates to the Realm of the Fair are open. I summoned your brother too."

Fury flashed in her dimming eyes. She'd underestimated me and finally realized it.

"Castian will come and if you're still breathing, he'll take care of you himself." Laughter bubbled up from my gut at the shock in her expression. I winced as the pain in my back redoubled. "It's over for you, bitch."

The two of us sank to the stage floor. Purple blood pooled onto the stage floor and I had never seen anything more beautiful.

"You may have won the battle, child, but the war is yet to come. Revel in your victory. It will be short lived."

Like a living horror movie, the wound in her gut exploded in a blinding glow. Golden mist spewed straight into the air. A moment later, it was gone and I was left with the empty shell that was once my mother.

I wanted to scream, to somehow change what the evil of the realm had put into motion, but the world went dark.

249

CHAPTER THIRTY-THREE

*D*eath was a cruel bitch and largely predictable. Except for when she exercised her malicious sense of humor. I opened my eyes a crack, not sure what to expect. No glorious white light surrounded me in warmth, no clouds, harps or angels, nor was Alyssa there to escort me into the legendary gardens of the 'After'.

Nope. Navy sheets twisted around me, as I lay crowded and hot in Rowan's bed.

Coal, curled like a kitten, balled up tight against my chest and belly. He had both his hands wrapped around one of the wooden training dirks we used with the younger students at the Academy. A smile twitched at the corner of his mouth making him look younger than he did when he was awake.

I blinked and swiped them clear and blinked again. Was I dreaming? Were we both dead? I didn't care as long as he was with me.

Warm, soft fingers brushed my cheek and I tore my gaze away from my boy. Jade spooned around him, facing me, her emerald green eyes glittering like two backlit gems. "He hasn't left your side. He's been so worried about you."

"How," I croaked.

Jade smiled. "We stormed the city searching for you. Bruin,

Cowboy, and Savage were lead group and making their way to the palace when they saw the first body fall from the amphitheatre wall. They didn't get there fast enough for your friend . . . but when the two kids went over, Bruin and Cowboy materialized and snatched them right out of the air."

I ran my fingers through the crazy cockerel comb of ginger-red hair and thanked Castian, all the gods, and even the Fates, that Weres had been part of the lead group. No race could materialize with the accuracy of the Weres, and probably no men other than Bruin and Cowboy would have attempted a mid-air rescue.

I shook my head, trying to wrap my head around it, Coal and Elani had been saved. Not Terran though. I died a little thinking about him never mashing up sayings again, never playing hide and seek with me or being teased by his parents.

"And Rowan? Have preparations been made for him?"

Jade propped herself up onto her elbow. "Not necessary. Castian restored him for what you suffered at the hands of his sister. A life given for a life taken, he said."

I swallowed as the room spun. "Rowan's alive?"

"A little browbeaten by Reign, Bruin and Julian, but he's held his own and is still breathing." The weight from her pregnancy had crept into the rounds of her cheeks. I hadn't noticed it before, but it was plain.

The deep grumble of Bruin's bear, snoring and huffing at the back of my neck startled me. The heat from his long, lush fur warmed my back. He'd come. After all that had been said and all the anger, he'd come when I needed him.

"Nobody browbeat him," someone mumbled from behind Jade. I saw it then, over her hip hung the arm of my other brother. I knew that beautiful shade of brown anywhere, deep mocha with a hint of cream. But—Julian *never* left Haven. I mean in the fifteen years he'd lived on our mountain he had never left the grounds. *Ever.*

"What about Rheagan and Abaddon?"

"We'll find them," Julian said, stretching and rising to his feet. "I should actually get back to it. You good, shrimpboat?"

I chuckled at the nickname I'd long forgotten. "Yeah. I'm good. Thanks for coming."

"Hey, Trouble, you're finally awake." Rowan's whisper came from the doorway as he strode over to our football field of a bed. He looked at the ensemble cast hunkered down around me and chuckled. "Good thing my parents believed in oversized furniture."

"Very good thing," I chuckled and raised my arm, ready for my husband to extricate me from the Shitstorm Survivors love-in. Bruin growled as I ruffled his fur and Rowan paled. "It's okay. He sleeps like a bear."

Rowan leaned over the sleeping mass of thick brown fur and squeezed my hand. "So, this is your family?"

"Yep. Except—"

"Your father's downstairs. He's been grilling me about Rheagan and Estes . . . or Abaddon, I guess . . . and my intentions." A crease formed between his brows as he frowned. "You said the man was scary, Lexi. That didn't begin to give me enough warning. He looks at me like he wants to chew my arms off for touching his daughter."

I snorted. "You just don't know him yet. His angry face and his happy face are the same. I'm sure you've charmed him and the rest of them."

Rowan shook his head, not looking convinced, then glanced to Coal. "How great is that?"

I nodded. "Jade told me about Terran. But Elani's safe?"

Rowan's eyes glowed. "Fine. Your friends really saved the day on that one."

"Help me up, will you? I'm stuck." Rowan pulled my hand to his mouth and kissed it. "There's something I need to tell you first."

A chill snaked down my spine. "What? What happened?"

"Nothing terrible." He squeezed my hand tighter and leaned over Bruin so he could see me better. "Do you remember when I told you that Faery traits either emerge at puberty or sometimes in stressful situations?" I nodded and he licked his lips. "Well, I think with every-thing that happened, the trauma of Tham and then witnessing Zale

and the soldiers throw Terran and the kids over the wall . . . well, triggered a change in you."

Bruin growled again and flexed his claws in his sleep.

Rowan paled and waited until he settled before continuing. "Now
don't freak out."

"Screw that, saying 'don't freak out' makes me lose my shit." My
breathing came shallow and fast while I took inventory, arms, legs—
"You are seriously fucking with my tranquility here, Rowan. What
kind of change?"

His grip loosened. "Lexi, look at me. Everything is all right. You're
beautiful. Stunning. It's just that now—you have wings. Your Air trait
is that your wings developed late, instead of you being born with
them. They couldn't break free and I had to operate to release them."

"Oh. My. Gods." My head whirled with that one as I whipped my
gaze from shoulder to shoulder to see. "Wings?"

Rowan nodded and eased me up, first to a sit and then I scootched
to the end of the bed. He lifted me up and over the footboard and set
me on my feet. I was wearing a backless halter top and yoga pants.
When he stood me in front of the mirror, tears welled.

"Hey, don't cry, baby," he said, sliding in behind me so he could
watch my reaction in the mirror. "You're stunning. Breathtaking."

I swallowed, but my mouth remained dry. "I feel like I Sigourney
Weaver'd, but my alien came out the back." Shifting first one way and
then the other I checked out the black velvety wings that hung sleek
and tight against my back and rear. Black was cool. And as I studied
them, they unfolded behind me. "Hey, did I do that?"

Rowan nodded. "You'll feel odd at first and your balance might be
off. But whatever happens, we'll deal with it.

His gaze met mine and his expression tightened. "That is, if you
still want this—me, I mean. Your family wants to take you home. You
have choices. So, if you want to rethink. . ."

"You're talking out of your ass, Doc."

"Yeah, well, I'm losing my mind."

Staring at the panicked reflection of my husband my vision grew blurry again. "Do you ever worry when things work out a little too well?"

"What do you mean?"

"Well, like, I walked through hell and managed to get to the other side, but a funny thing happened on the journey, I sprouted wings." I stretched my wings out and they fanned and flapped creating a little breeze. "You, Coal, Elani, and I are alive, my family is here and we are in love and married. It's all kind of miraculous, don't you think?"

Rowan broke into a brilliant smile and pulled me tight against his chest. "Yes *I* do. I was just afraid you might not. Lexi, you don't have to—"

My fingers on his lips stopped his ramble. "I'm right where I was meant to be, Doc. You should have clued in by now, it's not easy to get rid of me."

He dipped his head and kissed his way down the column of my neck. I moaned. He smelled perfect, the warmth of his lips on my skin was divine, and he held me like we were the only two people alive. "Come with me, Trouble, I've got a surprise I want to show you."

"Spoiler alert." Bruin yawned, producing clothes to cover his naked self as he rolled off the bed in his human form. "When a man says he has a surprise for you . . . that would be his penis."

Normally I would have laughed, but I couldn't. So much had gone wrong between Bruin and me. I waited, watching as he sauntered around the mammoth of a bed in ripped jeans and a slogan T-shirt that had a double-pointed arrow across his chest and read, *'Don't need a permit for these guns!'*

As my heart pounded faster, Bruin opened his arms and I ran. He caught me low on my hips and hugged me tight, one of his spine-cracking, bone-crushing hugs where you wonder if your lungs would ever re-inflate. In a flood of apology and genuine regret for my actions, the two of us made our peace.

If Bruin loved Mika half as much as I loved Rowan—and I knew he did—I didn't blame him for his anger.

"Fuck, Princess," Bruin growled, "don't ever disappear on us again."

"I promise," I said, swiping away my tears.

Movement on the bed had me turning just in time to catch Coal flying into my arms. His little body slammed into mine and it was only Rowan's hand on my back that kept us on our feet. I didn't care. I squeezed him tight and gave him a million kisses. "Oh, buddy, I'm so glad you're here. Are you all right? Estes didn't hurt you, did he? Nobody hurt you?"

The frantic head shaking was the best thing I'd 'heard' all day? Night? Coal pulled back and I set him back on the floor so I could see his hands. The more he rambled in his patchy, disjointed signing the more air I drew into my lungs.

"Okay, buddy," Rowan said. "How about we give your mom a minute to freshen up and we'll take her downstairs? I bet she's hungry."

I nodded. Coal took my hand and escorted me to the bathroom. When I opened the door, he assumed his stance against the bedroom wall and raised his dirk. He looked so serious and grown up. Before I started blubbering again and embarrassed the kid, I kissed the top of his head and stepped in the bathroom.

The kitchen buzzed with chatter and the clink of cutlery to plates. Leda refilled platters of food for Ydorus, and Eury. The rich aroma of her cooking made my stomach rumble. Both of my Strati men had seen better days, but considering the forces we'd come up against, the good guys had definitely come out on top.

It hurt that Terran wasn't sitting at the table, laughing with the others. I would miss him forever.

Coal ran to the table and knuckle-bumped the two warriors like he was one of the guys.

I would have marveled about that longer had an icy blast not hit me from behind me. I knew before turning who was there. Reign. People often remarked about his cold, dark eyes, but as his gaze met mine, I read all the hurt and anger and worry the others didn't see.

My first memory for my whole life had been me as an eight-year-old little girl afraid of the monolithic warrior glaring down on me when he found me that day in the forest. Little did we know Balor had chosen him as my mentor with the hopes that I could grow strong enough to defend Attalos. He'd been more than my mentor . . . he was my father.

"I always suspected you were a royal, Princess. I just thought it was just the *pain in the ass* variety."

My tears fell as I slammed against his chest and laid my cheek against his leather vest. His long, brindle hair brushed my cheek as his huge frame enveloped mine. "You look like road kill, old man."

He squeezed tighter. "I almost lost my baby girl. You know how fucking angry that makes me?"

"By the way you're squeezing the air from my lungs, I could guess."

Reign eased up on the welcome hug and set me back on my feet. "Don't you ever walk away from us again. You hearing me? Do you know how frantic I was not knowing what the fuck happened to you?"

While he cursed, and barked, and ranted, his arms remained locked around me.

"—and Zophia tells us about Tham, but won't give us any intel on where you are or how to get to you—"

Reign in a full on rage was the best thing . . . ever. I stood there, inserting my 'I'm sorrys', 'it won't happen agains', and 'yes sirs' where appropriate and had never felt more loved.

Once the air cleared, I formally introduced him to Rowan and tried to smooth some of the raw edges on that one. Despite his grumblings about Rowan being a civilian, and a Noble, I think he liked him or was starting to. Funny, most fathers would have been thrilled their daughter married a wealthy doctor, but in Reign's eyes, Rowan's only star quality was that he was a swordsmith.

Go figure.

Julian gave me a proper hug and offered me a cd case. "I downloaded the surveillance feed from your cam and made you this."

I'd forgotten all about my third eye recorder and rolled my eyes. "I lived that nightmare, bro, I don't need a reminder."

He scrubbed a hand over his cheeks and chuckled. "Uh . . . this footage was taken earlier in the evening. It's your wedding and the hours that followed."

I snatched the case out of his hand and my cheeks warmed. "You didn't watch it, did you, pervert?"

He made a face. "No, I edited it out before Reign saw it and killed the man. I will say, the time stamp from start to finish impressed the hell out of me. Your man's a machine. Well done, Princess."

I laughed and left my brother to go join my sex machine husband. After slipping the cd case into Rowan's pocket, I cupped his ass. "So, Doc, what's my surprise?"

"Despite what your brother thought it's not my penis."

He led me by the hand, past the colored glass doors of the library, past the entrance with the glass wall and the fish, and into an area of the main floor I had discovered during hide and seek. The double doors to a ballroom were open and when I saw who was inside, I jolted to a stop.

"*Tham!*"

I launched myself across the room and into his arms. He felt whole and warm and real and I let myself believe the past five days had been nothing but a cruel trick. "You're here. Castian gave you back to us. Gods, I'm so sorry. I never meant—"

Tham pulled back and wiped my tear-stained cheeks with his thumb. "*Shh*, I know your heart. I made peace with what happened and accept my passing."

"Made peace? Screw that. You're back now and that's all that matters."

Tham shook his head. "No, little one, Castian has allowed me to say my goodbyes and fulfill my promise but that is all. He will not undo what has been done. That time has passed and my body has been burned. I am grateful he allowed me this much."

"What? No? If I speak to him—"

"A life for a life, *sweeting*. You have your Rowan back. With Coal and Elani, your family is restored."

"But you're my family too. I need you." I could see in his Highborne blue eyes that the deal was done. I had only this moment with Tham to say our goodbyes. "Will you still come to me? Still visit me in my dreams? I need our time together."

The sharp intake of breath behind me made me wince. Shit. I'd never told Rowan about the nocturnal get togethers Tham and I shared.

"If I am able," he said. "I shall always watch over you and Galan and our Haven family."

I exhaled, glancing back to where Rowan stood over my shoulder. There was hurt and tension in his gaze, but love too. I turned back to Tham. "I'm so sorry this happened to you, Hotness. This is all my fault."

Tham shook his head and his flaxen waves rustled against the suede of his vest as it always had. "Mayhap this is where my *Ambar Lenn* was leading me all along. We cannot know what my path was meant to be. Whether my future lay in the hands of Castian, or the Fates, or my own free will, this is where we are and I accept it."

"You're such a fucking martyr," I said with a quiet laugh. His perfect features blurred behind my tears. "Only you could take being dead and make it sound like a new and exciting adventure."

He bowed his head and gestured to our family filing into the ballroom behind us. Reign corrected Coal's grip on his dirk. Tham smiled. "If I spend a lifetime watching your futures unfold, *neelan*, it will be a full life indeed. With Rheagan and Abaddon together and on the loose, the war with the Scourge will escalate. You will need someone watching your back."

"You're pretty determined for a ghost, you know."

"I am aware." He smiled at me with an ease that only Tham could muster and my heart ached. "Do you remember what you told Galan, Aust, and me the morning we left our village and headed to Haven?"

I shrugged. "Something profoundly inspirational?"

"Naturally." Tham laughed, running his fingers down the side of my cheek. "You said not to hold back when facing Fate's Journey, that starting anew is the perfect opportunity to strike a fresh path and create a life only dreamed of."

"So, what now?" I asked.

"Now, I fulfill the last promise I made to you. A dance on your birthday." Tham nodded to someone over my shoulder. The music came up and Bruno Mars started singing, "Count on Me". Tham waggled his finger, coaxing me, and I went to him, tears streaming, my heart filled to bursting.

"Happy birthday, *neelan*." Tham kissed my forehead and whirled me into his arms. My feet barely touched the tiles.

I memorized everything about those three magical minutes. The grace of Tham's movement as we glided across the polished floor, the way his dimples showed when he laughed, the aroma of suede mixing with the scent of his smooth, ivory skin. And as the song ended, the way his arms felt around me as he hugged me goodbye.

"*Amin mela lle*, Alexannia Grace."

"I love you too, Hotness." He waited while I gathered myself and then led us to our watching family. His smile softened as he raised our joined hands to Rowan. "You are a truly blessed male. Take good care of her. And be patient."

Rowan cleared his throat. "I absolutely will. And good luck to you."

I couldn't watch as Tham walked away and Rowan seemed to know it. He turned me back towards the dance floor and I kept my gaze focused on the windows on the far wall.

"I hate to admit it," he said, "but that guy is pretty great."

"The best." Realizing how insensitive my words were, I glanced up. "I'm gutted by losing Tham, but it's you I love. You know that, right?"

Rowan nodded, and for the first time I saw that the doubt and hurt he'd carried with him was gone. His eyes burned with the most beautiful flecks of gold and green. "I do."

I pressed my cheek to Rowan's side and he draped his arm across my shoulder. The chatter of our family dissipated and we were left alone. I don't know how long we stayed there, me listening to the thrumming rhythm of his heart beneath my ear. Eventually though, he gathered my hand in his and led me out a door in the opposite direction everyone else had gone.

"Back to what Bruin said earlier . . . I do have another surprise I desperately want to show you."

The chemistry sparking between us from that first moment ignited once again. My skin tingled to awareness as I jogged to keep up with his determined strides.

"Yay. And as the birthday girl, I get to unwrap my surprise, right?"

THANK YOU FOR READING

I hope you enjoyed Torrent of Tears, Book 3 of the Scourge Survivor Series. I sincerely hope you enjoyed Lexi and Rowan's adventure. If you'd like to share your thoughts on the series, please leave a rating or review at your favorite retailer.
Reviews help other readers find books.

If you're ready for more sexy adventures with the Haven gang, continue on with Book 4 –Blind Spirit

BLIND SPIRIT

As the war against the Scourge gains momentum, Lia struggles to cope with Abaddon and his plans for her. Faced with the horrifying truths of her capture the summer before, she re-evaluates everything she knows about herself, the people around her and her future. Lost and disenchanted, she finds strength in her friendship with the Celt wizard, Samuel, her brother's nemesis and the male destined to guide her toward her destiny.

<u>**Author Notes**</u>
Written on 09/09/2018

Thank you for reading Torrent of Tears, and here you are, still with me reading this. As a novelist of many genres of romance—fantasy, paranormal, timeslip historical, and sci-fi—I love to twist Alpha heroes and kick-ass heroines into chaotic, hilarious, and magical situations, and make them really work for a Happily Ever After.

To have you enjoy it enough to gift me with your time and attention is a true gift.

Thank you. I hope my imagined adventures continue to live up to your expectations.

All the best to you and yours.
Blessed Be,
JL

ALSO BY JL MADORE

<u>Find Me:</u>

Social Media – Facebook, Twitter, Instagram

Web page – www.jlmadore.com

Email – jlmadorewrites@gmail.com

Reader Group – JL Series Updates

<u>JL's Reverse Harem Titles</u>

Guardians of the Fae Realms

<u>Guardians of the Phoenix – Calli's Harem</u>

Book 1 – Rise of the Phoenix

Book 2 – Wolf's Soul

Book 3 – Bear's Strength

Book 4 – Hawk's Heart

Book 5 – Jaguar's Passion

<u>Darkness Calls – Keyla's harem</u>

Book 6 – Dark Curse

Book 7 – Dark Soul

Book 8 – Dark Crown

<u>Guardians of the Crown – Honor's Harem</u>

Book 9 – Honor Restored

Book 10 – Honor Guards

Book 11 – Honor Bound

Book 12 – Honor Empowered

<u>Rise of the Amberloq – Lark's Harem</u>

Book 13 – Find the Fallen

Book 14 – Rise from Ruin

Book 15 – Trust and Triumph

<u>Exemplar Hall – Jesse's Harem</u>

Book 1 – Captured by the Magi

Book 2 – Jesse and the Magi Vault

Book 3 – The Makings of a Magi Knight

Book 4 – Clash with the Magi Council

Book 5 – The Unstoppable Storme

<u>JL's More Traditional M/F, M/M, or Menage</u>

The Watchers of the Gray Series (Paranormal)

Watchers of the Gray Boxset – Complete Series

Book 1 – Watcher Untethered – Zander

Book 2 – Watcher Redeemed – Kyrian

Book 3 – Watcher Reborn – Danel

Book 4 – Watcher Divided – Phoenix

Book 5 – Watcher United – Seth

Book 6 – Watcher Compelled – Bo

Book 7 – Watcher Unfeigned – Brennus

Book 8 – Watcher Exposed – Taharqa

The Scourge Survivor Series (Fantasy)

Scourge Survivor Series Boxset - Complete Series

Book 1 – Blaze Ignites

Book 2 – Ursa Unearthed

Book 3 – Torrent of Tears

Book 4 – Blind Spirit

Book 5 – Fate's Journey

Book 6 – Savage Love – epilogue novella

Aliens of Atlantis Series (Sci-Fi)

Book 1 – Taryn's Tiderider

Book 2 – Kai's Captive

Book 3 – Alyandra's Shadow

9 798201 434380